PRAISE FOR KATE CARLISLE'S FIXER-UPPER MYSTERIES

"An immensely satisfying page-turner of mystery."
—*New York Times* bestselling author Jenn McKinlay

"I fell for this feisty, take-charge heroine, and readers will, too."
—*New York Times* bestselling author Leslie Meier

"Carlisle's second contractor cozy continues to please with its smart, humorous heroine and plot. Fans of Sarah Graves's Home Repair Is Homicide series will appreciate this title as a solid read-alike." —*Library Journal*

"Highly entertaining. . . . Quick, clever, and somewhat edgy. . . . Shannon's not a stereotype—she's a person, and an interesting, intelligent, likable one at that, which makes it easy to become invested in her tale."
—Smitten by Books

"An engaging cozy, including a complicated mystery woven throughout." —Mystery Suspense Reviews

"A great read, and I recommend it to both cozy and other mystery readers alike." —Open Book Society

"The Fixer-Upper series is a fan favorite, and for good reason. The characters are the kind of people many of us would love to have as friends and neighbors, as well as coworkers and family." —The Cozy Review

OTHER BOOKS BY KATE CARLISLE

BIBLIOPHILE MYSTERIES

Homicide in Hardcover
If Books Could Kill
The Lies That Bind
Murder Under Cover
Pages of Sin
(enovella)
One Book in the Grave
Peril in Paperback
A Cookbook Conspiracy
The Book Stops Here
Ripped from the Pages
Books of a Feather
Once upon a Spine
Buried in Books
The Book Supremacy
The Grim Reader
Little Black Book
The Paper Caper

FIXER-UPPER MYSTERIES

A High-End Finish
This Old Homicide
Crowned and Moldering
Deck the Hallways
Eaves of Destruction
A Wrench in the Works
Shot Through the Hearth
Premeditated Mortar
Absence of Mallets

DRESSED TO DRILL

A Fixer-Upper Mystery

Kate Carlisle

BERKLEY PRIME CRIME
New York

BERKLEY PRIME CRIME
Published by Berkley
An imprint of Penguin Random House LLC
penguinrandomhouse.com

ISBN: 9780593201350

First Edition: May 2023

Printed in the United States of America
1 3 5 7 9 10 8 6 4 2

To Joanne H, who named Mac's movie

Chapter One

Hollywood, California

"Camera's rolling, Chloe," Paul, the director, shouted, then shot a glance at the crew. "Settle down, people."

My sister, Chloe, stood out of camera range casually sipping the caffe latte that the production assistant had just handed her. "Be right there, Paul. Shannon, you ready?"

"Yes," I said a bit too loudly, and followed it with a light cough in a vain attempt to disguise the edge of terror in my voice. After all this time, I was still a little freaked out about being on camera. I didn't know how Chloe could drink coffee. My stomach was jittery enough already.

But Chloe loved every anxious bit of it. She was the producer and star of *Makeover Madness*, the number one home improvement show on the Home Builders Network. Not only that, but she had a bestselling book on home decor that had sold zillions of copies and had at least a few dozen print runs by now. So she wasn't just a TV superstar, but also a multimedia superstar.

She was movie-star beautiful and apparently had a cast-iron stomach lining, unlike me.

My boyfriend, Mac, and I had traveled to Hollywood to attend the world premiere of the latest film based on his bestselling Jake Slater novels. When Chloe found out we were coming, she invited me to appear on her show and do some home improvement work with her. And when her fiancé, Police Chief Eric Jensen, realized we'd all be in Hollywood together, he knew he had to come along, just in case. He figured—rightly—that whenever Chloe and I got together, trouble seemed to show up unbidden.

It was the last day of filming at a spectacular ten-thousand-square-foot mid-century modern home in Trousdale Estates, a high-priced enclave in the hills north of Sunset Boulevard. Chloe and her crew had been renovating the house for several months. I had arrived a few days ago to help with the finishing touches on the updated kitchen and the main bathroom.

Once Chloe was finished filming these last few segments, she and her crew would take a six-week hiatus while her editing team worked to put five full shows together featuring this one house. Until then, Chloe was on vacation in Lighthouse Cove.

When the shows were completely edited, she would fly back to Hollywood to tour the home and describe the amazing work she and her crew had done to turn a faded old house into a sparkling new showcase home for the homeowners.

And that was the magic of television.

"I'll stand over here," Chloe said to Paul, pointing to the far end of the massive walk-in shower. Bob the cameraman joined them for a quick rundown of the scene we were about to do.

"Shannon and I will explain things as we go along," Chloe said. "But Shannon will do the actual work, so keep the camera on her and maybe zoom in on the power drill if you can."

"I can," Bob said with a grin.

"Don't forget, Chloe," Paul reminded her. "This is the last day we'll be shooting at this house, so give us a quickie teaser about the next show at some point."

"Got it," Chloe said.

Meanwhile, my job, if I chose to accept it, was simply to attach a safety bar to the shower wall. This was something I'd done a hundred times, so it sounded like a piece of cake, right? But I was about to point out some very specific rules to follow in order not to damage the tile. And I would be doing that while running the power drill and looking and sounding professional the whole time. Like I said, piece of cake.

Chloe gave me a look. "You ready?"

I'd done Chloe's show before, a couple times, and I'd even done a scene or two by myself when Chloe was otherwise engaged—or in jail, as I recall. But it had been about a year since I'd worked on her film set, so yeah, I was feeling a little shaky.

Never let 'em see you sweat, my father used to say. Those were words to live by, especially in Hollywood. So I rolled my shoulders and stretched my neck around to loosen up, then smiled at Chloe. "Let's do this."

"Ready to roll," she said to Paul, and took her place at the end of the walk-in shower.

This shower space, by the way, was roughly the size

of my house. I'm exaggerating slightly. But seriously, there was at least enough space to play a quick game of basketball. Ten feet wide by sixteen feet long with a ceiling that went up twelve feet, it contained two rainfall shower heads plus six jet-spray nozzles on each side. I wasn't even sure what those were for, but they were definitely deluxe. The teak bench at the far end was elegantly carved and wide enough to seat two people very comfortably.

While I was admiring the huge space, Paul counted us down and cued Chloe to start talking.

"We've just about finished remodeling the main bath in this gorgeous mid-century modern home," she said to the camera. "The owners love bright colors, so we've added this beautiful gold-hued mosaic tile to this massive walk-in shower."

She gestured as she spoke. "But at the last minute, the owners asked us to install a safety bar on the shower wall. They explained that they're not getting any younger and wanted the security of having something to grab onto, just in case."

She held up the newly purchased safety bar, still in its packaging, and as she spoke, she walked toward me. The camera followed her. "It's not a bad idea to have one of these sturdy bars installed in your own home bath or shower, no matter how old or young you are. We can all use something to hold on to when standing on a wet, slippery surface. Am I right?"

I could tell that the camera lens had widened to include me in the shot.

"You're right, Sis," I said with a smile.

She winked at the camera. "Now Shannon's going to give you some step-by-step instructions to ensure that you install it correctly and, most importantly, that you don't crack the tile."

"The first thing you need to know," I said, "is that tile is a completely different animal than drywall or wood or even concrete. Mainly because, if you crack the tile, it's not going to be an easy fix. Unlike drywall or other surfaces where you can just patch it and keep going, that section of tile would have to be replaced. And that's a big pain in the neck."

"I'll say," Chloe chimed in.

"So here's how to get it right the first time."

"What tools have you got there?" Chloe asked.

My tools were gathered at one end of the teak bench, and I lifted my power drill. "This is my trusty cordless power drill that's been fully charged. And I'm changing my standard masonry drill bit to a diamond-tipped bit. I usually drill a small pilot hole using a one-eighth-inch bit and move up to the final size, which in this case will be a half-inch bit."

I held up the thin cylindrical drill bit for the camera. "I don't want you to be intimidated by the fact that it's a *diamond* tip. They're only slightly more expensive than a regular drill bit but totally worth it, because they're the best way to safely drill through hard materials. They work well on mosaic glass, ceramic, porcelain tiles, marble, granite, quartz—whatever."

As I attached the diamond bit to the drill, Chloe said, "I see you've got a level with you, too."

"It's always a good idea to have a level nearby." I held up my twenty-four-inch level. "We want this safety bar to be installed perfectly level."

Chloe grinned. "Yes, we do."

I smiled back at her, then continued. "In addition,

according to ADA requirements, grab bars should be mounted thirty-three to thirty-six inches above the shower floor, measured at the entry."

"That's pretty technical," Chloe commented.

I grinned. "Yeah, sorry about that. Now, the most secure way to anchor a safety bar is to find a stud. And the best way to do that is with one of these handy-dandy stud finders." I held up my own bright yellow stud finder. "You can locate studs by sliding this gadget along the wall and—wait for it." As the stud finder passed over a stud, the gadget beeped loudly and its light turned bright red.

"Pretty easy, right?" I said. "If you don't have a stud finder, or you have difficulty locating the studs, we have some additional tips on our website for various situations and solutions."

Chloe jumped in. "And in case you haven't heard me mention it a hundred times already, our website is MakeoverMadnessTV.com." She looked at me. "So now we're going to mount the safety bar. What happens first?"

"Okay," I said. "After we've carefully measured where we'll place our mounting brackets, I've marked a small piece of painter's tape and placed it over the spots I want to drill into. That'll add one more layer of protection, because I really don't want the drill to slip or skate across the surface and crack this beautiful tile."

Chloe grinned into the camera. "That's smart."

"So now we're ready to drill. Place the end of the drill bit on the mark on your tape. You'll want to start out slowly and keep the drill bit as steady and straight as possible. Then you can gradually increase the speed." I turned on the drill and demonstrated.

It took about ten seconds before the drill made it through the tile, the cement backer board, and the stud beneath. Then I turned off the power and set the drill down on the table. "It takes a few extra seconds to get through all those layers."

"I promise this gets easier each time you do it," Chloe said, smiling at the camera. "Once again, you can find detailed instructions for all our projects on our website. And when we come back, we'll show you the newly mounted safety bar as well as the rest of our mid-century modern main bathroom remodel."

There was silence for five seconds, then Paul shouted, "We're clear. That's lunch, everybody. Crew, we want you back on set in thirty-five minutes."

"Yo," someone shouted.

"Yes, boss," someone else said.

"Thanks, Paul," Chloe said, and grabbed my arm. "Let's take a break."

We walked down the hall and ran into two gorgeous men, namely my boyfriend, Mac Sullivan, and Chloe's fiancé, Police Chief Eric Jensen.

"Hey, did you catch any of the show?" Chloe asked.

"We did," Eric said. "You were both brilliant."

"And did you get to see Jason at all?"

"Yeah, I ended up going over to his place for coffee. He's good. They've got three kids now." Eric shook his head. "That was sort of a shock, but he's a great dad."

"That's nice to know," Chloe said.

"It is." Eric had told us all about his buddy Jason. The two men had joined the army together, and when they got out, they both joined the LAPD. Now Jason was a detective, still with the LAPD, and Eric was Lighthouse Cove's chief of police. "I was just telling

Mac that Jason has some ideas about Homefront that we might find helpful. I'll set up a conference call next week, and we can chat about it."

"We're always open to new ideas," Mac said.

Homefront was the veterans' village we had built on five acres in Lighthouse Cove. My crew and I had constructed fifty tiny homes, along with a community center that was now thriving, with all sorts of amenities for veterans. Eric and Mac, along with two of Mac's marine pals, had arranged all the backing and funding over the last few years. All of us considered it one of our proudest accomplishments.

While Eric was meeting with his old friend Jason, Mac had driven to the studio to talk to one of the producers of the Jake Slater movie.

I gazed up at Mac. "So how was your meeting?"

"Very productive," he said with a grin. "I'll probably go to New York for a few days later this month for more meetings."

He pulled me close and gave me a quick kiss. "Eric's right, your segment was great. And you look beautiful."

"Thank you. Chloe was my makeup and wardrobe consultant."

"Contractor Barbie at your service," Chloe said with a smart salute.

I frowned at Mac. "Could you tell I was nervous?"

"A little," Mac said, "but you relaxed after a few seconds."

"I'm not sure why she still gets nervous," Chloe said. "She's a natural."

Mac nodded. "I agree."

The four of us walked into the spacious kitchen, where dozens of sandwiches and five different bowls of salads were set up buffet style. There was a big tub of ice with all sorts of soft drinks and several trays of desserts.

"This is nice," I said.

Chloe nodded. "We like to keep the crew fed and happy so they don't wander off."

I shook my head. "Why would anyone wander away from all this?"

"Yeah, that would be dumb," she agreed. She grabbed a sandwich, then turned as more of the crew walked in. "Hey, Buck. You did a great job lighting that space."

I turned to look at Chloe's lighting director. He was tall, tan, and broad-shouldered, with sandy blond hair, amazing blue eyes, and a beautiful smile. He was a few years younger than us, maybe in his late twenties, and was the epitome of a California surfer, whether he surfed or not.

Buck grinned. "Thanks, Chloe. It's the first time I've ever been asked to light a shower stall."

With a smile, Chloe said, "You've got to admit, it was a pretty deluxe *stall*. But still, it wasn't easy. You made us look fabulous."

"That wasn't hard," Buck said, then winced. "Sorry. Was that too much sucking up?"

She laughed. "I'm really going to miss you. Don't get me wrong, it'll be wonderful to have Reggie back on the crew, but you've been such a great help. And you've got a fun sense of humor and a good work ethic, which I appreciate."

"Thanks," he said with a nod. "If you ever need an

extra lighting tech again, please call me." He grabbed a sandwich.

"How is Reggie?" I asked. Reggie was Chloe's regular lighting director, but he'd been involved in a car accident two months ago and had broken his leg badly.

Bob, the camera guy, reached for a can of cola. "He's been in physical therapy for six weeks."

Chloe nodded as she nibbled on a potato chip. "I talked to him last week. He sounds a lot better."

"He improves more and more every day," Bob said. "Should be good to go in another week or two."

"I hope so," Chloe said. "With luck, he'll be able to come back to work when we start on the next house."

Bob nodded. "He will."

"Hey, Buck," Chloe said, turning back to her temporary lighting tech. "Seriously, if you ever need a referral, let me know. I'll be glad to rave about you."

He flashed that perfect smile again. "I'd really appreciate it, Chloe."

"It's the truth. Your work is stellar."

Something occurred to me, and I stared at Chloe.

She brushed her chin. "What? Do I have mustard on my face?"

Mac was watching me. "You've got something on your mind. What is it?"

I looked at him. "Remember I told you about the job we're starting on the Lighthouse Church?"

"Of course," he said.

"That's a gorgeous old building," Chloe said.

"It's amazing," I said.

Chloe sipped her bottle of water. "You're turning it into some kind of museum, right?"

"An art museum," I said. "But it's so dark in there,

and there's so many nooks and crannies all throughout the place, I'm concerned. I've got a couple of great electricians on my crew, but I need someone who really knows lighting. Because, you know, it's tricky when you're trying to illuminate artwork in all those odd spaces."

"Don't I know it." Chloe's eyes narrowed. "Hmm. Buck, you studied theater, right? And . . . what else did you study in school?"

He gave a mock scowl. "You mean you didn't memorize my résumé?"

Chloe laughed. "Sorry."

He sobered up. "I went to UCLA. I have a master's degree in electrical engineering and a bachelor's in theater lighting and cinematography."

"Wow," I said. "That's specific."

He nodded. "I grew up on a horse ranch, which has nothing to do with anything, except that my mom wanted me to do more with my life than ride horses. So the electrical engineering degree is for her. But my dad was a stuntman for television and movies, and I used to visit him on the job all the time. That's how I got the showbiz bug. So the lighting and cinematography is for him."

"That's really nice," I said. "I'm impressed."

Chloe gave me a long look. "Well?"

"Well." I turned to Buck. "Okay, I need a lighting guy to start in two weeks. But you'd have to relocate to Lighthouse Cove, at least temporarily. That's in Northern California. North of Mendocino." I frowned. "It's a small town, and it's kind of a long way to go for a temporary job, although we'll probably need you for a full year, maybe longer, but . . ."

"I know Lighthouse Cove," Buck said. "I have an aunt who lives there."

"You're kidding," I said. "That's amazing."

"I'll say," Buck said. "Are you really offering me a job?"

"We can talk salary and benefits later, but yeah, I'm offering you a job."

"Holy smokes." He shook his head in happy shock. "I'll take it."

In the car on the way back to the hotel, Eric said, "I wish you hadn't told all those people about the church project."

"Why not?" I asked.

Chloe rolled down the window to let in the clean, warm breeze. "You think it's a problem?"

He frowned. "I think the less said about future plans, the better."

"Are you being paranoid?" I asked.

"Of course he is," Chloe said. "He's a cop. He's got a suspicious mind."

"You're darn right I do," he said. "For good reason. There were eighteen people in that lunchroom, and they all heard about the new church project. These days, it's just not safe to let people know your business."

"But it's not like she announced it on the show or on Facebook," Chloe argued. "My staff and crew are the only ones who heard us talking, and they're all trustworthy."

"Not everyone is trustworthy," he insisted. "All it takes is one word whispered to the wrong person, and all hell can break loose."

Chloe elbowed him. "You're such a cop."

But Eric's words reminded me that Chloe's former director and some of her staff had come up to Lighthouse Cove to film the makeover of one of our beautiful old Victorian homes a couple years ago. They definitely were not all that trustworthy. In fact, a few of them were downright awful, and Chloe's life had been threatened several times.

I shook off those memories because they had nothing to do with our current situation. "Even if the news does get around, it's just a construction job. On a church. And it's hundreds of miles away from here. Do you really think it's a problem?"

He frowned. "It's a dangerous world out there. And you are two beautiful women. People notice." He shook his head. "Look, it's probably nothing, guys. Don't mind me."

Chloe stared at him. "What's going on? Did you get some kind of a vibe back there?"

He narrowed his eyes. "I'm a cop, Chloe. I don't get *vibes*."

"Fine," she said with a laugh. "Let's call it your Spidey sense."

He thought for a moment, then nodded. "I'm okay with that."

The rest of us laughed, then Eric met my gaze in the rearview mirror. "Look, I shouldn't have said anything, mainly because I don't want you guys to worry about it. But generally, you shouldn't say so much about your personal plans in public places."

Back in our hotel room, Mac and I dressed for the evening. And I mean *dressed*. We were attending the world premiere of Mac's new movie, and we were going formal. Like, red carpet formal. The film company had put us up in a beautiful hotel suite in the hills with a view of the ocean. It was totally amazing.

I stared at the full-length mirror and wondered for a minute who that person was looking back at me. She had red hair and lots of curls, so it had to be me, because nobody I knew had that huge mop of hair. Except me. But, wow, I looked pretty good.

I had pulled some of my hair back and caught it in two silver barrettes. The rest of it curled over my shoulders and down my back. And I was wearing makeup. Not like the stuff I'd worn for the camera on Chloe's show. This was subtle and smoky.

The dress was stunning, and, yes, I had borrowed it from Chloe, who lived in Hollywood and went to events like this all the time. She had formal dresses to spare, so we picked one out that was perfect for me. It was the color of pewter with a hint of pink, and it sparkled with sequins. I felt sexy and glamorous, a feeling that didn't come over me too often, mainly because I worked in construction. Denim jeans, heavy boots, and a tool belt was about as provocative as I got.

The neckline of the dress was off the shoulder with the tiniest cap sleeves, which I loved. It fit me like a glove all the way down my torso, then it loosened up enough to make it easy to walk in, thank goodness. The front of the dress was slit halfway up my thigh. It was ridiculously sexy.

Mac, who had attended these premieres every time a book of his was made into a movie, seemed to appreciate the way I looked—if his being rendered speechless was any indication. He opened his mouth, but no words came out. Then he blinked several times, and I thought maybe he was stroking out. Finally he whispered, "Wow."

"Same to you," I said, smiling. The man had really nailed the James Bond *Casino Royale* tuxedo look.

He approached me slowly from across the room, like a panther on the prowl. "You take my breath away."

I held out my arms. "Come here."

With care, he pulled me close and whispered, "We don't have to go to the movie."

"It's tempting," I said, "but there's no way I'm missing that movie."

I could hear his laugh as he buried his face in my shoulder. "I had a feeling you'd say that."

I wrapped my arms around him, and we stood like that for a long minute. "I happen to know that you're dying to see it, too."

"I can think of a few other things I'm dying to do."

Then he kissed my neck and then my jaw and then my cheek, and then he stepped back. "Well, since we're all dressed up anyway, we might as well go to the movies."

I smiled. "As dumb as it sounds, I'd also really like to walk with you on the red carpet."

"Then that's what we'll do."

"I think it'll be memorable, don't you? Even though nobody will know who I am."

"Believe me, Irish, that's a good thing." For one brief second his eyes clouded, then he smiled and tucked a strand of hair behind my ear. "Let's go."

Chapter Two

"I've never seen anything so fabulous," Chloe gushed as the limousine driver pulled to a stop right at the edge of the red carpet.

"This crowd is huge," I said. "It's like we're going to the Academy Awards or something."

The movie studio had arranged for the four of us to be driven by limousine to the movie theater. There was a party afterward in the theater lobby. Then after that, the driver would pick us up and take us to some fabulous restaurant for dinner. We all stared out the windows at the crowd of moviegoers, reporters, and cameras filling the wide plaza in front of the theater. Along the side of the plaza were bleachers filled with cheering fans.

Bleachers. Cheering fans. I took in everything and thought, *Girl, you're not in Lighthouse Cove anymore.*

The driver turned around and looked at us. "Please wait in the car until I'm given the okay to open the door."

"No problem," Mac replied.

A moment later, the driver slipped out of the car and circled around to the passenger side. He didn't open the door yet, but stood and waited for instructions.

"Amazing," I murmured, still awed by the crowd size.

"This place is packed," Chloe said. "Not that I'm surprised. After all, it's Jake Slater."

Mac grinned. "Pretty cool, huh?"

"The coolest," she said.

Eric frowned. "I hope they've got their crowd control issues worked out."

Chloe, Mac, and I laughed, but Eric simply shrugged. "Hey, with a crowd this size, it's something to think about."

"That's just one of the many reasons why I love you," Chloe said. Her smile was dreamy as she leaned in close and kissed him. "You think about those things so we don't have to."

Mac and I beamed at each other as the driver finally opened the door for us.

I started to step out onto the carpet.

"I'll help you, ma'am," the driver said, taking hold of my arm.

"Thank you."

Mac touched my shoulder. "I'm right behind you, Irish."

"I hope so." I could use all the help I could get, I thought, considering the fragile, skintight dress I was wearing and these killer shoes.

As I waited for the others to climb out of the limo, I took note of the expansive courtyard with its giant Chinese pagoda, red dragon, and two Ming Dynasty lions guarding the entrance. And then I saw the famous hand- and footprints memorialized in cement.

"This is awesome," I murmured.

"Pretty cool, huh?" Mac said.

I grinned with excitement. "It sure is."

The early June evening was mild, thank goodness, and I was able to stroll without having to wrap myself up in the glittery pashmina Chloe had lent me.

Once the four of us were standing together on the red carpet, I began to hear the shouts. "Chloe! Chloe!"

Chloe turned and a woman shouted, "Who are you wearing?"

"Oh my God," someone else cried. "That's MacKintyre Sullivan! He writes the Jake Slater books!"

"I know!" A woman screamed. "Mac! I love your books!"

"Hey, Mac!" some guy shouted and hustled up to join us. It was clear that he was a reporter when he shoved a microphone in Mac's face. "Have you seen *The Edge of Danger* yet? What do you think?"

Mac was kind enough to stop and talk for a moment instead of shoving the microphone back at the guy.

"Chloe! Who are you wearing?"

"Is that Christian Dior?"

As Eric, Chloe, and I continued our slow trek along the red carpet, my sister leaned in close to me and said, "It just figures. They ask me what I'm wearing, but they ask Mac his opinion of the film. It's so wrong and sexist."

I slipped my arm through hers. "Do you want me to kick someone's butt for you?"

She laughed. "Let me get back to you on that." She squared her shoulders as the cameras continued to follow us along the red carpet.

"Nobody asked me who I was wearing," Eric said, and we laughed some more.

Watching Chloe glide easily along the carpet, I was reminded to straighten my spine and stand tall so I wouldn't trip over my hem and embarrass myself and everyone around me. "How do you walk in this getup?"

Chloe huffed at me. "It's not a *getup*, little missy. It's an incredibly gorgeous designer gown created by a brilliant artist with magical hands."

I squeezed her arm. "And it's sensational, the most beautiful thing I've ever worn. I owe you big-time."

"Yes, you do. Because you look fabulous, and the paparazzi are already chomping at the bit to start hounding you."

I had to laugh at that. "Oh, right. Because they love talking to nobodies like me."

Mac joined us and took my hand in his. Seconds later, a reporter called out, "Hey, Mac, who's the lady?"

The question sounded oddly confrontational, and I turned to get a look at the speaker. She was a very pretty blonde, and her voice was deep and sultry. Was she trying to sound enticing? *Oh well,* I thought. *Wait in line.*

Mac clenched his teeth and grabbed hold of my arm possessively. "Let's keep walking."

I took a quick peek over my shoulder. The woman was smirking at Mac now. Or was she looking at me? Hard to tell, but either way, that was not a friendly expression on her face.

"Who was that?" I asked.

"A local reporter," he said tightly.

Chloe had caught the interaction as well. "Celeste Simmons. Hotshot reporter for *Entertainment Daily*."

Mac turned to Eric. "Let's get off this stupid carpet and go inside."

"I'm all for that," Eric agreed, staring at the crowds as if he might be expecting a sniper attack.

I realized he had been doing that, scrutinizing the entire area, the whole time we'd been out there. He met my glance and I said, "I'm so glad you're here."

He winked at me, then continued scanning the crowds. And within seconds, we were inside the lobby.

It was so opulent, I had to catch my breath. Massive marble pillars stood sentinel at each of the corners while Chinese murals covered the walls and ceiling.

"Beautiful," I said.

Chloe just nodded as we both tried to take in everything at once.

"Mac." A tall man in an elegant black suit approached and spoke quietly to Mac for a moment. He signaled an usher, who rushed over. "Jess, show Mr. Sullivan and his friends to row ten, seats six through nine."

"Yes, sir."

"Thanks," Mac said, shaking the man's hand.

"We can talk after the film," he said.

"Looking forward to it," Mac murmured, and we all followed the usher into the theater itself.

"He looks familiar," Chloe said.

"Studio head," he said briefly. "Nice guy. I'll introduce you later."

"That would be nice," she said, intrigued.

When we were settled, Eric said, "Good seats."

Mac nodded. "Got the sweet spot."

"What's the sweet spot?" I asked.

"It's the spot in the audience where the sound is the most perfect."

"Huh," I said.

"Of course," he added, "this theater has state-of-the-art acoustics, so the sound's going to be good almost anywhere you sit. Still, I was told that these seats are the best."

Chloe frowned. "For a big premiere like this, aren't all the seats assigned?"

"Yes, they are," Mac said.

I gazed at Mac. "You seemed anxious to get inside. What was going on out there?"

He smiled and ran his fingers along my jawline. "It just got a little weird."

I almost let it go, but I had to ask. "Because of that reporter?"

He breathed deeply, and I wasn't sure he would tell me. But then he said, "Yeah. I've run into her before. She's not a nice person."

Chloe leaned over. "Are you talking about Celeste Simmons?"

Mac frowned. "You know her."

"Do I ever," Chloe said flatly, glancing at me. "She's a snake. Avoid her at all costs."

I hated to think that Mac had to deal with someone like that. And Chloe, too. "I will. Thanks."

I put the troubling thoughts aside and settled in to people-watch as members of the audience took their seats. Hollywood seemed to be made up of really good-looking, beautifully dressed people. I wondered how many of them showed up for events like this on a regular basis.

Both Chloe and Mac moved to the aisle to chat with

people they knew, while Eric and I remained seated. He asked more about my upcoming church renovation project.

"I'll stop by and check it out when I get back to town," he said.

"I hope you will," I said. "And don't worry. I'm not expecting any trouble because, you know, it's a church."

He chuckled. "I don't expect any trouble, either, but you know me. It's my town, so I'll want to check things out, see who's doing what and whether you're all getting along."

I patted his arm. "I appreciate that, Eric. And anytime you want to pick up a power drill and give us a hand, you're always welcome."

He smirked. "Unless I'm forced to use it as a weapon, that's not going to happen."

A minute later, Chloe returned to her seat next to Eric.

"Everything okay?" he asked.

"Sure. It's always a little frantic, though, meeting and greeting people at these events."

A few seconds later, Mac joined me and leaned over to kiss my cheek. "Next time I have to get up and talk to anyone, you're coming with me."

"As long as they don't gush over the fact that I'm a building contractor."

He laughed. "I'll try to keep them from fawning over you."

"Well now, MacKintyre Sullivan," a voice from the aisle said. "Is it really you?"

He whipped around, blinked once, and then jumped up. "Siobhán!" He moved quickly to the aisle, where he gave the woman a big hug and a kiss on her cheek. "How are you?"

Her smile was bright and friendly, and she held on to Mac's hands and squeezed. He simply grinned.

"Who the hell is that?" Chloe whispered.

"I don't know," I whispered. She was lovely, and her Irish accent was charming. Her dress was a stunning emerald green that accentuated the red hair that she'd pulled up and off her face in a classic updo.

I was starting to hate her, and I was itching to smack that goofy grin off Mac's face. Then I blinked and shook my head. Where had those thoughts come from? I didn't know the woman well enough to hate her. And I would never hurt Mac. Well, unless he continued aiming his googly eyes at this woman.

"Do you want me to scratch her eyes out?" Chloe asked quietly.

I smiled. "Thank you."

"I'm here to help."

At that moment, the woman, Siobhán, waved at me and smiled brilliantly. She looked at Mac. "And now I can see where you got your inspiration for Shana."

Mac turned and looked at me. "That's my Shannon."

That's my Shannon. His words warmed me all over. And as soon as I had that thought, I wondered if I was as big a fool as I sounded like in my head. First, I wanted to smack him, and now I was getting all googly-eyed myself. Idiot.

"Ah, the beautiful Shannon you've said so much about." She nodded slowly, still smiling. "And isn't Shannon the most lovely name?"

Mac's grin was wide as he waved me over. "Come and meet Siobhán, the costar of *The Edge of Danger*."

I took a deep breath, stood up, and made my way out to the aisle.

He took my hand. "Sweetheart, this is Siobhán O'Leary. She plays Shana in the movie."

I began to breathe again. "It's nice to meet you, Siobhán. You, um, you're exactly as Mac described Shana in the book."

"And so are you," she said with an impish smile. "'Tis a pleasure to meet you, Shannon."

A man in the third row was waving frantically and finally caught Siobhán's attention. He beckoned her to join him.

She waved at the man, then turned back to us. "I believe Terence has found our seats."

"Let's talk afterward," Mac said. "I'd like to say hello to Terence and catch up with the two of you."

"Aye, we'd both love that." She shook my hand. "I hope you enjoy the film, Shannon."

"I know I will."

After she walked away to join her husband, Mac finally turned and gazed at me. "Seeing the two of you together is mind-blowing."

"I suppose it's the hair," I said lightly.

"I think it's a little more than that." He moved in and gently kissed my cheek, then leaned his forehead against mine. "I'm afraid I'll smudge your lipstick if I kiss your mouth."

I smiled. "I wouldn't mind, but Chloe might."

He nodded and kissed my other cheek. "Can't piss off Chloe."

I managed a laugh, and then we made our way back to our seats. "Did you have anything to do with the casting?" I asked.

"I know why you're asking, and no, I didn't have anything to do with it," he said. "But seeing Siobhán here tonight and then looking at you standing next to her, it makes me realize how absolutely brilliant our casting director was. She cast Siobhán based solely on my description of Shana in the book."

Mac had written the description of Jake's new love interest shortly after he and I met.

I still remembered how much his character Jake loved Shana's tangled red hair and wide green eyes the color of seagrass.

And, yes, he could've been describing me.

Remembering those early days, I realized I had no right to be jealous. I smiled at him. "Siobhán is beautiful."

"Yes, she is. And that Irish accent of hers really helped nail the character."

I loved his enthusiasm, even when it was directed toward another woman. "Have you seen the whole movie put together yet?"

"This'll be the first time." He grinned like an excited little kid. "I'm really psyched."

I squeezed his hand. "Me too."

The lights began to dim and the audience cheered. But before the movie could begin, a man walked onto the stage holding a microphone. It was the same well-dressed fellow Mac had pointed out when we first walked into the theater lobby. The head of the studio, Mac had said.

"I'll just take a moment to welcome you all and to thank you for being here. We're very excited about the newest Jake Slater thriller, and we think you'll love it, too. I want to make sure you all know about the party in the lobby after the film is over. At that time, I'll take a minute to introduce some of the very important folks who made this all possible."

There was polite applause, then he said, "For now, please sit back and enjoy the film. And we'll talk later."

This time the applause was more enthusiastic, especially when the lights dimmed completely and the film began.

"That was the best movie I've ever seen," Chloe gushed when the lights came up.

"I'm exhausted," I said. "And exhilarated. I swear I thought he was going to die in that helicopter. And I've read the book! I know how it ends!"

"Me too," Chloe said with a laugh. "Wow, I'm not even sure I can stand up."

Mac laughed. "So it was good, huh?"

"Good?" Chloe said. "It was absolutely fantastic."

"It was incredible," I agreed.

"Damn good," Eric agreed. "I've liked all of the Jake Slater films, but I'd say this one was a few notches above the rest."

"Because he fell in love," Chloe said with a sigh.

I gazed at Mac, who smiled back at me. "That makes all the difference."

Eric thought about it. "Guess that's true. Luckily, though, he still killed a bunch of bad guys and saved the planet from thermonuclear destruction. But, yeah, sure, it was kind of nice that he met a beautiful woman who didn't die in the end."

Chloe laughed and elbowed Eric. "So romantic."

"Hey, come on," Eric protested. "Jake's women usually die a horrible death in the end. Right?"

Chloe rolled her eyes. "Yes, you're right."

"I'm glad you all liked it," Mac said. "I thought they did a really good job."

"They didn't change much of your original story line," I said.

"You noticed that?" he asked.

I smiled. "Well, I've only read the book five or six times. So, yeah, I noticed."

"That's my girl."

Back in the lobby, I was finally introduced to Stephen Dane, the amazingly good-looking man who played Jake Slater. Mac called him Dane, and it seemed that everyone he talked to called him Dane, too. He was smooth and funny, tall and dashing, and really very nice. After doing four movies together, he and Mac had become good friends.

"He's never invited me to Lighthouse Cove," Dane said. "And now I know why."

I gave Mac a quizzical look.

"He's too slick," Mac said, but his lips twisted into a sardonic smile at Stephen. "Women fall at his feet."

I smiled at Dane. "Is that true?"

He scratched his head. "Uh, hmm. Hey, if Mac says so, it must be true."

We all laughed and I said, "Well, I hope you'll visit sometime. Lighthouse Cove is a charming little town with world-class sensibilities."

"That's the perfect way to describe it," Chloe said.

"Mac seems to love it there," he said. "I was completely shocked when he told me where he was moving. He's always seemed like a big-city guy to me. New

York, London, LA. But I guess I was wrong, because he seems pretty happy in your little town." He cast an admiring glance at me. "And I can understand why."

We spoke about the film for another minute, and then he moved on to mingle with a new group.

Mac and Eric went to the bar to get us all another glass of wine, and Chloe and I had a chance to talk.

"You know," she began, shaking her head, "it's a good thing Eric is so gorgeous, because otherwise, I could really fall for Stephen Dane. He's so good-looking, isn't he?"

"He seems nice, too," I said.

She glanced around the room, spied Eric laughing at something Mac said, and sighed. "I think we're both pretty lucky."

"I absolutely agree."

We watched as a couple of people stopped to talk to Mac, and the whole group chatted while they waited for the bartender.

"Mac seems to know everyone here," Chloe remarked.

"I guess he does. A lot of them have worked together on all four of the Jake Slater movies, so that's, like, eight years or more."

I watched him talking earnestly to another couple, and then he threw his head back and laughed. I couldn't help but smile as my heart soared at the sight. At the same time, I felt a niggling sense of anxiety.

"Look at him," I said softly. "So happy. He loves being here. These are his people."

Chloe followed my gaze and nodded. "Despite what you hear about the showbiz, there are mostly nice people around here." She shrugged. "I love working here, too, but I love Eric more."

"You're one of the lucky ones," I said. "You can have it both ways."

When Chloe had taken on the duties of executive producer last year, she made some changes to the production schedule so that she could take more time off to be with Eric in Lighthouse Cove.

"Yeah, I can have my cake and eat it, too," she said, and gazed across the room at the slow-moving line to the bar. "And so can Mac."

"Yes, he can. But I sometimes wonder why he sticks around Lighthouse Cove. It's such a small town and there's not a lot to do."

She laughed. "Well, when he's not helping you solve murders and catch criminals, he spends his time writing books. He can do that anywhere. And now he's got the veterans' village. And you. Let's face it, Sis. You're his comfort zone."

"But you know what I mean, Chloe. We don't have a lot of big-city attractions in Lighthouse Cove. We've got one movie theater, one playhouse, and as far as fancy stores and restaurants go, I can count them on one hand."

"Don't forget our gambling dens and houses of ill repute," she added with a laugh and an eye roll. "Oh, and I wouldn't tell your best friends Jane or Emily, or our Uncle Pete, that we don't have any good restaurants."

I winced. My friend Jane Hennessey owned the most elegant restaurant and hotel in the state. Uncle Pete owned a fabulous winery in the Anderson Valley, a mere hour's drive away, plus an Italian restaurant and wine bar in town that was a big hit with locals and travelers alike. And my friend Emily had the most delightful tea shop in Northern California.

"Okay, you're right about that," I said.

"Look, Mac is not exactly stuck in Lighthouse Cove," she argued. "He can travel anytime he wants to and go anywhere he wants. But he loves our town and he loves you. He's happy."

I stared at her for a long moment. "So you're saying . . . I'm being an idiot?"

"Kind of," she said with a smile. "But I love you anyway."

I gazed across the room at the small group that had gathered around Mac and Eric. Siobhán and her husband, Terence, had joined them. Mac was telling them a story, and they were all listening and laughing. Siobhán wrapped her arm around Mac's waist, and he gazed at her fondly as he continued the story. Terence looked on with a good-natured smile. Everyone laughed when Mac reached the punch line. He was in his element, clearly having the time of his life with his very good showbiz friends.

My sister took hold of my hand and gave it a little squeeze. "Don't read anything into this, Shannon. He's not Tommy."

"Oh God, I know that." Tommy Gallagher had been my beloved boyfriend all through high school, until newcomer Whitney Reid deliberately tried to break us up. She was the classic mean girl, and as it turned out, it had been alarmingly easy for her to accomplish her goal. Tommy's betrayal broke my heart, but I got over it—after a few years.

Obviously, my feelings for Mac went way beyond high school. He was the love of my life. But as I watched him chat with other members of the Jake Slater crew, I had to wonder if he missed this fast-paced life he'd given up in exchange for Lighthouse Cove and me. For the past few years, I had thought that he and I were totally solid together, but every so often, these doubts jumped up to bite me. It was stupid, really, because Mac and I had recently moved in together. We loved each other. I was just being silly.

Silly or not, though, the one thing I didn't doubt was the fact that if Mac Sullivan broke my heart, I would never get over it.

I shuddered involuntarily and had to give myself a quick, stern warning. *Don't be a wimp! You're stronger than that,* I said to myself.

A few minutes later, Mac and Eric finally returned, carrying two wineglasses each. "Sorry for the long wait," Mac said, handing me a glass.

"No problem," I said, taking a sip of wine. "You looked like you were having a good time."

"Yeah, it's great to see everyone."

Shortly after that, Siobhán and Terence joined us, and I was able to learn more about them. They were both born and raised outside of Galway. Terence was the star of a popular Irish television series, in which he played a warrior from ancient times. *He would be perfect in that role,* I thought. They had been married for two years.

At that very moment, Chloe gave me a look that I interpreted to mean, *He's so hot!*

Siobhán laughed at the look on Chloe's face. "I know what you're thinking."

"I hope not," Chloe said, frowning.

Siobhán sighed dramatically. "Let me assure you that it's not easy to live with someone like Terence. I've taken to carrying a big stick in order to beat the women off him."

"You know she's exaggerating," Terence said, taking a sip of beer from the bottle he held. "The stick isn't all that big."

We laughed, and I found myself enjoying the two of them very much. In the end, as we waited outside for the limousine to pick us up, I joined Mac in inviting them to visit us in Lighthouse Cove. Mac had spent the last ten minutes talking up the town and everything it had to offer. I wanted to kiss him when he talked about all my fabulous construction projects around town, including the veterans' village and Jane's beautiful new hotel and restaurant up at the Gables.

As Siobhán and Terence jumped into their own limo and took off, I began to think that maybe Chloe had been right. When it came to worrying about Mac, maybe I really was an idiot.

Chapter Three

Lighthouse Cove, California

Mac walked into the house, set down our suitcases, and flopped onto the living room couch. "It's good to be home."

I flopped down next to him. "I couldn't agree more."

Thanks to Mac's publisher, we had flown in a private jet from Hollywood to Mendocino, yet another ridiculously extravagant treat that I would've loved to become accustomed to. We had picked up Mac's car at the airport and then driven an hour up the coast to Lighthouse Cove.

We sat on the couch pressed up against each other for at least ten minutes before either of us moved or said a word. I was afraid we might fall asleep right there, and I didn't want that to happen. It was just noon, and I still wanted to get some work done. I needed to do payroll and talk to my foremen. I was hoping to confirm schedules and check up on my crew.

But finally I just sighed. "That was really fun."

Mac wrapped his arms around me, and I snuggled

even closer to him. "Yeah, it was. It was great seeing all those people, and I've got to say, I was real happy to have you there with me. I just hope you had a good time, too."

"I was with you and Chloe and Eric, so that's always fun. And I met some really nice people that I hope we'll see again. Working with Chloe was a blast, as always. The movie was outstanding, and that whole evening was magical. And it was fun to drive through Hollywood and Beverly Hills and go shopping with Chloe." I smiled at the memory. "Now *that* was an education."

I could feel him smiling when he said, "And now it's nice to be home."

"So nice," I murmured.

He pressed a kiss to the top of my head. "What do you say we go pick up the kids? They'd probably love to be home, too."

I beamed up at him. The "kids" he was talking about were our animals: Robbie, our West Highland terrier; Tiger, our orange marmalade cat; and Luke, short for Lucifer, an adorable black cat that Mac had rescued as a kitten when he first moved to town. They were such good, well-behaved pets that one of our animal-lover neighbors was happy to babysit them for the week we were gone.

"I say that's a wonderful idea."

"And then what do you say we walk over to Bella Rossa, bring home a pizza, and hang out and watch TV?"

I rested my head on his shoulder. It occurred to me that maybe I wouldn't get any work done that afternoon, but I was okay with that. "You have all the best ideas."

Chloe and Eric had decided to rent a car and take a leisurely weeklong drive up the coast. Mac and I didn't have that kind of time to spend on this trip, and we were both okay with it. I knew he had to get back to his latest manuscript, and I had a company to run—specifically that big church project to prep for.

Every few hours, Chloe would text me quickie updates about the places they were seeing and the wonderful meals they were enjoying. She took pictures of everything, and I knew she was having the time of her life. She assured me that they would be back home before I started work on the church renovation.

It seemed that both Chloe and Eric were interested in checking out my church job. Eric had indicated that he wanted to check up on my team and make sure things were going smoothly. He always liked to know everything that was going on in "his town."

And Chloe wanted to get pictures and videos to feature on her show. Her audience enjoyed seeing unusual renovations with all the fun details included. And the truth was, I really liked having my sister working with me on my job sites. We had always worked well together, and I planned to coerce her into putting some time into my latest project.

Having been away for an entire week, I knew the first job I would have to tackle was the payroll. The number of crew members working for me had tripled in the last year, and my company and its bank account were thriving. Unfortunately, that meant it took a lot longer to get everyone paid, including our vendors. But I managed to get through it all, and within twenty-four hours of starting the task, everyone had received their checks by electronic transfer. I proudly considered that a modern-day miracle, given the fact that for the past seven years, I'd been writing out actual checks and driving around town to hand them out.

A few years ago, one of my crew members had accused me of using an abacus to add up figures. It was a rude, libelous claim. I was a thoroughly modern girl, just a little slow on the uptake when it came to the world of technology.

That was then. Now I was a wiz at the whole business technology thing, and strangely enough, I really enjoyed it.

For the next week, it was business as usual around our house. Mac had settled back into his writing schedule, which consisted of waking up early, usually while it was still dark; starting a pot of coffee; and then heading to his office over the garage to work on his latest book for an hour or two. By the time I got myself out of bed and dressed for the day, Mac was back in the kitchen and usually at the stove, making bacon and eggs or pancakes or whatever struck his fancy.

This morning, I couldn't tell what he was making, only that it smelled wonderful. Robbie was scurrying for joy at the sight of me while Tiger and Luke watched him with such disdain, I wanted to laugh. Meanwhile, Mac stood at the counter preparing their meals.

I gave Mac a kiss on his cheek. "Good morning."

He turned and kissed me on the lips. "Very good morning."

Robbie barked, and I acceded to his demand for

attention. As soon as I was seated at the table, both Luke and Tiger moved in to twirl themselves around my ankles.

It was such a domestic scene, I thought. Despite their antics, all three of them were watching Mac's every move. Robbie grew fidgety and I pointed to the floor. He sat instantly, and I gave him a light back scratch for his good behavior. "That's my boy."

"Here you go, you crazy beasts," Mac said, setting their food bowls down on their individual feeding mats, then carrying their water bowls over from the sink and placing them next to the food.

Without a second glance at me, the little ones raced away to their respective stations and commenced gobbling.

"I think they like you best," I said, watching them bolt down their morning meals.

"I'm a likable guy," Mac said. He walked over, put his arms around me, and kissed me. "Hi again."

"Hi," I said.

After a moment, he whispered, "I made bagels. We have cream cheese. And there's sausages."

I smiled. "Mm, I like you best, too."

Monday finally arrived, and I left the house early to get to the old Lighthouse Church for the first official meeting of key members of my crew and the artistic director of the museum project. Outside on the front steps, I gathered with the group, which included my two foremen, Wade Chambers and Carla Harrison; my head carpenter, Sean Brogan; my stonemason, Niall Rose; and my wood-carving expert, Amanda Walsh. Since the interior walls of the church were almost completely made of stone and wood, Amanda and Niall would be key players in this project.

I was also glad to see that Buck Buckner was here this morning. I knew that Chloe's Hollywood lighting director, with his electrical engineering expertise, would be an invaluable addition to the crew and the perfect person to have on hand during this walk-through. He would be able to nip any lighting problems in the bud as soon as they arose.

We would be joined shortly by the new artistic director of the art museum of Lighthouse Cove, Madeline Whistler, and her assistant, Sarah Spindler.

I was hoping Mac might show up as well, just to take a look around the church. He loved checking out the odd location in case he could work it into his latest plotline. At dinner the night before, he'd told me he would try to stop by and take a look at the place.

"The outside of the church is awesome," he'd said. "But I've never been inside."

"It's even more intriguing than the outside," I'd assured him, and could see his mind starting to spin ideas around.

"I could use it for a hostage situation," he'd mused. "Or maybe just blow it up, you know?"

I had observed him cautiously. "You're still writing fiction, right?"

He'd laughed. "Yeah. Just fiction. But don't you love the visual? Those Gothic lines are so magnificently creepy."

"That is a perfect description," I had agreed.

For a small-town church, the Victorian Gothic influences were impressive, with radically tall spires, pointed arches, flying buttresses, lacy moldings, and fancy finials. There were gargoyles, too. And that was just on the outside of the building.

Besides Mac, I was also hoping that Chloe would show up today. I'd expected to hear from her over the weekend, but she hadn't called. I left a message that she was welcome to join the walk-through anytime.

My head foreman, Wade Chambers, and I had already been through the building a number of times with Madeline and our architects. We had gone over the blueprints a dozen times and had made countless lists and taken a gazillion notes and snapped innumerable photographs of everything Madeline had shown us.

We'd also had numerous meetings with our structural engineer in order to flesh out any flaws that might show up at some point during the project. I still had some questions for Madeline, specifically concerning the church basement. The small space down below the wide altar platform didn't seem to jibe with the old blueprints, but she had assured us that the rest of the space had been completely filled in and walled off. The structural engineer had given us his blessing to start the job. I was pretty sure we were on solid ground, so to speak, but it always helped to consult with experts to make sure.

This would be a fascinating and difficult job and would probably take a full year to complete, but in the end, this beautiful old Victorian Gothic church was going to be transformed into an amazing new art museum that our town and Madeline Whistler would be proud of.

In anticipation of the project ahead, I had studied dozens of designs of repurposed churches from all around the country. Several of the churches had been turned into museums and art galleries, but there were also restaurants, B and Bs, offices, shops, and private homes. It was always fun to see what someone with a little imagination could come up with.

In the case of our particular old church, we were starting with an intriguing building that was both lovely and fascinating. It wouldn't take much to fashion it into a world-class museum with universal appeal.

From the church steps, we could look out at the town square and beyond it: the beach, the pier, and the ocean. I had never realized what a beautiful view the churchgoers enjoyed from these steps.

I glanced around. "It looks like everyone's here except Madeline and her assistant. So I'll take this moment to officially introduce you all to Buck Buckner." I put my hand on Buck's shoulder. "He worked as the lighting director on my sister Chloe's show, and he was awesome. He's got an impressive résumé and mad skills, and Chloe loves him, so that's good enough for me. And he's also a good guy."

"Thanks, Shannon," Buck said with a grin. "Nice to officially meet you all."

"Great to meet you, too, Buck," said Sean Brogan, my head carpenter and one of my oldest friends. "Officially, that is."

The others joined in welcoming Buck to the team. They were chuckling at my "official" introduction because I had "unofficially" introduced everyone at the pub last week. My guys had given Buck high marks, especially when he picked up the tab.

"Here comes Madeline," Sean called from where he stood near the side of the bottom step.

The woman cleared the building and walked toward us looking like she belonged on Madison Avenue in

New York City rather than the quaint town square of Lighthouse Cove. She wore an elegant black pantsuit with a white silk shirt, lots of gold jewelry, and shiny black pumps. She was lovely, with dark brown hair cut short and sleek. She carried a very chic black leather tote bag, and when she saw us standing here, she smiled and waved.

I took in my own outfit of blue jeans, denim shirt, and steel-toed boots and had to bite back a groan. But then I had to let it go. This, after all, was my signature look. Besides, my boots were really nice, as practical and as comfy as steel-toed boots could get. Same went for my jeans. What could I say? It all worked for me.

We watched as the new director of the art museum hurried over to join us on the steps. "I'm sorry I'm late. Have you all been waiting long?"

"We got here a few minutes early," I said, "so you're actually right on time."

Madeline let out a breath. "Oh, thank goodness."

I walked down the steps and shook her hand. "I know you've met Wade, but let me introduce you to a few of my crew that you might not have met yet." Turning to Carla and Sean, I introduced my second foreman and my head carpenter. They both greeted Madeline cheerfully with smiles and handshakes. Then, looking at my newest crew members, I began, "This is Niall Rose, our master stonemason. He's an artist with glass and stone and tile. Niall, this is Madeline Whistler."

Niall shook Madeline's hand. "'Tis a pleasure to meet you, Miss Whistler."

"Oh, please, it's Madeline," she said with a smile. "And it's nice to meet you, too, Niall. Are you . . . Scottish?"

"Och, aye," he said, going full Scottish and making me grin.

"And this is Amanda Walsh," I said, indicating the pretty brunette standing on my left. "She's brilliant when it comes to anything having to do with wood, including carving and cutouts."

"Nice to meet you," Amanda said.

"You, too, Amanda," Madeline said. "The church has a lot of wood surfaces, so I'll be happy to hear what you think."

"I look forward to checking it out," Amanda said.

Finally, I turned to our brand-new crew member. "And this is Buck Buckner, our electrical engineer and lighting designer."

The two greeted each other and shook hands, then Madeline checked her wristwatch. "Have any of you seen Sarah yet?"

"Not yet," I said, scanning the area. "Maybe she's inside already."

"I know she had one stop to make this morning, but she should be here any minute." Madeline smiled brightly. "We might as well get started."

We all followed Madeline up the wide stone steps. Like many churches throughout the ages, our Victorian church had its entrance facing west, which meant that when churchgoers walked inside and sat to pray, they would be facing east toward the altar. It was one of many little-known facts that I had come across while researching churches over the past few months to prepare for this job.

At the top of the steps, I took one more moment to enjoy the view of the picturesque wide blue cove that gave our town its name. Then I turned and followed the group through the beautifully carved heavy wooden doors of the Lighthouse Church.

"Don't close the door yet," Madeline said. "I've got to find the light switches first."

"I'll hold the door open," Amanda said. "I want to get a closer look at the carvings on these door panels."

Ten seconds later, my sister, Chloe, rushed in through the open doorway. "Hey, Sis."

"Hey." I hugged her. "I wasn't sure you'd be here, but I'm glad you made it."

"Me too." She smiled at everyone. "Hi, gang. Hope you don't mind if I join you." Then she saw Buck and grabbed him in a big hug. "Buck! How are you?"

"I'm great, Chloe. Thanks again for the glowing reference."

"You earned it," she said, and hugged him again. Then she turned to Madeline. "Hi. I'm Chloe, Shannon's sister. You must be Madeline. I've heard so much about you."

"Oh my God, I love your show!" Madeline said. "I'm a big fan."

Chloe beamed. "Then we'll be new best friends."

Madeline applauded like a fangirl.

Chloe laughed at me rolling my eyes, and said to Madeline, "It's great to meet you. And now I promise I'm going to shrink into the background and just listen to everything you have to say."

"Oh, no," Madeline said. "Please join in whenever you have any thoughts about what we're doing here."

Chloe winked at me and I just laughed. She knew I would be happy to have her help on any project, anytime.

Madeline reached for the light panel and flipped

several switches. "The good news is, we have lights and plenty of power. Amanda, you can close that door whenever you're ready."

"Ready," Amanda said, and pulled the door closed.

Wade glanced around. "Hey, looks like you cleaned up the place."

Madeline smiled ruefully. "We're getting close, but we've got a way to go yet. It practically took an act of congress to get Reverend Patterson and his wife to clear out all the years of junk they'd piled up around here." She waved her hands as if to erase her words. "I don't mean to complain. They worked here for over thirty years, so it's natural that they would have stacks and stacks of documents and schedules and correspondence and papers and tchotchkes and doohickeys and God knows what else." She stopped and frowned. "Well, it's a church, so I guess God really does know." She laughed at her own joke. "But there were so many other things shoved into drawers and cabinets and stuck inside closets and cubbyholes. And a lot of them are still there."

"What kinds of stuff?" Wade asked.

"Oh, old altar cloths and dozens of vestments and all the other things that the reverend wears when he's up on the altar. And there were chalices and cruets and incense holders and other stuff that I thought was, well, frankly, sort of sacred, you know? And they were all just shoved inside that huge cabinet inside the sacristy."

Carla's eyes narrowed. "Do you think the reverend is a hoarder?"

Madeline thought for a moment. "Oh, no. He's a lovely man, very kind and smart and practical. He's got a real spiritual vibe about him."

He sounds wonderful, I thought. "What about his wife?"

"She's as sweet as she can be, although I'll admit, I don't know her really well. But she seems charming and very upbeat. The two of them have been living here for such a long time, I suppose it's natural that they would've been collecting things all this time. And according to the church secretary, their people give them gifts all year long, so that might account for the buildup."

"That's reasonable," Wade said.

"Yes," Madeline said. "Many of the old vestments are practically threadbare, but I suppose they don't want to simply throw them away. Or maybe they're not allowed to. I really don't know the procedure for getting rid of things like that."

It was my turn to frown. "But Reverend Patterson's new church is just a few blocks away. Couldn't their congregation help with packing and moving their things?"

"They've helped a lot, truly, but Mrs. Patterson wouldn't let them touch the stuff in the sacristy." Madeline shrugged, then glanced at me. "I'll show you. I assume everything's still in there. And by the way, their new church really is just beautiful. Very modern and filled with light. So I wonder if maybe they just didn't want to take all their old things over there."

"That's possible," I said.

"On the bright side," she continued, "some of the interesting old relics and traditional vestments will become part of our permanent exhibit in the new art museum."

"That's a clever idea," Amanda said.

Madeline nodded. "I thought so, too. A few of the pieces are antiques. It'll be a nice touch."

"And by the way," Sean said, "we can handle any additional cleanup if you need it."

She breathed a sigh of relief. "That makes me very happy. Thank you."

She reached out and touched my arm. "Forgive me for going off like that. Reverend Patterson and his wife are good people. I'm just so anxious to get the ball rolling."

"We are, too," I assured her.

She turned around and spread her arms out to indicate the area we were standing in. "So let's get on with the tour. We're standing in what is properly known as the *narthex*. You might think of it as a lobby or a foyer, but I plan to continue referring to it as the narthex, even after it becomes the art museum." She smiled at each of us. "I have an affection for the old terms, so you might want to write them down. There might be a quiz."

Buck's eyes were wide. "Good to know." He looked around the space and gazed up at the ceiling.

I followed his gaze and looked up at the heavily paneled ceiling that rose some twenty feet above us. Once we stepped into the main part of the church, the ceiling would soar even higher. But above this section was the choir loft, so the narthex ceiling was naturally lower.

"The word *narthex* sounds really old," Carla said. "Like medieval, maybe."

"Oh, it's at least that old," Madeline said.

I smiled at Carla. "Good Scrabble word, huh?"

She wiggled her eyebrows. "You know it. I could get seventeen points at least." She and her husband were rabid Scrabble players.

I turned to Madeline. "You and I have taken this walk-through a number of times over the past few months, but most of my crew are seeing it all for the first time. I'm hoping as we move through the church, you'll explain what you'd like to have done in each area."

"I'll be happy to," Madeline said. She checked her watch again. "I probably shouldn't worry about Sarah since she did mention that she might stop at the tea shop for pastries."

Carla grinned. "That's the absolute best reason to be late."

Madeline chuckled. "You're so right."

Sean rubbed his stomach. "Now you've got me hungry for a cheese Danish."

"You're always hungry for a cheese Danish," Wade said.

Sean ignored him and turned to Madeline. "Would you mind calling Sarah and telling her to speed it up a little? I missed breakfast."

I was about to explain to Madeline that he was joking, but she had already started laughing out loud. "I'm going to enjoy working with this group."

And I thought for the thousandth time how lucky I was that I worked with the best, funniest, smartest people in the world.

Chapter Four

Madeline was still chuckling when she said, "Okay, on with the tour. And please feel free to make your own notes or ask questions if you see a particular area that calls out for attention." She pointed to the doors we'd just come through. "This, of course, will be the main entrance to the art museum. And most of this area, the narthex, will obviously act as a lobby of sorts. This is where we'll collect the admission fees. We'll also have a cloakroom, where we'll check bags and coats and packages."

"Oh, right," Amanda said. "These days, you can't allow certain devices or bottles or even food."

"So true. But there'll be benches along the wall for people to sit and wait for friends or to take a short break. The ticket counter will be over here." She pointed. "Some of you have already seen the blueprints, so you have an idea of the design of the ticket counter. It'll be a large three-sided counter in which some of my staff will work, along with a member of security. We'll greet visitors, take money, hand out brochures, provide information, et cetera."

"You've planned a gift shop in here as well," I added.

"Oh, yes," she said, and pointed at the north end of the narthex. "The gift shop will be located down there, and I'm very excited about it. Honestly, don't you just love a museum gift shop?"

"I do," I admitted.

"My wife does, too," Wade said. "I'm more partial to a museum pub, myself."

We all smiled at that. Then Madeline said, "Any other questions about the narthex?"

"How about you, Buck?" I asked.

He was staring up at the ceiling. Finally, he pointed out the three thick wooden beams that crossed from the church's outer wall to the inner wall separating the narthex from the main part of the church. Each held a large wrought iron chandelier that gave off a nice decorative light. "We can hang spotlight cams on each of those beams without too much trouble." He looked at Madeline. "And we can regulate the brightness and darkness from the lighting board. We'll also be able to aim the spots in any direction and change them if necessary, right from the control room or from an app."

"Wow," she said. "There's an app for that?"

"Sure is," he said, grinning. "I have it on my phone and it'll save lives, for sure. I assume you'll be changing the art installations throughout the museum on a regular basis, right? So, yeah, we've got this Wi-Fi system that will allow your lighting person to realign and redirect the pin spots from down here."

Madeline shot me a glance. "You never mentioned a Wi-Fi system."

"I wanted to let Buck tell you about it," I said. Buck and I had barely discussed the system, but I was familiar with it and had planned on discussing it in detail with him soon. It made me happy to see that he was taking the initiative to explain the process to the art director.

"It sounds fantastic," she said.

"It really is," Buck said with a grin. "So whenever you want to change up the artwork, we can readjust the lighting in a few minutes instead of taking hours to climb a scaffold and fiddle with the equipment from fifty feet in the air."

"I'm very impressed," Madeline said.

So was I, but all I did was smile at Buck and consider giving him an immediate raise in pay.

Madeline checked behind her to make sure everyone in the group was keeping up before pushing open one of the huge wooden double doors. "Let's enter the nave."

She held one of the doors open for us to walk through to the main part of the church. "As I said, this main area of the church is called the *nave*."

The first thing I noticed when we stepped into the main body of the church was the silence. Nobody spoke for a minute, and it somehow seemed proper that we would share this brief moment of contemplation before moving on. I was eight years old when my mother died, and my father dealt with it by throwing all of his time and energy into his work. He brought me and Chloe with him to his construction sites, and that's how we grew up.

It was funny that I had never gotten involved in anything too spiritual despite the fact that Lighthouse Cove was considered to be a magnet for every mystical, otherworldly discipline known to humankind. If you walked around our town square, you'd find that at least a third of the shops and spas offered stuff like sacred stone healing, chakra cleansing, and aura color enhancement.

The closest I'd ever come to doing something spiritual was the time I took a meditation class with Lizzie and Jane. We drove out to the Sanctuary of the Four Winds, which was a famous Buddhist retreat by the redwood forest outside of town. The six-hour class consisted of lots of chanting, a marathon meditation session, and a healthy lunch prepared by the Buddhist monks who lived there. I must confess, the meditation put me to sleep. But the lunch was good.

Buck stared up at the ceiling again. "Wow, this gets really high, really fast."

"Will you be able to use your Wi-Fi system in here?" Madeline asked.

"Oh, sure," Buck said. "We'll just need some extra long ladders or scaffolding to run the initial wiring and install the lighting and equipment."

"We've already designed the scaffolding plan," Sean said. "I'll go over it with you after we're through here. But we've also got the use of an articulated boom lift, so that'll be a big help when we're placing the lighting."

"That's awesome," Buck said with relief.

We walked down the main aisle, and Madeline explained her ideas. "These pews are beautiful, aren't they?"

"I love this dark wood," Amanda said. "It's so rich and smooth. From so many years of use, I imagine."

"Yes," Madeline said. "We plan to keep some of these pews in place so that visitors can sit and reflect on the artwork, or just take a quick, quiet break. But the rest of this area will be cleared away for the artwork. We'll install a number of pedestals for displaying sculptures, as well as several long glass cabinets to show smaller pieces of art and sculptures. We'll also have some display cabinets mounted on the walls that will feature our collection of antiquarian books, many with jewel-encrusted bindings."

"Can't wait to see it all," Carla murmured.

"I'm excited, too," Madeline said. "Now let's proceed to the *apse*."

"The apse?" Wade repeated.

"Yes." Madeline spelled it for us, and Wade tapped the word into his tablet.

"Is the altar part of the apse?" Wade asked.

"Yes. The apse encompasses most of the front section of the church, including the altar, the sacristy, and the smaller chapels behind the altar. You also have the *transepts*, which are the two aisles that run crosswise and lead to the outer doors at each side of the church."

She pointed first to the right aisle. "The south transept." Then she pointed to the left. "The north transept." She glanced around at the assembled crew. "As you can imagine, all of those individual sections can be divided into even smaller parts with specific names, but we'll keep it simple for now."

"Thank you," Wade muttered in relief.

As we continued walking down the main aisle, Madeline pointed out the heavily carved stone columns whose archways led to a wide hallway that circled around the back of the central platform that held the altar.

At least a dozen stained glass windows stood at intervals high above the stone columns.

"Will you keep the stained glass windows?" Buck asked.

"Oh, absolutely," Madeline said. "Aren't they gorgeous?"

"The colors are amazing," Carla said, then studied them more carefully. "Wait. Are those the stations of the cross?"

"Yes," Madeline said brightly. "I know we've had discussions about getting rid of the religious symbols so that we don't offend anyone, but I truly can't bear to part with the windows. I'll be doing a bit more research on them, but I believe I've tracked down the group of glass artists who created them back in 1867."

"Wow, that's some researching," Buck said.

Madeline smiled. "That's part of my job."

"And that way," I said, "you can talk about the windows as artwork and not purely religious works."

"Exactly." She looked pleased that I understood.

"Maybe I'm hallucinating," Carla said, "but the closer we get to the altar area, the more I think I can smell incense."

"I smell it, too," Madeline said. "It makes sense, though, doesn't it? Reverend Patterson was saying mass in here up until a few months ago. And he used incense in a lot of his ceremonies."

"And others were doing the same thing for a hundred years before that, right?" Sean said. "After all that time, the incense has probably permeated the wood."

Wade sniffed the air. "I get a waft of it every so often."

"Isn't it fascinating how it still lingers?" Madeline said.

Amanda took in a deep breath, slowly exhaled as she spoke. "Yeah."

At the foot of the steps that led to the central platform and the altar itself, Madeline pointed. "We talked about removing the altar but decided against it. It's made of extremely heavy stone, and it was built into the platform, so removing it would be costly and difficult. We'll simply incorporate it as a piece of artwork all on its own."

"It is an amazing design," Carla said. "So . . . stark."

Madeline smiled. "Isn't it?"

"If you don't mind, Madeline," I said, "before we get into the apse and its features, I wanted to touch on some security issues. Carla is our expert on everything to do with security, and she'll be supervising the installation of the security system as part of the control room we'll be designing in the basement."

"Wonderful," Madeline said, aiming her brilliant smile at Carla. "I've been anxious to hear your plans."

"I'll keep it brief," Carla said. "I think you're already aware of most of this, but for the sake of everyone else involved, we plan to install state-of-the-art closed-circuit cameras and sensors in every sector that will indicate motion, temperature, and changes in moisture levels. Their range will encompass every possible inch of the museum."

"And a backup plan?" I asked.

"Naturally," she said with a smile. "We'll have backup power for security as well as an emergency lighting system." She glanced at Buck. "Do you have any expertise in that area?"

"For sure." He grinned. "I've gotcha covered."

I maintained my composure even though I wanted

to grin, too. The synergy of my crew was making me very happy and proud.

Madeline smiled at each of us. "At the risk of repeating myself, I'm very impressed."

I turned to Wade, who was my HVAC expert. "Speaking of moisture levels and temperatures, can you talk a little bit about the HVAC system we'll be installing?"

"You bet," he said. "It'll work in conjunction with the security monitors and include an air filter system to minimize dust and air impurities that could degrade the artwork. We'll map out each of the sectors of the museum so we can allow for individual requirements of heat and humidity levels, depending on the artwork being displayed and the levels of exposure to light and air."

"That's exactly what I was going to ask for," Madeline said. "Thank you for making my job so much easier."

"It's our pleasure," I said, very happy with her reaction.

We continued walking toward the altar area.

"Wow, that dome is spectacular," Buck said.

"I love it," Chloe said.

The ceiling above the altar was a beautifully painted dome, and the walls surrounding the space were arched.

We all stared up at the huge half dome that hovered over most of the platform. The wall behind it was curved as well, following the lines of the platform.

"Isn't it great?" Madeline nodded enthusiastically. "As far as I'm concerned, it's the highlight of the entire space."

"I'll bet Reverend Patterson wished he could take it with him."

“You know he did,” Madeline revealed with a smile.

“It’s so beautiful,” Carla said, and continued making notes on her tablet. Wade and I did the same, and we each took pictures as we moved around the church. I wanted to get every possible angle of all the areas so we would be able to easily refer to each sector and make changes as we went along.

“Can you tell us any details about this dome?” Wade asked. “Or half dome, actually. Either way, it’s really impressive.”

Madeline stared up at the dramatic structure that hovered almost thirty feet above the altar. “Technically, our architect refers to it as a semidome. And the pastoral painting is so charming, isn’t it? Trees and flowers and sheep. And the good shepherd, of course. And you can see blue sky and fluffy clouds along the top section.”

“Are those camels?” Sean asked, pointing at one of the panels.

Madeline laughed. “Yes. And palm trees. I think it’s just marvelous.”

“From the back of the church, it looks like a painting,” Wade said.

“It’s actually made up of thousands of tiny mosaic tiles,” Madeline said.

“I worked with a mosaic artist for a short time last year,” I said. “That’s hard work.”

Carla tried bending over to get another perspective. “The artists must’ve been working upside down for a while.”

Madeline seemed to enjoy our enthusiasm. “I want to demonstrate something now, and the tiles have something to do with it. Wade, will you help me?”

“Sure.”

"If everyone else will remain here," she said, then took Wade's arm and led him up the three steps. Then she turned. "As you must know by now, so many things in a church are symbolic of that particular faith. This is one I only learned recently, and it's simple, really. The three steps that lead up to the altar are said to represent the holy trinity."

"Interesting," Carla said.

"Yes," Madeline said. "And honestly, I can't verify that one. But I can verify that the altar must always be built at a higher level than the rest of the church."

"Oh yeah," Wade said. "That makes sense."

Madeline looked at my foreman. "Okay, Wade, we're going to walk toward that wall."

"Deeper under the dome," Wade said in a formidable baritone voice, making us all laugh.

We watched them walk toward the altar and beyond to the back wall. Then Madeline and Wade began a quiet conversation about the latest restaurants they'd been to.

And we could hear every word!

"Whoa!" Sean said.

Carla began to laugh. "You guys, we can hear every word you're saying."

"I'll have to try that restaurant," Sean said.

"That wasn't really the point." Madeline laughed. "My point is that the shape of the dome and the arched wall behind us create a phenomenon that some scientists call 'whispering walls' or 'whispering arches.' It's fascinating and a little eerie, don't you think?"

I turned around and gave my crew a meaningful look. "Did everyone hear what happened? Do you understand what it means?"

"Uh, yeah," Sean said. "Don't talk to anyone under the dome because we'll all hear you."

I chuckled. "Okay, yeah. But there's also an architectural phenomenon happening here."

Chloe leaned in to whisper in my ear. "And any renovations in this area will have to be done with care so as not to hinder said phenomenon."

"You got that right," I murmured.

Wade looked a little dazed as he crossed the platform and joined us. "Could you really hear every word?"

"Oh yeah," I said. "She asked you what you had for dinner last night. You told her you went out to a new restaurant and had an amazing steak."

He was taken aback. "Um, yeah. I said that. And also, this is crazy."

"I've heard that some really old churches in Europe have that feature, too," Chloe said.

Madeline said, "True, but you don't actually have to go that far. I once went to a trendy restaurant in Los Angeles that had inadvertently created the same phenomenon in their domed dining room. And Grand Central Station in New York City has some spots where you can stand across the corridor and hear someone whispering in a corner twenty feet away." She pointed to the arches along the side that led to another passageway. "Be careful about sharing secrets around here."

Looking around, I could see a number of dazed expressions on people's faces. A few others just snickered at the news.

"So much for the confession box," Buck said. "Just stand under the dome, and the whole world will hear your transgressions."

"But will they forgive them?" Sean asked, chuckling.

Carla frowned. "You might want to post a sign to let museumgoers know about that little design quirk, Madeline."

"That'll take all the fun out of it," Wade said.

There were more laughs as Madeline walked toward the group.

"Are you all ready to move on?" she asked.

I looked at the notes on my tablet. "How about if you show us one of the corridors beyond the arches and then take us into the three smaller chapels?" I knew those areas would present some interesting challenges in terms of lighting and security.

"Good idea," she said, and stepped down off the platform. "Let's go this way."

We followed her along the transept aisle to the north side of the church and under one of the archways. "Please be careful. There are no lights along these passageways."

"I kind of noticed that," Buck said wryly.

"It's a bit odd, isn't it?" Madeline said. "I was told that Reverend Patterson preferred to use candlelight to illuminate this space."

"That's . . . quirky," I said, picturing it all going up in flames. I looked at Buck. "Any thoughts?"

He turned back to Madeline. "I assume you'll be displaying artwork along these walls."

"Oh, yes. It's such an intriguing space."

"Then we'll need to have lights," he declared. "Nothing too bright, right?"

"No," she said quickly.

With tongue in cheek, he said, "Okay. So we won't order klieg lights."

She laughed. "Since it won't be a Hollywood movie premiere, maybe we could go for something more subtle?"

He grinned. "I'll bring some samples to show you."

"I appreciate that." She pulled her phone from her tote bag and turned on the flashlight. "This way to the chapels."

As we followed her along the dark passageway, I had to wonder why anyone would think that candles were the best lighting choice inside a 160-year-old building. Yes, the church walls and floors were made of stone, but much of the building was held together with wood.

Because it was another aspect of my construction business, I had rebuilt dozens of old homes and buildings that had been damaged by fire. With fire damage came water damage, and that was often worse. So, needless to say, I wasn't a big fan of using candles to light up a room or set a mood. I would rather try to create a mood using lamps and pin spots. I suppose, in that regard, I had something in common with Buck, who seemed to do the same thing on a larger scale.

"The church has three small chapels behind the main altar," Madeline was saying, "and each is simply charming. We'll use them to display smaller works of art or collections of miniature artwork. I'm already planning which pieces I'll initially highlight in each of the chapels."

"I've seen these rooms," I said to the group. "The stained glass windows alone are worth a visit."

"And since they're all facing east," Wade added, "they'll get quite a bit of sunlight in the morning hours."

"It's going to be so beautiful," Madeline said.

I looked at Wade, then glanced at Buck. "We'll need to discuss some type of UV filtering in order to protect the artwork."

Buck spoke up. "I've been sourcing some museum-specific filtering systems because it's important to illuminate the art correctly but also to make sure that the pieces are not damaged by direct light. Some art is so fragile that even a small wattage lightbulb is capable of inflicting further harm."

Madeline wore a worried frown. "Actually, I think *every* piece of art should be considered fragile."

"Absolutely," Buck said. "That's why I'll be following the IES guidelines." At the blank looks, he said, "Oh, sorry. That's the Illumination Engineering Society's guidelines when it comes to the parameters and standards for museum lighting design, in order to ensure safety, preserve artifacts, and provide the best visual experience for your patrons."

We all stared at him for a long moment.

Then Sean murmured, "Whoa, dude."

Wade held up his hand. "High five, my fellow geek."

I watched Buck turn red, smile sheepishly, and then return the high five. "I do tend to go off on the occasional geekish tangent. Sorry about that."

"No," I said quickly. "I'm impressed that you're familiar with exactly what's required."

Madeline shook her head and I thought I saw moisture in her eyes. Was she crying? Was she upset?

"Are you all right, Madeline?" I asked.

She gave all of us a watery smile. "You know, this museum has been the project of my heart for almost two years now. To be honest, I was worried that I wouldn't choose the right construction company to do the work. But I can see now that I've chosen well. Thank you, Buck. Thank you, Shannon, and all of you. I'm so happy to see that you all show the type of dedication to the work that this project really needs."

"That is lovely of you to say," Carla said.

"Yes, thank you, Madeline," I agreed. "We really appreciate hearing that from you."

She was still smiling as she shook herself back to the moment. "Okay. Shall we take a look at the chapels?"

"Yes," I said. "Lead the way."

Madeline turned to Niall. "I especially want you to see the stone flooring. There's some deterioration, and I'm concerned that there might've been some water leakage."

"We'll be fixin' that, of course," Niall said.

"That is music to my ears," she said, sounding reassured.

I rewarded Niall with a big smile, and he grinned. I wasn't sure what Madeline had been expecting, but my guys were the best in the business. No matter what problems arose, we could make them go away.

The passageway curved, and I realized we were walking directly behind the central platform where the original altar had stood under the half dome. Madeline opened the door to the first chapel, and a few of us stepped inside. The room couldn't hold more than four or five people.

"It's so precious," Carla said reverently.

"This is known as the Rose Chapel," Madeline said.

"Makes sense with that beautiful rose-colored stained glass," Chloe said.

Buck scanned the small area. "This room should be

easy enough to light. And I'll use a filter over the window that will protect the artwork but won't hide the stained glass."

"That's perfect." Madeline glanced at the group. "The other two chapels are almost identical to this one, so we don't have to look at them today if you'd rather save some time."

"I'm okay on time," I said after taking a quick glance at my wristwatch. "I'd like the guys to see exactly what they look like since I imagine they'll each have their own idiosyncrasies and issues."

"Yes, of course they will." She led the way to the next small chapel. As she reached for the door handle, she said, "We call this room the Blue Iris Chapel for obvious reasons, as you'll quickly see."

She pushed, but the door was stuck. She used her shoulder to apply more pressure, but it wouldn't budge.

"Is it locked?" I asked.

"No, the handle works, but the door itself is just stuck. I think I can get it." She continued to push.

"Let me help you," Wade said.

"Thanks." She stepped out of the way.

He gave the door one strong shove, and it still wouldn't move. "It's not locked, but it feels like there's something blocking its way."

"Hold on," I said, and studied the doorjamb along the top of the door and then crouched down to check the sides. "Look at this."

Wade knelt down beside me. "What is that?"

"Some kind of lacy material is stuck in there."

"Yeah," he muttered. "It's acting as a shim."

"Let me try and pull it out." I managed to get hold of the edge of the lace and tugged it, trying to be gentle so it wouldn't tear off. But I could only get a few inches before the thing deteriorated.

"Very weird," Sean said.

"Maybe Reverend Patterson or his wife left something in there that caught in the door," Madeline suggested.

"That's possible." Wade put his shoulder into one hard push, and the door popped open a few inches. "Now it's scraping the floor. It probably needs to be rehung."

I saw a piece of lace flutter to the floor. "What the heck?" I reached for it and held it up. It was a round piece of delicate tulle with narrow lace trimming about ten inches wide.

"It's a chapel veil," Carla declared. "I went to Catholic school, and all the girls used to wear them in church."

"As a head covering," I said.

She grinned and touched the edge of the lacy veil. "Yeah."

"I'll hold on to it," I said. "Mrs. Patterson might want to keep it." I folded the lace and slipped it into my bag, then pushed the door open all the way.

And jumped back in shock.

The body of a young woman was sprawled on her back on the floor. She wore a white linen tunic over black tights and boots. Her long blond hair covered half of her face and was splayed across the hard marble surface, almost as if she were posing.

"Oh no." Chills swept through my body. "This can't be happening."

"What is it?" Madeline asked, then spotted the woman and started to rush over to her. "Sarah? It's Sarah!"

I held my arm out to block her from entering the room. "Madeline, no. Stay back."

She glared at me. "But she needs help."

She is beyond help, I thought, but couldn't say it. Instead, I said firmly, "Don't come any closer."

Madeline struggled to pull away from me, then simply gave up trying. She stared down at Sarah, and all of a sudden, comprehension hit her. Her tote bag slipped from her grasp and she began to scream.

Chapter Five

"Let go of me!" Madeline screamed, her pretty face contorted with pain. "Is she ill? I have to help her!"

"I'm so sorry, Madeline," I said. "We can't help her."

I glanced over my shoulder and looked at Wade. That was all it took for him to immediately come forward and take hold of Madeline's arm. "Come on, Madeline. Come with me."

"But . . . but Sarah!" she cried. "Oh my God."

Sean stepped forward and took her other arm. "The police will be here soon, and they'll take good care of her."

"She can't be dead!" She sobbed loudly. "Oh God!"

"Come on, let's go sit down." Wade glanced around. "Hey, Amanda, can you come with us?"

Clearly he wanted another woman for backup. I understood.

For a moment, Madeline refused to budge, simply stood sobbing helplessly in the doorway. But then

Wade and Sean were able to lead the inconsolable woman away from the small chapel and down the hall to one of the pews facing the central platform. Amanda sat down next to her and clutched her hand. We could hear Madeline's sobs echoing throughout the church, and I couldn't blame her. This was terrible.

Despite the horror of the moment, I was so grateful that I worked with people like Wade and Sean, who were both amazing. Amanda too. Now that I thought about it, I could count on every one of my people when it came to handling difficult emotional situations.

I realized that some of them were still gathered around the chapel doorway, unable to look away, so I finally said, "The police will be here soon and they'll want us out of the way."

"For sure," Carla said, and took a few steps back. "Do you think they'll want to halt our work for a few days?"

I grimaced. "Absolutely. We'd better be prepared for that."

Carla sighed. "Let's go this way so we don't screw up any more evidence than we already have." She pointed in the opposite direction from the way we'd come, but eventually, it led around the central platform and back to the main aisle.

"Thanks, Carla," I said. My heart felt heavy as I watched the rest of my team walk away from the chapel. Alone, I turned and stared down at Sarah one last time. It occurred to me that I'd better make sure the poor girl was dead, so I knelt down and felt her neck for any sign of a pulse.

Nothing.

She wasn't breathing. There was no sign of life. This

poor girl was gone. But how had this happened? And why?

Except for our group, the church was deserted. It had been that way for the last month. There was rarely anyone around whenever I'd walked through the church with Wade and the architect or the engineers. Most people who belonged to the Lighthouse Church had switched over weeks ago to their beautiful new building a few blocks away. The only people I'd seen working here during those visits were Reverend Patterson, his wife, and one or two other members of the church who were helping the reverend pack up and move things to the new church.

I realized I was shaking and had to take a few seconds to catch my breath. *Damn it! Who would want to hurt Sarah? How could this have happened?*

A tiny voice inside my head rephrased the question. *How could this have happened . . . again?*

I was still on my knees when I noticed a small puddle of blood on the floor by her head. With a gasp, I quickly scooted back a few inches to avoid getting it on me. I knew I should stand up and walk out and leave this horrible situation to the police chief, the CSI team, and the medical examiner. Yes, that was the right thing to do. For sure.

Who was I kidding?

Instead of scurrying away, I leaned in close and looked carefully at the source of the bleeding. I could see several large, circular welts on the side of her head, just above her ear. Someone had hit her so hard that the strands of her hair were coated in blood, and I could see a pattern of deep lines indented on her skin.

I sat back on my heels. The lines must've been caused

by whatever was used to bludgeon her. Something hard, obviously. A pipe? Or a baseball bat with protruding lines? I'd never heard of such a thing.

I looked around on the floor for a discarded weapon but didn't see anything. That's when I saw something else that both confused and intrigued me.

Before I could investigate further, Chloe sidled up beside me and whispered, "I called Eric. He and Tommy are driving back from some big police conference in Ukiah. They'll be another forty-five minutes at least, so he said he'd send Lucy Timmons over to handle things until he gets here."

Lucy Timmons was the newest police officer to join the Lighthouse Cove Police Department, working with Chief Eric Jensen and the rest of the squad. I had met her last fall when the veterans' village first opened and a friend of mine was brutally murdered. Despite being the newest member of the force, Lucy was smart and experienced.

"How soon can she get here?" I asked, standing up.

Chloe exhaled. "She's clearing up an accident over on the highway, so it'll be at least twenty minutes. Eric said to tell you to keep everyone away from the body."

"I will." It gave me a feeling of confidence to know that Eric trusted me that way.

"Oh, and he also said to tell you, 'Don't even think about playing Nancy Drew.'"

I blinked. "Well, that was rude."

She grinned. "Yeah. He knows you."

I grimaced. "Guess so."

"There's more," she said. "He'd like you to make a list of every single person in the church this morning."

"I can do that."

"And he asked if we could look around for at least three separate areas they can use for interviewing the witnesses."

"Oh, good idea. Okay." I thought of three right off the bat: the narthex, the central platform area, and maybe one of the pews at the back. I figured these first interviews would just be for gathering contact information, so they wouldn't need a private room. If they did run across someone suspicious, they would take them over to the station and conduct a formal interview there.

Chloe leaned in, trying to see over my shoulder. "So, what the hell happened, Shannon?"

I tried to shield her, but she wasn't having it, so I just sighed and moved out of the way. "I have no idea. But that's Sarah Spindler, Madeline's assistant. Obviously, she's dead."

She stared at the body, then frowned at me. "Why does this keep happening to you?"

I was shocked and angry, and I glared at her with so much intensity that I wondered why her head didn't explode. "Seriously? How should I know?"

"Okay, okay. Sorry. But you know what I mean." She gave an apologetic shrug, then made it better by hugging me. "Really, I'm sorry."

It was easy to curb my temper, because it was mostly made up of fear and worry. "That's okay. I'm kind of used to it."

"You shouldn't have to be."

I shrugged off the comment and watched as she stared at the body for a few more seconds. And then her face turned ghostly pale. "Oh hell."

"What is it?" I asked.

"Sarah Spindler. I just realized I went to school with her. We were both on the volleyball team. She had a wicked spike."

"I vaguely remember her from high school, too, but I didn't realize she was in your class."

"Yeah." Chloe looked dazed.

"Have you seen her since you moved back?"

"No. I had no idea what happened to her." She winced. "Well, now I know. Ugh."

I rubbed her shoulders in sympathy. "I'm sorry, Sis. Listen, I need to check on something before Lucy or Eric gets here. Could you go out there and see if my crew is okay? Let them know they can't leave until the police get here and talk to each of them. I'll join you all in, uh, just a minute."

"Okay, Nancy. Just don't let Eric catch you."

"Ha ha," I said dryly.

Once Chloe was gone, I went back to examine what I'd noticed before she walked in here. There were marks on the floor around Sarah. It looked like someone had recently swept the floor with a wide broom or some kind of cloth, but they'd done a bad job, because the sweep marks looked as though most of the dust and dirt were still on the floor. Along with something else. On closer examination, I saw some minute smears of red.

Red dust? Not likely. I squinted to focus my eyes and realized the tiny smears could be . . . blood? Sarah's blood? How in the world had someone swept blood into the chapel, right where Sarah had ended up?

Guiltily, I jumped up, knowing that Eric wouldn't be happy to see me on my hands and knees studying

Sarah's body like this. Of course, he wouldn't be here for a while, but Lucy might walk in at any moment. I wasn't worried about one of my team walking in and finding me staring at blood particles on the floor. They were used to seeing me involved in murder investigations. Still, I didn't want the whole world to know what I was doing.

When Eric got here, I would show him all of the weird evidence I'd found. He wouldn't be thrilled, but he would be glad I'd showed him. I hoped.

And speaking of Eric again, I really needed to get out of here, but I hated to leave Sarah all alone. Sadly, there was nothing I could do for her now, except tell the police what I'd noticed. And maybe, eventually, it would help them find some justice for her.

I walked out of the small chapel and closed the door, then stood in the hall and brushed the dust and dirt off my jeans. I shook my head and wondered again how Sarah had ended up in that tiny chapel. Staring down at the floor, I realized that thanks to all the dust that had accumulated there, I could see that something had been dragged down the middle of the hall, probably by a wide cloth of some kind. The marks were similar to those by Sarah's body. Had someone dragged her down the hall and into the chapel? Why would anyone do that?

But then, why would anyone kill her?

I followed the drag marks down the very dusty hall. They led to the sacristy door. I didn't go inside just then, but instead walked back to the Blue Iris Chapel. I had things to do before the police arrived.

I wondered again if someone had actually dragged Sarah down the hall and into this room. Had they then crammed that piece of lace into the door to jam it shut? Had they believed they could hide Sarah's body in this little chapel long enough to make it out of the church undetected?

That was sick and twisted, for sure. And it made me wonder if they had actually been in the church when we all walked in. Had they panicked? I thought about it for a long moment, then asked myself, *How did they get out of the church without us seeing them?* I froze as the possibility arose that Sarah's killer might still be hiding inside the church.

I glanced around, then crept back inside the blue chapel and knelt down to check Sarah's clothing. I had no intention of turning her body over, but I wanted to get a look at the back of her white tunic to see if it was dirty from being dragged down the hall.

I carefully tugged on her shirt just enough to see that there was no dirt on it at all. So how could she have been dragged all this way? Did the killer wrap her in a tarp to get her here?

That was just creepy, and I shivered at the thought, then forced myself to shake off my fears. I left the chapel and studied the drag marks out in the hall more closely. The thought of someone being so desperate that they would drag this lovely young woman around the church was hideous.

But it was a darn good clue. I followed the drag marks back around to the door of the sacristy.

On an earlier visit, Madeline had explained that the sacristy was where Reverend Patterson changed into his vestments and where he kept all the religious objects he used during mass. Others used the room as well, including the choir leader, altar boys, and several deacons. They all kept their ceremonial wardrobes in there, tucked inside the cabinets against the wall.

In the past, I had only been able to take a quick look inside the room, because until very recently, Reverend Patterson and his wife had still been cleaning and packing things up. Boxes and wardrobe crates had been stacked wall to wall, and it was hard to see what the room actually looked like. The small section I'd been able to view, though, was amazing. One wall was completely covered, floor to ceiling, by a massive antique cabinet made of mahogany and inlaid with satinwood. The entire piece had been built into the wall and couldn't be moved, much to Reverend Patterson's dismay, I knew. Down the middle of the cabinet were sixteen long narrow drawers similar to map drawers. On either side of those were another thirty or so drawers, cubbies, cabinets, and cupboards of different sizes and shapes. It sounded overwhelming, and it truly was, in a good way. It was magnificent.

The wall opposite the cabinet was half-lined in beautifully carved mahogany panels with stained glass windows above that afforded a view of the coastline and the blue ocean beyond.

The panels were just one of the reasons why I had specifically asked Amanda to work on this project. Since she was an expert in all things made of wood, I knew she would be enamored by this room in particular. But then, the rich wood timbers and beams that filled the main sections of the church were probably just as enticing to her.

Now I reached for the door of the sacristy and found it unlocked, so I took a chance and peeked inside. A few boxes still remained in the corner, but for the most part, the room was empty. And then I saw the drag marks. They continued halfway across the room, then stopped abruptly in front of the wall opposite the big cabinet, right under one of the stained glass windows.

Was this where Sarah was killed?

I took a close look around, stared down at the floor, and spotted blood.

It wasn't much blood, just one drop that had formed a tiny puddle right next to the wood-paneled wall. I could tell it had already coagulated, and I knew from past experience that blood tended to clot within two to three minutes. I shivered again. That was another grisly but useful bit of knowledge I'd picked up over the years. So, yes, this was most likely where Sarah met her demise.

It wasn't much to go on, but I already had a theory. It was a good one, and I couldn't wait to run it by Eric.

For now, though, I needed to check on my team to make sure they were doing okay. I wanted to let them know exactly what was going on, as if they didn't already know that a murder had occurred. Still, they needed to be kept informed.

Most of them had been working with me for years, so they knew how often I had stumbled upon a dead body or a skeleton on one of my construction sites. It was almost as if it came with the job—which was a terrible thought. It wasn't like I asked for this kind of trouble. In fact, I really hated it.

My heart was still beating a little too fast as I closed the door to the sacristy. I stood in the hall, and without another thought, I pulled out my cell phone and called Mac.

When he answered, I whispered, "Mac."

"Shannon," he said. "Are you at the church? How's it going?"

I took a deep breath, let it out, and realized I was shaking again. "How's it going? It's, um. Well, it's going . . . oh, jeez, Mac. We found a body."

"What? Who? How? Hell, Shannon, what happened? Wait."

He stopped for a moment to take it all in and to give me a chance to breathe some more.

"Shannon, do you want me to come over there?"

I leaned against the stone wall. I hated to sound so wimpy, but I quickly said, "Yes, please."

And all he said was, "Give me twenty minutes."

He hung up. I closed my eyes and just breathed some more.

Mac was another hero. I had a lot of them in my life.

I thought about Sarah Spindler and knew that she hadn't deserved to be killed. She was a sweet young woman with an art history degree who loved her job and enjoyed working with Madeline. She had friends, a great attitude, a cute boyfriend, and a nice family.

"Damn it," I muttered, and slapped my hand against the cold stone wall. There was no reason for this perfectly nice woman to be dead. So, what in the world had happened? Why had she been so brutally attacked? Had she arrived early to impress her boss and instead had surprised some maniac so badly that he had killed her?

Some maniac? I shook my head and stared up at the ceiling. It hadn't even occurred to me to ask myself, *Who did this?*

I wasn't going to get any answers just yet, so I quietly headed out to join my team in the main aisle of the church. But before I made it as far as the transept, another scream rang out. And it came from the direction of the Blue Iris Chapel.

"Oh no!" I ran back down the hall to the chapel. An older woman stood at the open door, one hand on the doorknob and the other covering her mouth. She began to murmur, "Oh God, oh God, oh God."

She was beautiful, probably around sixty years old. She didn't appear frail, just truly frightened. She wore comfortable blue jeans, a UCLA sweatshirt, and sturdy tennis shoes. And she wore a round piece of white lace held to her head with a bobby pin. The lace was very similar, if not identical, to the piece I'd found stuffed in the door earlier.

Her skin was smooth and pale, a classic peaches-and-cream complexion. Her eyes were bright and blue and she wore her blond hair in a short, wavy bob.

"Ma'am?" I said, slowing down my approach so as not to startle her.

"Oh!" She blinked. "Oh dear. Hello. Did you know there's a woman lying on the floor?"

"Yes, the police have been called."

"So she's dead." She nodded. "I thought so."

"Why don't you come with me?" I carefully pulled her hand away from the doorknob and slowly closed the door.

That's when I noticed the shards of green glass scattered on the stone floor by her feet. I could still see the sweeping marks, but now I was worried that they might be obscured by this woman's shoes and the scattered pieces of glass.

"Did you drop something?" I asked.

"Oh gosh," she said. "Yes, I dropped a vase. It broke."

"Would you like to sit down?"

"I should get a broom and clean up this mess."

"No. The police wouldn't want you to do that."

"Oh." Her eyes widened. "Right. Evidence might be erased."

Yikes, she sounded just like me. Another *Law & Order* crime scene junkie?

"Shall we go sit down so you can catch your breath?"

"I'd better do that." She patted her chest. "I've really had quite a shock."

As I led her around the wall toward the row of pews facing the central platform, she asked, "Do you know who that woman was?"

"Yes," I said. "Her name is Sarah. She was the assistant to the new artistic director of the museum."

"Oh, mercy. That is tragic. How did it happen?"

"We're waiting for the police. They'll investigate."

"Of course." She pointed to the steps leading up to the central platform. "I can sit right here." And she hunkered down on the first step.

I sat down beside her, unsure whether she was recovered from the shock or not.

"I'm Flora," she said. "They call me the flower lady. That's because I take care of the flowers here at the church. I make sure there are flowers on the altar for every occasion and make sure they're fresh. You'd be surprised how many flowers we need every week. I do all the ordering and arranging and the cleaning up."

"That must keep you busy."

"Oh, it's a full-time job, for sure," she said. "Well, just today, I realized I'd left a few things over here when we moved. So that's why I was looking for that green vase. I found it, then realized I'd better go through the small chapels in case I was missing anything else." She shook her head. "That green vase was one of Mrs. Patterson's favorites. I don't relish telling her it's broken."

"Will she be angry?"

"Oh, no, she's a lovely woman. But I feel bad. Although you can't really blame me. I had the shock of my life seeing that woman on the floor." She patted her chest again.

"Aunt Flora? Are you all right?"

I looked up and saw Buck standing in front of us, staring down at the woman.

"Oh, Mickey, sweetie," Flora said. "I didn't realize you'd be here today."

"Yeah, Aunt Flora," he explained softly. "Today's the day we're doing a walk-through with the crew, remember?"

"Mickey?" I said, staring at him.

He looked back and forth between his aunt and me, and grinned. "Everybody calls me Buck except my aunt. Aunt Flora, this is my boss, Shannon Hammer."

"Oh, now I thought you looked familiar," she said, patting my knee. "I've known your father, Jack, for years."

"Really?" I looked at Buck. "I remember you saying you had relatives in the area, but I didn't realize they'd be this close."

He shook his head in amazement. "It's a small world."

"You can say that again." I turned to look at his aunt. "So, you know my dad?"

"Sure do," she said. "Jack and I went to school together. I know your uncle Pete, too."

I could hear sirens in the distance and stood up. "I've got to go talk to the police. It was very nice to meet you, Flora."

"You too, Shannon. You'll probably see me around, here and there. I've still got a few things to go through in the old sacristy, so I might be around for a few more weeks."

"It'll be nice to see you," I said, then leaned closer to Buck. "She found the body in the chapel, so she might need some comforting."

"Oh hell! Thanks for telling me, Shannon."

"And please don't let her leave," I added. "The police will want to talk to her. They'll want to talk to all of us."

"Got it." He sat down in my place and gave his aunt a one-armed hug.

The police would be here soon, and that realization brought back the image of Sarah Spindler flashing through my mind. Twenty minutes had passed by too quickly. Or maybe I had been too wrapped up in protecting the evidence and had lost track of time.

"Protecting the evidence?" I muttered. I was definitely pulling a Nancy Drew. Good grief. I really needed to stop finding dead bodies.

Before I joined my team, I hurriedly jotted down the names of everyone here so Eric would have them when he arrived. At the last minute, I decided to include Flora the flower lady since she had walked into the Blue Iris Chapel and had probably left her fingerprints on the doorknob. Not only that, but her tennis shoes had invariably left their pattern in the dusty floor.

I found Chloe sitting next to Madeline in the pew,

and I slid in and sat next to my sister. We were both trying to console the artistic director when I heard the staccato sound of stiletto heels *tip-tip-tapping* on the marble floor. And they were coming our way.

I had a moment of queasiness as I realized who had entered the church. Could this day get any worse?

"Madeline! Where are you?" The voice was whiny and demanding, and my queasiness increased.

Chloe gripped my arm, looking horrified. "Is that who I think it is?"

I groaned. "I'm afraid so. Don't turn around."

"Madeline Whistler," the woman demanded, her tone growing louder and shriller. "Are you here or not?"

"She's so annoying," Chloe whispered. "What's she doing here?"

"Tempting fate." I shivered. "She shouldn't be allowed inside a church. Watch out for lightning strikes."

Chloe snorted a laugh.

Madeline was still sniffling and dabbing at her tears, so she didn't seem to hear our conversation.

"Damn it, Madeline, you said you'd be here." She took a few more steps, and then the woman known as Whitney Reid Gallagher stopped abruptly and stared at Madeline. "There you are. Why didn't you . . ." She gasped. "What happened? Why are you crying? Did Shannon Hammer hurt you?"

Madeline shook her head but couldn't speak.

I stood and walked out of the pew. "Of course I didn't hurt her, you numbskull."

"Oh, Whitney," Madeline whispered. "It's Sarah. She . . . she's dead."

Whitney let out a scream that banshees would envy,

and everyone turned to look at her, which was exactly what she wanted, of course. "Oh my God!" she screamed again.

Madeline was taken aback by Whitney's reaction, but the rest of us just rolled our eyes.

"For God's sake, Madeline!" Whitney shrieked. "Didn't I warn you? I told you Shannon Hammer would bring death to your door!"

I mentally slapped her upside the head. This woman had been my worst nightmare since high school. Today she was dressed in the height of fashion—if you were attending a retro disco party. Her black leggings and off-the-shoulder angora sweater gave her that sexy slutty look that was always perfect for church. And there were the aforementioned stiletto heels, of course. Her short black hair revealed a pair of diamond earrings as big as my thumbs.

As soon as Chloe and I exited the pew, Whitney scurried in and cuddled up next to Madeline, causing the artistic director to sob a little more. Whitney joined her, moaning and emitting the occasional high-pitched scream that caused Madeline to jolt in shock.

I shook my head. Whitney was as awful as ever, and I really wanted to punch her.

"Be quiet!" Carla suddenly shouted from the next pew over.

Whitney stopped just as suddenly, and I could've kissed Carla.

Now I could hear the sirens coming closer and knew that the police would be here momentarily.

I walked into the pew behind Madeline and touched her shoulder. "Will you be all right for a little while? I'm going to go outside and wait for the police."

"Of course," she said. "I'll be fine." She sniffed and touched her eyes with the tissue she clutched. "Thanks, Shannon."

Whitney glared. "Now that you're leaving, she'll do a lot better."

Resisting the urge to smack Whitney like the annoying gnat that she was, I smiled at Madeline and gave her shoulder a light squeeze of support. "I'll be right back."

I flashed Chloe a look, and she immediately joined me. We walked quickly up the aisle and through the narthex, pushed open the outer doors, and stood on the steps, breathing the clean fresh air.

Chloe stared out at the horizon. "I don't think I ever realized what a stunning view they've got here."

"It's beautiful, isn't it? Amazing to realize that we're only a block from the beach."

"I guess I forgot that after being inside for a while."

Our town plaza was the heart of Lighthouse Cove, a gathering place for parades and parties all year long. A beautiful green lawn covered most of the central area, and a plethora of flowers lined the little pathways that led to the large gazebo where concerts were held every summer.

Surrounding the park on four sides was a pretty brick walkway. People strolled along, taking in the views and visiting the several dozen shops and restaurants that lined three sides of the square. The fourth side was dominated by the Lighthouse Church, which had stood on this spot for over 160 years.

The sirens stopped abruptly.

"That must be Lucy," Chloe said. "Are we standing out here to usher her into the church?"

"Well, yes."

"You didn't think she'd find her way inside?"

"I just thought it would be good to greet her at the door and then introduce her to everyone inside."

"That's nice."

"I also wanted to escape from Whitney."

"Ah. Now it makes sense." She grinned at me. "If I recall, you used to be in charge of the high school welcome wagon."

"Hey, I've always been a helper."

"And you always will be."

"Probably." In high school, my friends and I had made a point of reaching out to make the new kids in town feel welcome. I found out later that my gesture of friendship had really annoyed mean girl Whitney Reid and had set her on the path to destroying my life.

And she was still trying. But she hadn't broken me and she never would. So, yeah, I was still playing the welcome-wagon girl, and I didn't have one damn problem with that.

Chapter Six

We were still standing on the steps waiting for the police to arrive when I turned to Chloe. "I've got to say something."

"What is it?"

I narrowed my eyes and stared into the distance. "I'm pretty sure Whitney warned Madeline not to hire my company to do the renovations on the church."

Chloe thought about it. "After hearing what she said just now, I think you may be right. She is, after all, the manifestation of Satan on Earth, so it makes sense."

I grinned. "I like that."

She scowled. "She's just so evil."

"Yes, she is. And unfortunately, she and Madeline appear to be friends. I didn't see that coming."

"I can't figure that out." Chloe shook her head. "Madeline is so professional and sophisticated. Whitney isn't, but she puts on a pretty good act."

"She's still riding on her father's name."

"Didn't he go broke?"

"Actually, he was swindled out of millions, but Whitney still pretends like they've got all the money in the world."

"She's the worst," Chloe said. "You just remember that Madeline *did* hire you, so ignore Whitney. Otherwise, you'll drive yourself crazy."

"I'll try, but you know how Whitney gets under my skin."

She rolled her eyes. "Boy, do I! I got chills when I heard her voice just now. And let's not forget that I'm engaged to Eric, so I actually have to see her sometimes."

Whitney's husband, Tommy, was the assistant chief of police under Eric. The two men were good friends. Luckily for Chloe, though, Eric knew how she felt about Whitney and didn't push her to be friends.

It was too bad, because Tommy was a good guy. His wife, however, was another story.

"I guess I'm still an easy target for her."

"You're stronger than that," Chloe insisted. "But I know what you mean. So, whenever you start to feel that way, just look in the mirror and say, "Not today, Satan. Not today."

I laughed. "Thank you, Church Lady."

"Hey, it works." Chloe looked around. "So where'd Lucy go?"

"I don't know. I thought that siren we heard was her car. Maybe she's grabbing stuff from her trunk to carry inside."

"Maybe. So, while we're waiting, can you tell me how Sarah Spindler started working for Madeline Whistler? How did this happen?"

"All I know is Madeline adored her, and she was

really nice to me and my guys. Anytime we had to get any paperwork or random tasks done, Sarah took care of it. A few years ago, she went back to college to get her master's degree in art history, and then Madeline hired her about six months ago. And I know that they got to be really close friends, even though Madeline was her boss."

"No wonder she's so upset."

"I don't blame her. It's just tragic. I know Sarah has a boyfriend, and her parents still live here."

"And she was killed right there inside the church?" Chloe shook her head. "Who in the world would do that?"

"Good question." And I planned to find some answers. But I wasn't going to admit that out loud in case Chloe happened to mention it to Eric. Or in case Lucy was lurking around the corner. Not that I was paranoid or anything.

"Oh, hey, you the lady I should talk to about the construction going on in the church?"

We both turned and saw an older man wearing baggy jeans and a faded plaid flannel shirt.

"I'm in charge," I said. "Can I help you?"

"Flora says I should talk to you about bringing up some ladders and sawhorses and other thingamajigs from the basement."

"We usually bring our own, but it would be nice to have some equipment on-site." I held out my hand. "I'm Shannon Hammer, the general contractor, by the way. What's your name?"

"I'm Brindley. Mitch Brindley. I'm the handyman around here. Well, I was, until we moved to the new church. But I know where everything is, so Flora told me to track you down and offer my assistance if you need it."

"I appreciate it." I glanced at Chloe. "This is my sister, Mr. Brindley. Her name is Chloe Hammer."

He tipped his baseball cap. "Ma'am."

I was just guessing, but the man looked about seventy years old. He was tall and still looked strong and agile, which was a good thing for a handyman who might be climbing ladders and using power tools on a regular basis.

"I don't know if you've heard," I said, "but there's been a death inside the church. The police will be shutting us down for a few days."

He scratched his neck. "I heard something about that from Flora."

"But once we're back inside, I would really appreciate your help."

"Good enough." He nodded. "I'm here and there, but I'll find you in a day or two." He tipped his cap again and walked away.

"A man of few words," Chloe said.

"That's all right," I said. "If he's willing to help us out, he's okay in my book."

A few minutes later, we were still standing on the steps when Lucy Timmons came walking around the corner looking strong and confident.

"Hi, Lucy," I said. "We heard the siren but didn't see you. We were starting to worry."

"Hey, Shannon. Sorry. I had to finish up my report on the traffic incident. So how are you?" Then she grinned. "Chloe. How're you doing?"

"I'm good. It's great to see you."

I grabbed the handle to the door, and we were about to step inside the church when Mac ran up the steps.

"Wait for me," he called.

Despite the somber moment, I smiled as he approached. I could tell he'd been running all the way from our house, which was only a couple of blocks away, but still. I was gratified to know he'd hurried over to see me.

"Hi." I started toward him, but he put up his hand to stop me. "Don't hug me unless you want to get all sweaty."

I held up both hands. "Uh, no. Thanks for the warning, though. Consider yourself virtually hugged."

"I can go with that."

I smiled up at him. "And feel free to hug me when you're all dried off."

He grinned. "You know I will."

At that moment, another siren blasted the air, and we all waited to see what was going on. Two minutes later, Eric and Tommy came running over.

"You made good time," Chloe said, and gave him a big kiss. I had to give her props for that. Eric tried to discourage her from showing affection in public when he was in uniform, but she simply ignored him.

The thought made me smile for some reason.

"Hey, Shannon!" Tommy called jovially. "Great to see you."

"You too, Tommy."

Only Tommy could be this buoyant at a murder scene, I thought. The man was just too cheerful and friendly to hate, so even though he had cheated on me with Whitney, then gotten her pregnant and married her, we were still friends. It was a longer story than that, but the bottom line was that I figured he had suffered enough just by living in the same house with Whitney.

Eric led the way to the church doors, and Lucy and Tommy followed close behind. As he swung the door open, Eric turned and looked at me. "Shannon. Have you got something for me?"

"I do." I pulled out the slip of paper with everyone's names on it and handed it to him. "I also listed a few areas I thought would work for interviewing purposes."

"Thanks," he said. "Do me a favor and stay close."

"Sure." I shot Mac a look of intrigue and he gave me one of his cockeyed grins. He knew I usually got a kick out of helping with the investigations.

We walked through the narthex and into the nave, making enough noise to alert my crew. Wade turned, then stood up and said, "Hey, everyone, the police are here."

The assembled crowd stopped talking and whipped around to watch as Eric, Tommy, and Lucy strode up the aisle. They were followed by Chloe, Mac, and me.

"As some of you may know," Eric began, "I'm Police Chief Eric Jensen." His voice was so commanding that everyone immediately sat up straight and stared at him. It was no hardship, because he happened to be big and tall and very good-looking. When I first met him, I mentally called him Thor. The image of a Viking god still worked for me.

"I appreciate your patience," Eric continued, "and I thank you all for your cooperation. We'll try to make this process move as swiftly as possible and get you out of here as soon as we can. But we need to interview each of you, and that will take time."

He leaned over to me and whispered, "Who's in charge of this project?"

"Madeline Whistler," I said.

He asked, "And where's the body?"

"In the Blue Iris Chapel."

He nodded, then said loudly, "Madeline?"

"I'm here." She stood and waved her arm.

Eric glanced around and found her. "I'm very sorry for your loss."

She sniffed. "Thank you."

Eric nodded. "Please go ahead and sit down for now, Ms. Whistler. I'll need to talk to you in a few minutes, but we have some things to take care of first."

He took a quick look at the list I'd given him. Then he looked around at my crew. "Sorry to have to interrupt your jobs for the next few days, but as you know, a crime has been committed, and we've got a duty to the victim to find out what happened. We'll be searching the church for evidence and interviewing everyone who might've been a witness to what happened here."

Eric turned, found Tommy and Lucy standing nearby, and continued speaking to the assembled group. "This is Assistant Police Chief Tom Gallagher and this is Officer Lucy Timmons. They'll be conducting very brief interviews with each of you. Mainly, we're going to want your contact information, and we also might ask you a few questions. When one of them calls your name, please follow them. As I said, we'll try to be brief. And even though we know many of you already, we'll still want to get your contact information and some details of what you saw here today." He glanced around and made sure everyone was still paying attention.

With a nod, he added, "And thank you again for your cooperation."

He took a minute to speak in low tones to Lucy and Tommy, then handed my list to Tommy. I saw him point to the note I'd made about the different places they could use for interviewing.

Tommy nodded. "We got this, Chief."

"Good." Then Eric looked over at me. "Let's go."

I glanced at Mac. "Be right back."

"I'll wait here." He winked at me and I had to smile.

As I followed Eric down the aisle, I heard Tommy speak softly. "Whitney, honey, I need you to go on home."

I couldn't tell if she was happy that he'd singled her out or annoyed that he was making her leave. It didn't really matter, as long as she left.

I hurried to get ahead of Eric and then said, "It's this way."

When we'd rounded the central platform and were behind its circular back wall, he stopped.

"I'll take a brief look at the crime scene before Leo and Lilah arrive. They should be here soon."

"Okay." I pointed down the hall. "The Blue Iris Chapel is down this way." I led the way toward the three small chapels and stopped at the Blue Iris door. "She's in there, and I've got a few details I'd like to show you when you're ready for me."

He raised one eyebrow in a move meant to intimidate, but I'd known him too long to fall for it.

"It won't take long," I assured him. "And you'll want to hear what I have to say."

"We'll see." He reached into one of his pockets and pulled out two thin rubber gloves and slipped his hands into them. Then he carefully turned the doorknob and pushed the door open. He stared down at the body of Sarah Spindler and sighed. "Did you know her?"

I nodded. "She's Madeline's assistant, so I've met her a few times at their office and a few times here at the church. But she grew up in Lighthouse Cove, so Chloe and I both went to school with her."

He whipped around. "Chloe knew her?"

"She knew her in high school but hadn't seen her in years."

He spent another two minutes studying the body and looking carefully around the room. Then he stopped and glanced at me. "What did you want to tell me?"

"Okay. First, there's this." I pulled the chapel veil out of my bag. "This was stuffed between the door and the doorjamb. We couldn't get the door opened for a minute or two. It was obviously meant to slow us down."

He took the scrap of lace and examined it.

"It's a chapel veil," I explained. "I understand that women wear them on their heads when they go to church. Carla went to Catholic school, so she knows the routine. You can talk to her if you want more info."

"Where in the door was it stuck?" he asked.

I pointed to the exact place a few inches below the door handle.

He reached in another pocket, pulled out a baggie, and put the veil inside. "Okay, what else?"

I crouched down beside Sarah's body and pointed out the drag marks. "If you look really carefully, you can see tiny bits of blood. She was dragged here and left. Those drag marks and the bits of blood go all the way down the hall and inside the sacristy. They end at the paneled wall. There's a drop of congealed blood there, but nothing else. If you want me to, I'll show you that in a minute."

"I'd rather wait until Leo gets here."

"Oh, good idea."

"Thank you," he said wryly.

"The thing is," I continued, "I think she was killed in the sacristy and dragged down here. I think the killer wanted to hide her body because he heard us coming. It's just a theory. But I also wonder if she was still alive when she got to the chapel, because you can see the small pool of blood around her head. So her heart still must've been pumping while she was being dragged down here." I shook my head, suddenly feeling sick to my stomach at the thought. "Even if that's true, by the time we got in here, she was dead."

"You've been watching *CSI: Miami* reruns, haven't you?"

I'd known him too long to take offense. "That's one of my favorite shows."

We left the chapel and he closed the door. "What's all this green glass on the floor?"

"Oh, almost forgot. The church's flower lady came by to pick up some things. When she opened the Blue Iris door and saw the body, she dropped the vase and began to scream."

"Is she sitting out there with the rest of the group?"

"Yes. She's the aunt of my lighting technician."

"Who's that?"

"Buck Buckner. We met him in Hollywood, on Chloe's show. Remember?"

"Oh yeah. He took the job, huh?"

"Yeah. And he's great. Really smart."

"Good."

"One more suggestion."

"That's enough, Shannon. I have a job to do."

"Just hear me out. I think you should call Reverend Patterson and his wife over here for questioning. I haven't seen them today, but according to Madeline, they're in and out of here all the time because they're still packing up the old church stuff and taking it to their new place. So, you know, they might've seen something or heard something. You know what I mean?"

"Yeah, I know." He managed a half smile. "And that's a good idea. I'll take care of it right now." He pulled out his phone and hit a number. "Hey, Tom. Ask Madeline for the number of the reverend and his wife." He gave me an expectant look.

"Reverend Patterson," I said.

"Reverend Patterson," he said to Tommy.

He listened for a few seconds. "Yeah? Good. I'm going to want to talk to them. Thanks." He ended the call and looked at me. "The reverend and his wife are already here. Tom said the flower lady called them."

"Flora," I said. "Good for her."

"Yeah," he said, then added gruffly, "I've changed my mind. Show me the sacristy."

"All righty. It's this way." I glanced at the floor. "And watch out for the drag marks."

After I'd shown Eric the sacristy and pointed out the drop of blood I'd found, he walked me back to the nave. Reverend and Mrs. Patterson were sitting in the front pew chatting with Wade, Carla, Buck, Flora, and another woman I didn't recognize. Also, Leo Stringer, the crime scene investigator, and his part-time assistant, Officer Lilah O'Neil, had arrived and were standing near the back of the nave.

"I've got to get Leo set up in the chapel," Eric said, checking his wristwatch. "Would you mind telling the Pattersons I'll be with them in just a few minutes?"

"I don't mind at all." Mainly because it would give me a chance to meet and chat with them. I was a people person, after all.

Someone new was sitting with Flora, but since I was standing near the reverend and his wife, I stopped to say hello to them first. "Good morning, Reverend Patterson, Mrs. Patterson. I'm Shannon Hammer. I'm the contractor working on the church restoration."

Reverend Patterson stood and shook my hand. "Hello, Shannon. Everyone calls me Reverend Roy. It's nice to meet you, despite this tragic event that took place in our dear old church."

His big hand engulfed mine but didn't squeeze or pump too vigorously, for which I was grateful. The man was as tall as Mac and almost as broad through the shoulders. He wore his hair slightly longer than many men his age and brushed it back from his face. I would've guessed him to be an actor or a successful businessman, except for that white clerical collar he wore. But besides that little detail, he just didn't give off a businessman's vibe. He exuded humor, intelligence, and benevolence, and I wondered why I had never met him before. We lived in a small town, after all. But I supposed he spent most of his time working at the church with his congregation. And I had never been one of them.

"Nice to meet you, too, Reverend Roy," I managed to say after I reeled in my thoughts.

His wife smiled at me and reached for my hand. "I'm Lavinia Patterson, Shannon."

The woman was simply lovely with ash-blond hair and soft blue eyes. Her smile conveyed so much kindness and warmth, I was immediately drawn to her. I returned the smile. "Hello, Mrs. Patterson."

"Flora told me how kind you were and mentioned that she knew your father."

"It's a small world, isn't it?" I said. That cliché was going to get very old, very soon.

"It is, and it must be so comforting to know that you have such a deep connection to this beautiful town and its people."

"Yes," I said, and searched my brain for something a little deeper to say in return. "I, um, hope you've experienced that same feeling through your work with the church."

Her bright eyes radiated happiness. "That is lovely of you to say. I have indeed experienced that connection, and it quite simply gives me life. I'm truly blessed."

I happened to catch Madeline's gaze and saw her smile at me. I guess she had gotten to know the Pattersons pretty well by now and had been the recipient of these double-barreled shots of compassion and goodness the couple delivered.

It was powerful. Made me want to go out and do charitable works and stuff. I had to give myself a mental shake and remind myself to keep my eye on the ball. I couldn't forget that someone had been murdered this morning.

Besides, my company did charitable stuff all the

time. Like our veterans' village project. We had built fifty tiny homes for veterans in need. I felt really good about that. We donated our construction time a lot, and we always contributed to feed the families at Thanksgiving and Christmas. But maybe that wasn't enough. Maybe we should've been doing more. I'd have to think about it.

One thing was clear, though. The Pattersons had some strong magic working for them.

"Shannon," Mrs. Patterson murmured. "I'd like to ask you something."

"Of course."

"Did you know the young woman who was killed?"

I sighed. "I didn't know her that well. I had met her a few times with Madeline, and my sister, Chloe, was in her class in high school. It's just so terrible."

"Oh, it is." She gave my hand a gentle squeeze. "It's tragic. We met her a number of times with Madeline as well, and she was such a sweet young person. Reverend Roy led a moment of silence right here just a few minutes ago, and he's already scheduled an evening of prayer this coming Thursday in her memory."

"I'll be sure to attend," I said.

"Good," she said, and patted my hand before letting go. "I find that an evening of prayer always lifts my spirits, especially when something dreadful has happened. And spending the time with others is balm for our collective spirits. So glad you'll be there."

"Mrs. Patterson, does anyone ever tell you no?"

Her laugh was musical. "First of all, please call me Lavinia. And in answer to your question, very rarely."

We both laughed, and I said, "Thank you for talking with me. I feel a little better already."

"Isn't that wonderful?" Her smile was brilliant. "And your telling me that makes me feel better as well."

"I'm going to go talk to some of my crew, but I hope I'll see you again soon."

"You'll probably see me around here for the next few weeks because I'm still packing things up. Can you believe it? But we lived and worked in this church for over thirty years, so we've accumulated quite a lot over time."

"Oh, I can believe it," I said.

"Of course you can. In your business you must've taken on renovation jobs that were downright harrowing."

I chuckled. "That's a good word."

She smiled. "I'm looking forward to seeing the changes you make to our little church."

"Me too." I stood. "It was great talking to you."

She took my hand again. "You're a good girl, Shannon Hammer."

I walked away smiling, then quickly turned. "Oh, by the way, Lavinia."

"Yes, dear?"

"Chief Jensen wanted you and Reverend Roy to know that he would be out here to talk to you shortly."

"Then we'll wait for him right here. Thank you, Shannon." She started to walk away. Then something caught her eye, and she came back and whispered, "I just noticed that Colleen Sayles has arrived. You'll want to meet her." She glanced in the direction of the north transept, and I turned to see who she was talking about. I watched a stunning, dark-haired woman approach the main aisle wearing a drab gray business suit that didn't do a thing for her.

"She's a good worker and knows a lot of the church's history. Reverend Roy depends on her for all of his business needs, but . . ." She winced, then whispered, "I don't really trust her."

"Oh."

"I shouldn't have said anything," Lavinia murmured, and shook her head. "And I've made you uncomfortable."

"No, really, I'm fine," I insisted. "And I appreciate your honesty, especially when it comes to your own people."

"No, no. I admit I was being uncharitable, and it wasn't fair. Colleen is a lovely woman and always willing to lend a hand. We would be lost without her. So please ignore me. This horrible murder has me behaving very badly."

I chuckled. "I doubt you could ever behave badly."

Her soft trilling laughter sounded joyous. "I'll say it again, you're a good girl. Thank you again for your kind words."

As Lavinia walked away, I noticed that Colleen Sayles was speaking to Flora. That dull gray suit she was wearing had me wondering if she purposely toned down her wardrobe so as not to draw attention to herself. She was, after all, a very attractive woman.

The question was, could I trust her?

I watched her with Flora for another moment. Finally, I felt the urge to move around, so I turned and walked toward the narthex.

Halfway down the aisle, Mac caught up with me. "I saw you talking to the reverend's wife. What did you think?"

"Have you talked to her?"

He held up both hands in surrender. "I was ready to give up my worldly goods and follow those two."

"She's amazing, isn't she?"

"And the reverend's no slouch, either," Mac said.

"I haven't had much of a chance to talk to him."

"Oh, Shannon, dear. There you are."

We both turned, and I saw Flora the flower lady—and Buck's aunt—walking toward me. "Hi, Flora. Have you met Mac Sullivan?"

"Oh my. No." She patted her chest. "I was too timid to introduce myself. But . . . I have all your books, Mr. Sullivan, and I just love that Jake Slater."

Mac grinned and shook her hand. "Well, thank you, Flora. I really appreciate that. And you'd better call me Mac."

"Oh, that would be lovely. Thank you."

I looked at Mac. "Flora is the flower lady for the church."

She smiled bashfully. "That's what the kids call me, but I do have an official title. I'm president of the Ladies Society. And I also like to call myself the unofficial historian of the church. I've been working here for over thirty years, and I've kept records of everything that's happened, including all the construction work and minor remodeling jobs we've done over the years. So ask me anything."

"Oh, that's great," I said. "I have a feeling I'll need some of that information."

"Good. That's what I'm here for."

"I might need your expertise as well," Mac said. "I was thinking of writing a scene inside a church."

"A Jake Slater scene?" she asked cautiously.

"Yes."

She leaned in closer. "Will there be explosives?"

Mac laughed. "Of course."

"Oh, how wonderful." She giggled. "I'll be glad to help in any way I can."

"Flora is Buck Buckner's aunt," I explained to Mac. "Remember Buck? The lighting designer from Chloe's show?"

"Hey, I sure do," he said, studying Flora a bit more carefully. "Well, isn't that amazing?"

She smiled up at him. "It's a wonderfully small world, isn't it?"

Mac grinned. "You can say that again, Flora."

I had to smile, hearing that remarkably apropos cliché used once again.

Flora blinked, then grabbed my arm. "Goodness, I almost forgot why I was looking for you, Shannon."

"What can I do for you?" I asked.

"I wanted to introduce you to Colleen Sayles. She's a good friend."

Colleen. That was the woman Lavinia didn't trust. But it seemed that she and Flora were close. I wondered what the real story was.

Flora glanced around, her forehead furrowing with concern. "Now, where did Colleen go? I'll find her and get the two of you together."

"Okay. Who is she, by the way?" Lavinia had already given me a few details, but I wanted to get a second opinion.

"Colleen is the church secretary. She's been working for Reverend Patterson almost as long as I have."

"You have a lot of loyal employees around here," Mac said.

"We're all very loyal to the Pattersons because they're

such lovely people," she said. "Colleen is, too. And she's so smart. She'll be able to intercede if you need to get anything done around here. Or if you have any questions for Reverend Patterson, she'll make sure you get answers."

"She sounds like someone I'd like to get to know," I said.

Flora beamed. "Oh, she is. And of course, unlike myself, she is the true *official* historian for the church. So if I'm not around, you can always call her."

"Yoo-hoo, Flora!"

We all turned and saw a woman approach from the narthex.

"Talk about perfect timing," Flora said to us, then turned to the woman. "There you are, Colleen. Come meet these two."

From where I was standing, it appeared that Colleen's smile was forced. I guess I couldn't blame her. With murder and everything else that was going on here, who had time to make nice with new people?

But Colleen made the effort and walked over with her arm outstretched to shake hands. "Hello, I'm Colleen Sayles."

I smiled as I shook her hand. "Hi, I'm Shannon Hammer. I'm the contractor working on the church renovation."

"Of course. It's good to meet you."

Mac held out his hand. "Mac Sullivan. Nice to meet you."

"Oh." She blinked. "I've heard of you. You write books."

"Guilty as charged," he said with an easy smile.

"They're very good."

Now he grinned. "Thanks, Colleen. I appreciate it."

Colleen was about Flora's age, late fifties or maybe sixty. She was tall, about five foot ten, with big blue eyes and dark hair cut short and shaggy.

"I told them you're the official historian for the church," Flora explained. "And they might have some questions for you once they get going on the renovation."

"Call me anytime," Colleen said. "It was nice to meet you both. Now I'd better go find Lavinia and Roy."

"Good to meet you, too," Mac said.

As I watched Colleen hurry down the aisle, I mentally added her to my list of people who the cops needed to interview right away. Because in case anyone had forgotten, we had a murder to investigate.

Chapter Seven

I set my shoulder bag on the kitchen table and flopped down onto the nearest chair. "Why am I so exhausted? I hardly did any work today."

Mac stood behind me and rubbed my shoulders. "It's hard work focusing on everyone else's needs all day."

I groaned. His hands felt so good.

"It shouldn't be that hard," I murmured. "I like everyone there, especially my crew. I'm always happy to be around them."

Robbie immediately clamored for attention, but I was too distracted by Mac's strong fingers massaging my neck. Robbie simply jumped up and sat on my lap, which was fine with me.

Tiger strolled over and joined the party by twining herself around my ankles and finally making herself at home on my feet. Luke followed and curled himself up around Tiger. It was so lovely to know they were all friends. Well, until the food came out.

"You always seem pretty happy when you're working," Mac said. "But at some point during the day, you'd have realized that you were sitting in the same room with a killer. That's got to slow you down."

I winced and shut my eyes. "Thanks for that reminder."

He kissed the top of my head. "I'm always here to help."

"You sure are." I rolled my shoulders and stretched my back. "Thanks, Mac. That felt good."

"Anytime." He walked over to the refrigerator and pulled out the half-full bottle of Viognier we'd had with dinner the night before. "Hey, I never got a chance to hear what happened when you and Eric disappeared."

I sat back in my chair. Robbie took the opportunity to hop down to the floor and roamed the room looking for things to sniff.

"Well, first thing he wanted to see was the body, of course, and I knew which way to go. But since you know Eric, you won't be surprised to hear that he really didn't want to hear my opinion about anything."

"But I assume you convinced him to listen to you." Mac grinned. "Because you were both gone for a long time."

"I convinced him." I couldn't keep the self-satisfaction out of my voice. "At first, he was his usual hard-nosed chief-of-police self."

"I know it well," Mac said with a chuckle.

"Me too. But after a minute or two, he realized I had some important things to tell him, so he actually paid attention to what I'd found out."

"Wait." He pulled down two wineglasses, filled

them, and handed one to me. "I want to hear about all that, too."

I took a sip. "Mmm, thank you." I set the glass down on the table. "I was dying to tell you, but I didn't want to say anything inside the church."

He sat down and clicked his glass against mine. "Cheers, Irish."

I smiled at him. "Cheers, Mac."

We both took a sip of wine, then Mac said, "Now watch this."

Robbie barked once from across the room where he'd been waiting patiently for attention. Mac gave a signal—he patted the side of his leg—and Robbie sprinted across the room and leaped up onto Mac's lap.

I laughed. "Wow. Superdog."

"It's a little trick we've been working on," Mac said.

I frowned. "Is that where all the bacon went?"

"Rewards were required."

I reached over and gave Robbie a quick scratch behind the ears, then kissed Mac. "I love you guys."

"We're pretty crazy about you, too," he said, and Robbie barked in agreement. The dog jumped off Mac's lap and strolled over to his water bowl.

Mac took another sip of wine. "Okay, so tell me everything now."

We settled in for a long talk. I told him how I'd found the body of Sarah Spindler after struggling to get the door open. Then I went through everything that had happened with Eric. "Once everyone had talked to the cops, Eric shut down the church, and we all had to leave."

"I was there for that. But as soon as I talked to Tommy, I came back home."

"Right. So after you left, I had a meeting with my people to figure out alternate assignments and readjust everyone's schedules."

"Eric made it sound like it would just be for a few days."

"Yeah, but I'd like to keep everyone working and happy and making money in the meantime."

"Can't complain about that."

"I hope not." I thought for a moment, then admitted, "I spent some time in my truck driving around and feeling sorry for myself. I mean, it's happening again. My latest construction project has been halted by murder."

Mac was watching me. "I hope you're not blaming yourself."

"No, of course not. But it's a little weird, don't you think?"

"I do. But it can't be about you."

He said it kindly, so I reached for his hand. "I know. But a few times, I couldn't keep the thought from creeping up on me. The only way to make it go away was to remember Sarah. I pictured her on that hard, cold floor. And I had to ask myself, Why? What in the world happened? She was a good person. Why would someone do that to her? Why did they hurt her? Did she see something she shouldn't have seen? Did she interrupt some criminal act? Did she say something to the wrong person?"

Mac squeezed my hand in sympathy. "Those are good questions. And I know it won't do me any good to ask you not to try and find out the answers all by yourself."

I bit back a smile. "Probably not."

"Okay, so do me a favor. If you're tempted to track down some suspicious character all by yourself, promise me you'll call me first."

"I promise," I said.

"Good. Because you know how much I hate to miss out on the action."

I laughed and kissed him. "I know."

He smiled brilliantly. "Guess I'd better start the spaghetti sauce."

"Good idea," I said, rubbing my stomach. "I'm starving."

"Yeah, me too."

"I'll go pick some veggies and make a salad."

"And while you're making the salad, you and I can talk about criminal acts."

I grinned. "I'd better hurry up with those veggies."

Twenty minutes later, I stood at the kitchen island chopping lettuce for the salad. I had been growing vegetables in raised beds for years now, ever since high school when I'd needed to distract myself from a broken heart and decided to bring my mother's garden back to life.

This year, I was growing six kinds of greens: romaine, red leaf, butter lettuce, Swiss chard, elephant kale, and arugula. Okay, some considered arugula an herb, but my arugula had big fat green leaves and a fresh peppery flavor, so I was putting it in the greens category. I also had a huge batch of celery, plus carrots and green onions. And just for Mac, I dug up a garlic bulb for him to add to his sauce.

I'd planted one entire bed with cucumbers and zucchini vines, and put my tomato plants in separate pots because they tended to overwhelm the garden. And I had lots of herbs. Thyme, cilantro, basil, tarragon, mint, lavender, and more.

Back in the day, I would dry my herbs and bundle them together with string, then ride my bike around town and deliver them to all my best friends. These days, I was a little too busy with all my construction work, but I had always enjoyed delivering my little herb bundles. It was a good way to visit and make sure my friends were okay.

In the kitchen, Mac had filled a pot with water and put it on the stove to boil. The tangy, garlicky aroma of the marinara was causing my stomach to groan in anticipation.

As Mac stirred the sauce, he asked, "So, who do you suspect is our killer?"

"Isn't it a little early to be coming up with suspects?"

His smile was innocence personified. "It's just a game, remember?"

"Yeah, and I remember how cutthroat you are when you play it."

His laugh was a little wicked.

It was the Scooby-Doo game, and the two of us had been playing it ever since we met. He often used it as a writing tool when he was coming up with characters for his books. The game was based on the old cartoon show *Scooby-Doo*, in which four teenagers and a Great Dane tracked down the bad guys.

We had gotten to be pretty good at it.

"I'll have to get a pen and some paper to do this right." I always liked to make two columns in order to play the suspect list against a list of motives each one might've had.

Some couples went bowling. Mac and I solved crimes. At least, on paper anyway.

I put the salad bowl into the refrigerator and pulled pen and paper from the kitchen drawer.

"We're going to need more wine," Mac said, and poured the rest of the Viognier into our glasses, giving each of us about a half glass.

"And we're going to need cheese." I pulled out a hunk of rich Parmesan, grated a hefty portion into a small serving bowl, and put it on the dining room table. We both loved lots of Parmesan cheese sprinkled on our pasta.

Returning to the kitchen, I sat and drew that line down the center of the page to make my two columns. "I'm going to go ahead and write down everyone's names."

"Good start."

I wrote down all the members of my crew who were there this morning, then added Madeline Whistler; Flora the flower lady; Reverend Roy; Lavinia; Mr. Brindley, the handyman; and Colleen, the church secretary. For fun, I added Whitney's name because, hey, she was a suspicious character.

I added Mac's name, too, because I knew he would want to be included.

"Water's boiling," Mac said. "The pasta will take fourteen minutes."

"Okay. Do you want to hear the suspect names now or wait until we're sitting in the dining room?"

"Let's hear one name," he said.

"Okay. Madeline Whistler."

"Oh yeah," he said immediately. "She's obviously guilty."

I had to laugh. "Do you even know who she is?"

"She's the head of the new art museum, right?"

"Yes." I was impressed that he knew.

"She's older than Sarah, right?"

"Oh, for sure," I admitted. "Probably about fifteen years older."

"And Sarah was born and raised here in Lighthouse Cove, right?"

"Yes."

"What about Madeline?"

"She moved here three years ago. So what?"

"So everybody knows Sarah, and by the time the museum finally opens in a year or so, Sarah would've known all of the artwork, she'd have a list of all the contacts in the art world, and she'd know everything about running the place. And she would know every member of the town council who all know and love her, too. Because she's their hometown girl."

"So what?"

"So the council would have fired old Madeline—who makes way too much money, by the way—and put Sarah in charge. They'd give her a token raise and everyone would be happy."

"Yikes," I said. "Even knowing you made that up, it's a real possibility."

"I know, right? And believe me, Madeline could see the writing on the wall. She had to get rid of her pretty little assistant."

"That is cold," I said.

He laughed. "But reasonable, don't you think?"

I cringed, hating to admit it. "Yeah, kind of."

"So tell me what happened when you first saw her today."

I thought about it. "Okay. Madeline met us on the steps in front of the church."

"You saw her drive up?"

I thought about it for a few seconds. "No."

"Is it possible that she got there early and exited out the back way, then walked around to meet you all?"

I frowned. "It's possible."

"For all you know, she could've planned to meet Sarah an hour earlier. Then the two of them went inside to check out one of the rooms, and Madeline bashed her in the head and dragged her into the blue chapel."

"That's not . . ." I was still frowning. It was too easy to picture it.

He was delighted by my hesitancy. "You can see how it could've happened."

"Okay, yes. Maybe I can. But it's not possible. I seriously don't believe that Madeline killed Sarah." I was a little concerned that he'd gotten into it so quickly. "This is still a game, right?"

"Of course," he said with a laugh.

"Good." I rubbed my arms. "Because that gave me chills."

"I'm proud of you," he said, still grinning.

I shook my head. "You're a weirdo."

"I love you, too," he said fondly, and poured the pasta into the strainer.

"This sauce is so rich," I said, almost moaning in delight. "It's delicious."

Mac twirled pasta around his fork. "I think it's one of my best."

"Your sauce is always good, but this is really extra amazing."

"Thank you, ma'am." He held out his glass and I clinked mine against his. "Your salad is pretty awesome, too," he added. "I love that dressing."

"Thanks. It's basically lime juice and olive oil with salt and pepper and a few other little goodies."

"When you combine it with all those fresh veggies from your garden, it becomes extraordinary."

"Well, thank you," I said.

We toasted each other again and took another bite or two. Then Mac said, "Ready for round two?"

"Yes," I said, "because I really want to wash away the bad things you said about Madeline."

He grinned and rubbed my arm soothingly. "Remember, it's just a game."

"I know, but doesn't it feel a little creepy to talk about people that way?"

"That's because once we lay out all the motives, it can start to sound plausible. Anyone could commit murder under the right circumstances."

I frowned. "I don't want to believe that, but I guess it could happen."

"Let's just have fun with it," he said. "So who's next?"

"I'll do an easy one, and by that, I mean someone with no motive at all."

"A challenge," Mac said.

"That's right, because the next name is Wade Chambers."

"Your head foreman and one of our best friends." Mac nodded slowly and swirled his wine as he gave it some thought. "Okay, I've got it. Wade was secretly having an affair with Sarah. She threatened to tell his wife, and he had to kill her."

"Well, that was way too easy," I said. "And very wrong."

"Really? How well do you know Wade?"

I laughed. "Stop it."

"Those pesky extramarital affairs are always getting in the way, aren't they?"

"Not when it comes to Wade."

"But you're writing it down in the motive column anyway."

"Well, yeah. That's part of the game."

It was his turn to laugh. He took the paper and studied the list. "Let's go with Reverend Roy next."

"He was so nice," I said. "But then Sarah found a list of all of his offshore accounts and threatened to tell his wife and the bishop."

"See how easy it is?" Mac said with a laugh, and gave me a high five. "Let's do his wife. Lavinia, right?"

"Yes, and she's very nice, too. The two of them are such lovely people."

"They really are," Mac said. "You'd never know she had a gambling addiction. Sarah was at the racetrack with her boyfriend when she happened to run across Lavinia putting five hundred dollars down on Lucky Louie in the fourth race."

"I am shocked," I said. "I'll bet her husband doesn't know."

Mac shook his head. "No, he does not. Lavinia offered to pay Sarah to keep her mouth shut, but Sarah tried to blackmail her instead. Lavinia had to kill her."

"Wow, they're not such a lovely couple after all," I said.

"Nope."

I gave him a big smile. "We're getting pretty good at this."

"You're not feeling guilty anymore, are you?"

"I think I'm over it." I smiled and held out my glass. "Thank you."

"You're welcome."

I took a sip of wine. "I'm getting so full."

"Me too. But it was good, huh?"

"It was wonderful," I said. "And we have enough left over for two more dinners."

"We're pretty savvy when it comes to cooking, aren't we?"

I smiled at him. "Yes, we are."

"Okay, last name tonight." He put down his fork. "Flora the flower lady."

I stared at him. "You were suspicious of her this afternoon, weren't you?"

"You could tell?"

"Yeah. You had a funny look on your face when you were talking to her about Buck and what a small world it is."

"You picked up on that."

"Well, I'm getting to know you pretty well."

He reached for my hand and pressed a kiss onto it. "Likewise, I think."

I had to take a breath. "Um, you think it's too much of a coincidence that we met him in Hollywood and I hired him, and not only does his aunt live here, but she works at the church that we're refurbishing?"

"Yeah, that's just way too much." He sat back in his chair. "I'm not accusing her of anything. In fact, I can't imagine what her motive would be. But since we're playing the game, I think it would be smart to keep her on the suspect list and watch her."

"What about Buck? He seems like such a nice guy and a really good worker."

"I agree, he's a really nice guy." He thought about it for a long minute, then slowly smiled. "And that's why I think we'd better watch him, too."

The next morning, while sitting at the kitchen table drinking coffee, we talked about our plans for the evening. I was going to my friend Emily's home for our monthly girls' night out, and Mac was having his buddies over for their monthly poker party. He had already placed his order with our favorite Italian restaurant for pizzas and salads and garlic bread. One of the guys—my friend Lizzie's husband, Hal—would pick everything up on his way over since he worked right down the street from the restaurant.

Last weekend, we had shopped for all the other supplies the guys would need: beer, chips, dips, salsa, nuts, and cookies. They were set for the evening.

I poured another cup of coffee for each of us, then said, "I thought of something else I meant to tell you yesterday."

Mac was stroking Tiger's back and causing the lucky cat to purr loud enough for the whole neighborhood to hear. "Something to add to the Scooby-Doo game?"

I thought for a second. "Um, not really. It's more to do with the ongoing horror that is Whitney Reid Gallagher."

"Ah. Let's hear it."

I told him how Whitney had come screaming into the

church, and when she saw Madeline crying, she accused me of hurting her. "And when Whitney heard that Sarah was dead, she went ballistic." I shook my head and sat down again. "She was shrieking and moaning and crying, and of course, she was accusing me of causing Sarah's death. She said, or rather shrieked, to Madeline, 'I warned you that death follows her wherever she goes!'"

I had tried to imitate Whitney, and now I was developing a headache.

"Good God," Mac muttered. "That woman is unhinged."

"True."

"I had other words in mind for her," Mac admitted. "But that's the cleanest I could manage."

I gritted my teeth. "I wanted to pull out my hammer and whack her with it."

"I'm sorry you have to put up with her."

"Me too." I sipped my coffee. "I was wondering what she was doing there, but apparently, she's a friend of Madeline's. And that's just weird. I have no idea how the two of them got together."

"That's a puzzle," Mac said. "You want me to find out?"

I laughed in surprise. "You're too busy to bother with things like that."

"You're right. But I would love to figure out why she's always showing up when you're on a job."

I frowned at him. "She does, doesn't she?"

He shrugged. "Something to think about."

I thought about it for a few seconds, then remembered another moment. "Listen to this. Something else happened between Whitney and Carla."

"Carla? Really? What happened?"

"Well, first I have a disclaimer to make. I heard this secondhand because I went off with Eric to look at the murder scene."

Mac nodded. "Understood."

"So, according to Wade, Whitney was still whispering loudly to Madeline, and I guess Carla asked her to be quiet. Mainly because she was complaining about me. So that made Whitney mad, and she started accusing Carla of being my stooge."

"That's ridiculous."

"I know," I said. "So Carla told her to get out."

"She probably didn't take that too well."

"No. Apparently that really triggered Whitney, and she started yelling and swearing and stomping her stupid stilettos. And finally Carla shouted, "Show some respect, you heathen. You're in a damn church!"

Mac laughed. "You're kidding."

"Nope. And honestly, I've never seen Carla get pushy or angry or anything. She's totally calm. The most gracious woman I know."

"That's a good description of her," Mac said.

"Yeah. But lately she's been getting in Whitney's face more and more. Carla told me that the change started to happen when her little girl Keely ended up in the same class with one of Whitney's boys."

"Uh-oh," Mac said. "I've met Keely. She's a sweetheart."

"She is, and she doesn't put up with troublemakers."

"I almost hate to ask. Did it get ugly?"

"Oh yes, it got ugly. But only because Whitney was one of the mothers in the classroom that day, and she stuck her stupid nose into it."

Mac rubbed his hands together. "I've got to have details."

I laughed. "Okay, so Whitney's son Tyler was taunting Keely, and he just wouldn't stop. He was being a little jerk, probably because his mother was there, and he thought he could get away with murder."

"Did Keely clean his clock?"

"Only in the most gracious way, since she's Carla's daughter. She spoke very quietly and firmly to little Tyler, telling him that if he didn't stop, she would have to put him in his place."

"That's it? That's all she said?"

"That's all she had to say," I said. "Because she's the princess of calm. But Tyler kept giving her grief, and Keely told him he needed a time-out. And that's when Whitney turned to Keely and said, 'Why, you little witch. Don't you tell my son what to do. Apologize right now.'"

Mac's eyes widened. "Whoa. Whitney said that to Keely?"

"Yup. And then Tyler turns to his mother and says, 'Mommy, you're being unfair.' And Whitney tells him to shut up."

"You're kidding."

"Nope. So Tyler shakes his finger at his mother and says, 'Mommy, you're being a bully. You have to go to the principal's office.'"

"Uh, did Whitney turn on her own kid?" Mac wondered.

"Of course," I said, laughing. "Whitney repeats, 'Shut up, Tyler.' So then Tyler and Keely both turn to their teacher, who says very politely, 'Mrs. Gallagher, we have a zero tolerance policy for that kind of behavior in this classroom, so you'll have to wait in the hall.'"

"Go, teacher!" Mac said.

At his raised fist, I laughed again. "But then Whitney says to the teacher, 'Don't be ridiculous.' And the teacher says, 'Ma'am, you realize you're getting off easy, don't you? I could send you to the principal's office.'"

"No way!" Mac said.

"Yes way," I said. "And now all the kids are chanting, 'Send her! Send her!'"

Mac pounded the table. "I love it."

"And get this," I said. "When Carla came to pick up Keely that afternoon, the teacher was the one who told her the whole story."

Mac grinned. "Gotta love a teacher who's on the side of the angels."

His words made me smile. "Yes, you do."

An hour later, I was upstairs getting dressed for work when I realized I really didn't have any work to go to. I sat down on the edge of the bed and thought about it. I could go up to the Gables and check on the work we'd done for Jane's hotel. Or I could go up to the lighthouse and make sure everything was going well with my team up there. Or . . .

"Shoot," I muttered. I was all geared up to work on the church renovation. But that was impossible.

"What's wrong?" Mac said when he walked into the bedroom.

"I'm not sure where to go today. I mean, I have plenty of choices, but I was all psyched up to start the church project. I completely forgot that the church is now a crime scene."

"Why don't you come with me to Homefront?"

I gazed up at him. "What's going on there today?"

He gave a casual shrug. "There's some talk about building more tiny homes."

"Seriously?" I was excited to hear it.

"Yeah," he said, then grinned. "Actually it's more than just talk. The property still has enough space, and we have a whole bunch of vets on a waiting list hoping to move in as soon as someone else moves out. But nobody has moved out. I mean, why would they? Homefront is so nice, and the community center offers just about everything a veteran—or anybody, really—would need to live a good, healthy life. So we made the decision to add on some more houses."

"You didn't tell me that."

He sat down next to me and draped his arm across my shoulder. "Shannon, you've been inundated with details on getting the church renovation up and running, and I know it's going to be an important new addition to the town. I just figured I'd wait to mention it until we had a firm plan in place. But believe me, I'm not about to start this new addition to Homefront without you."

I believed him. "When would you want to start building?"

"It would probably take two to three months to get it going. Depends on how quickly we can have the equipment and materials delivered. I'd love to get your input on that. I remember you and your guys had a pretty well-oiled machine putting those homes together."

"That's for sure." My guys and I had worked it to the point where we'd been able to build five tiny homes a week from start to finish. And they were beautiful, if I do say so myself.

"So, I thought that once you got the church project going, you might be able to send a few of the guys over to Homefront, along with Carla or Wade. And we could get started on twenty new homes."

"Twenty?" I jumped up from the bed. "That's fantastic."

He smiled broadly as he stood and then slipped on a lightweight denim jacket. "Yeah, we're all pretty excited about it. We're just working out the details."

"Just give me ten minutes to get ready, and I'll go to your meeting with you. Okay?"

He leaned over and kissed me. "It's better than okay."

Chapter Eight

Driving onto the Homefront property always gave me chills in the best possible way. I had been working in construction most of my life, and when I looked around Lighthouse Cove in almost any direction, I could see my work and be proud of what my team and I had accomplished. In my head, I often ran my own personal highlight reel, which might sound a little crazy, but it helped to look at my completed projects to verify that we were doing a good job.

One that I was particularly proud of was Mac's lighthouse mansion, which I'd begun refurbishing shortly after he moved to town. There was the new barn and Ecosphere at Rafe and Marigold's farm. And who didn't love Jane's beautiful new luxury hotel and restaurant at the Gables? Of course, I was truly pleased that my friend Emily had hired me to renovate her haunted house. And the restoration of the old lighthouse north of town was something we'd been excited to take on.

Added to those jobs, I had dozens of home makeovers and remodeling jobs throughout the town. But I had to admit that I was proudest of my participation in the building of the veterans' village known as Homefront.

This was the sort of place that changed people's lives for the better. And I wasn't just referring to the veterans who lived here. Everyone who worked here or came to one of the workshops felt it, too. I had seen it happen before my eyes, and it was beyond inspiring to be a part of it.

Mac grabbed my hand and we walked into the community center together. It was heartening to see so much activity going on in this place.

The café was filled with people, some eating breakfast with neighbors, others sitting alone with a cup of coffee and a laptop. Some were writing or paying bills. Others were checking emails or simply sneaking a peek at the latest social media gossip.

Walking down the hall, we saw folks sitting in chairs, waiting for one of the many different counselors who were there to help with everything from mental health to job seeking to veterans' benefits. There were a couple of guys waiting outside the door to the barbershop and another waiting for the nurse who came twice a week. The place was humming, and it gave me a warm feeling to know that I'd contributed to its overall success.

Our meeting with Vince, the community project manager, was short, sweet, and productive. Mac laid out the ideas that had come out of his meeting with the Homefront board of directors, which consisted of Mac and Eric and two other partners as well as Vince and two of his team members, along with a number of residents. One of the guiding principles of the board was that residents should be involved in the decision-making process. It was just one reason why the community was successful on so many levels.

Vince himself was a combat veteran who had been a commander in the army. All of the residents respected him because he was a wise, caring guy with a devilish sense of humor.

We talked about schedules and permits and equipment needed, along with a dozen other topics, including the proposed budget that twenty more houses would require.

We walked up the main road from the community center to the far edge of the property and checked out each of the short streets. There were ten tiny homes on each street, homes that my team and I had built. Then Vince pointed out the area where twenty new homes would be located. Since the property was terraced, we would add two additional levels and build ten houses on each.

Along one edge of the property, we had built a park with picnic benches and shade trees. Now I noticed that someone had constructed three raised beds and had planted lots of vegetables. Each bed was filled with lush and verdant leafy greens, along with tall tomato vines and a dozen different pepper plants. I noticed that they had set up a drip-line irrigation system that looked clean and efficient.

"Who started the vegetable garden?" I asked.

"One of the vets," said Vince. "His name is Jerry, and he was a landscape architect in his former life. He got together with the cook in the café, and they set the whole thing up. The rule is that any of the vets who want to pick some veggies for their dinner are welcome to it. Naturally, the kitchen gets the most use out of it, and Jerry supervises the whole thing. He's a really cool guy."

"That's so smart," I said. "I'm impressed."

"Shannon has a world-class garden on her property," Mac boasted. "We're always making salads and cooking all those fantastic vegetables she grows."

"I've got to admit I was surprised," Vince said. "But the guys are really into it, and the vegetables are growing like crazy."

I nodded. "Our weather is conducive to a year-round growing season."

"It's great to see the vets take charge," Mac said.

Vince grinned. "And it helps that we've added on some new cooking classes."

"Now that's brilliant," I said.

As we strolled back down to the community center, and Mac and I prepared to leave, Vince said simply, "Good to see you guys again. Let's talk later in the week and firm up the schedule to get this done."

There were handshakes and good wishes, and then Mac and I drove off.

"He makes it all sound so easy," I said.

Mac turned onto Blueberry Lane and headed for home. "That's what I like about Vince. He's always on the ball with everything that's going on here. He's smart and innovative, yet totally easygoing."

"That's the perfect combination of qualities for someone in that position."

"Yeah," he said, "I'm glad he's in charge."

When Mac drove into our driveway and parked, I

grabbed my bag, then turned and looked at him. "What's next on your agenda today?"

"I'm going to call the partners and let them know how the meeting with Vince went."

"Why weren't any of them here with you today?"

"Well, Eric seems to be busy trying to solve a murder."

I gave him a wry look. "I heard about that."

He grinned. "And Sam and Dave both told me to handle the meeting and give them the details later."

Sam and Dave were Mac's Navy SEAL buddies who had joined with Mac and Eric to form the Homefront partnership. They both lived within an hour's drive of Lighthouse Cove, and they handled other things connected to the project, like advertising and marketing. But as far as feet on the ground went, they preferred to be silent partners.

As we slid out of the car, Mac turned my question back on me. "So what's next on your agenda?"

"First, I'll call Eric and see what's going on. I'm going to try and convince him to let us work on the outside of the church for a few days. Then I thought I'd try to get together with Wade and Carla. Is it okay if I tell them about the plans for Homefront?"

"It's fine," he said slowly. "They're your foremen, so they should know what's coming up."

"I hear a 'but.'"

He chuckled. "*But* . . . maybe the three of you could keep the news to yourselves for a while, just until we actually go public."

I smiled. "We can do that."

In the kitchen, Mac made another pot of coffee. He took half of it up to his office above the garage. Once he was gone, I grabbed my phone and called Eric.

"Shannon," he said. "What's up?"

He sounded busy, so I didn't waste any time. I explained that we had plenty of work we could do on the outside of the building for the next few days. "There are dozens of superficial cracks in the walls and on the front steps, so I'm hoping it'll be okay to take care of some of them while you and your guys are working inside."

He thought about it for a few seconds. "That shouldn't be a problem. Just don't step inside the church. Don't open the doors. In fact, don't even touch the doors."

"We won't do any of that," I said easily, fighting the urge to roll my eyes. "Thank you. I appreciate it."

"Do me a favor," Eric said. "Send me a text tomorrow when you get to the church so I'll know you're out there working."

"I will. And one quick question. Do you have any idea how long we'll be locked out?"

He paused, and I thought he might give me grief. Instead, he said, "Leo and our crew will need two to three days."

"Okay. Thanks again, Eric."

He ended the call.

An hour later, I met Wade and Carla at the pub and ordered a tuna sandwich and potato chips. Both of them ordered the cheeseburger and fries. Over iced tea and soft drinks, I gave them the news about the veterans' village. They both reached for their tablets and started making notes.

"That's wonderful," Carla said.

Wade nodded. "Totally good news. And let me add that I'm glad they don't plan to start construction for another two or three months. By then, we'll have been working on the church for a while and have a better idea of how to divide up the work schedules."

"That's what I was thinking, too," I said.

Wade swiped the screen and started calculating. "As soon as we get the go-ahead, we've got to order the supplies and equipment we'll need."

"The sooner, the better," Carla said. "Then we'll need a team to get everything loaded onto the site."

"And once we're ready to start building," Wade said, "we'll split into two teams of five guys each."

"If we work at the same pace as before," I said, "barring some reasonable interruptions from the church project, we should be able to have all twenty homes completed within three to four months."

Carla glanced up from her tablet. "At that point, we'll need to schedule some of our specialty artists, like Niall and Amanda, to work on kitchen tiles and outside embellishments."

Since the entire town of Lighthouse Cove was registered as a historic landmark, and many of the homes were individually listed on the National Register of Historic Places, we had made a point of adding at least one Victorian feature per tiny house. These included things like a miniature widow's walk on the roof, some gingerbread detailing around the front porch, and gables on the pitched roofs. Each house was a little different, and everyone appreciated the variety of styles that set each home apart from their neighbor's.

Our food was delivered, so we took a few minutes to enjoy the meal. Then I said, "I spoke to Eric a little while ago. He thinks it'll take his CSI team another two to three days."

Carla's breath whooshed out. "It's still a shock to realize they're in there collecting evidence to find out who killed Sarah. She was such a sweetheart."

"I know," I said. "It's just so wrong. I can't imagine why anyone would want to hurt her."

"There are bad people in the world," Wade murmured.

I looked at Carla. "How well did you know Sarah?"

"She and my youngest sister were best friends all through school. She was always over at our house, and she was really great."

"Your sister must be devastated."

"Inconsolable," she whispered.

I could see her trying to hold back tears. "I'm so sorry."

She nodded, and we were silent for a long moment. My mind flashed on what we'd seen the day before: Sarah's inert body on the floor of the Blue Iris Chapel, her head bashed in by some hard bludgeoning instrument, blood on the floor, drag marks along the hallway.

I had to take a few breaths and shake my head to get rid of those images.

I was thankful when Carla finally said, "I need to stop thinking about that and get back on track with the schedule." She still sounded a little winded. "Chief Jensen said two to three days, so let's plan for the cops to be out by Friday. That way, it's settled, and we won't get all anxious wondering if we can start Thursday."

"Good idea," Wade said. "We can get a lot done on the outside on Wednesday and Thursday."

We spent the rest of lunch selecting the limited crew we would need for the outside job.

"Niall can supervise the work being done on the steps," I said.

"Since he's the god of stone and tile," Carla said, "there's nobody better."

I laughed. "Agreed. I'll give him a call after lunch. Wade, you'll be there to help Niall supervise the work on the walls, right?"

"I'll be there." He stared at his small screen. "This is only the first phase, so let's talk to Niall before scheduling additional people. He's got his own crew that he uses on other jobs, so he'll have some thoughts."

"That's right," I said. "So depending on how many people he thinks we'll need, we've got his two guys, plus our own: Sean, Billy, Johnny, and Amanda." I thought for a moment. "I might be able to coerce Chloe into helping, but I don't know how long she'll last. She's, you know, a superstar."

Wade grinned. "We'll happily use her for as long as she's willing to stay."

"Carla, you're still in charge of supervising our other job sites."

"Yeah," she said. "We're a couple days away from finishing the Johnson kitchen remodel. And the Farbers' patio redesign will be a few more weeks. I've got Martin, one of Niall's guys, on the patio job with us. He does beautiful work."

"Oh, he's brilliant," I said. "And where are we on the Skinners' new roof?"

"Practically done. We'll wrap it up tomorrow."

"Okay."

Wade set down his fork. "Turns out, our timing was pretty good on all those jobs."

"Yeah, it was." I grabbed my last chip. "Sounds like we'll have most of our crew available for the church job by next Monday."

"For a few weeks, anyway," Carla said. "Then I'm stealing a couple of the Mendocino guys and getting them started on the Anderson rehab."

"Right." We had booked that job a few months ago, but the Andersons hadn't been ready to pull the trigger. Now they were.

Mendocino was an hour away, and there were plenty of good workers down there who didn't mind the drive. Carla had worked with them in the past, and they all got along pretty well. "Are your Mendocino guys aware that the Anderson job might take up to six months?"

"Yeah, they're psyched."

"Good." We always liked to have several jobs going on at one time because it kept people employed and happy.

Carla sipped her soda. "And once the Homefront gig starts up, I'd like to make myself available at least a few hours a day. I love that place."

I smiled. "I think we all feel that way. We might switch things up and put you in charge of the church restoration while Wade and I work on the tiny homes and then switch after a couple of weeks."

"Sounds good," she said.

"We'll work it out," Wade said. "But yeah, I'd love to get back to the village. It was a lot of fun."

"The whole place has a good vibe going for it," Carla agreed. "I think it's the veterans themselves. They're good people, and they're really grateful to have us there, which always means a lot."

We were all excited about building the new homes at Homefront. Yes, I loved having lots of work to do, but it was extra gratifying to know that the people you were working for were appreciative.

Once lunch was over, we walked to my house a block and a half away. The first thing I did was call Niall to ask him if he could work for a few days on the outside of the church. I put him on speakerphone so we could all talk.

"Since we can't get inside the church for a few days," I said, "I thought we could start repairing the mortar around some of those loose stones on the front of the church. And we could also smooth over the pitted surfaces of the outside steps."

Niall immediately agreed. "But eventually, we'll have to replace the steps altogether because of the water damage."

"I agree," I said. "But for now, we'll do some cosmetic work so someone doesn't catch their heel on those steps and twist an ankle. And I'd like you to supervise since you're our expert."

"That's not a problem," he said jovially.

Wade moved closer to the phone. "Hey, Niall, it's Wade. I'll be going to the hardware store this afternoon to pick up whatever you think we'll need for the job. Can you go with me?"

"I can," Niall said. "If you're making a list, you'll want to add mortar, and we'll need two London trowels. One standard ten-inch and one seven-inch pointer."

"Got it," Wade said.

"I'll bring my own mixing tubs."

"Okay." And then, because it was Niall's show, I asked, "What would you like for the steps?"

"We can temporarily seal those pitted areas with fast-drying cement."

"I'll add that to the list," Wade said.

"Oh, and we can pick up two six-and-a-half-inch masonry brushes."

"Will do," Wade said.

"You know, Shannon," Niall said, "I noticed some excess moisture along the base of the church on the north side. I fear there may be some foundational damage."

I looked at Wade and grimaced. "That sounds bad."

"We can dig down and get an idea," Niall said, "but we won't know for sure until we can get into the basement."

"Sorry," I said. "We won't be able to do that for a few days."

Niall thought for a moment. "I'd like to give those steps and walls a closer look before we spend too much money."

"Do you have time right now to meet me at the church?" Wade asked. "We can take another look and confirm what needs to be done."

"That would be best." Niall paused, then said, "I can be there in fifteen minutes."

"Sounds good," Wade said. "I'll see you then."

They ended the call and I had to smile. "Good. I'm glad we set that up. And you and Niall will pick up everything we'll need for the outside jobs."

"Great," Wade said. "I'll call you from the church in case anything changes."

"I would appreciate that," I said. As he started to leave, I added, "Save your receipts."

He grinned. "Yes, boss."

I'd been telling him to save his receipts since the day we started working together, and he'd never forgotten, not once. At this point, it was almost a joke.

"I'm going to take off, too," Carla said.

"Okay." I walked with them to the front door. "Just a quick reminder not to mention the Homefront job. It's our secret, for now."

They both assured me that mum was the word, then left the house.

In the kitchen, I sat down to play with Robbie for a few minutes. Tiger sauntered in and simply sat and watched, while Luke ambled in like the royalty he was and allowed us to play with him, too. I gave all three of them treats, and they settled down to munch on them.

Twenty minutes later, Wade called. "Niall's hunch was correct. We've got a drainage issue along the north wall. I'd like a few extra guys to bring the backhoe so we can do some exploratory digging."

"Get in touch with Sean," I said. "He'll arrange it. And I'll contact Madeline to let her know what's going on."

"Got it. We'll keep you posted."

"I appreciate it. Thanks, Wade."

He hung up, and I texted Mac to let him know I would be leaving in a little while to see my girlfriends. "Hope you have a manly time tonight."

A minute later, Mac texted back. "Have a great time with the girls. Bring me back some good gossip." And he added a laughing face.

I sent back a kiss and a row of pretty red hearts.

An hour later, I drove over to Emily Rose's house to meet my girlfriends for our monthly dinner and discussion group.

"Dinner and discussion" sounded so much more refined than "gabfest."

Emily opened the door and grabbed me for a big hug. "I feel like I haven't seen you in months."

"It's only been a few weeks," I said with a laugh. "But I'll admit I've been busy. And I've missed you, too."

"You left town for a week. Where'd you go? Was it fun?" Her soft Scottish brogue slipped out a few times as she led the way into the kitchen, where her big farmhouse table was set for six. She had come to town years ago with her fisherman boyfriend who tragically disappeared on a boating trip. She had thought about returning to Scotland, but by then, she had made a few good friends, and we saw her through the sad times. Then she met Gus Peratti and the rest was history.

A few years ago, Emily convinced some of her Scottish family to come to Lighthouse Cove, and the result was that her brother Niall, a stonemason, joined my construction crew.

"Am I the first one here?"

She turned and smiled at me. "You're always the first one here."

I winced. "Sorry."

"Don't be," she said as she eased the cork out of a nice-looking bottle of champagne. "You're right on time. Everyone else believes in being fashionably late."

"I just never got how that works," I confessed. "Is it ten minutes? Twenty?"

She chuckled. "You just keep doing what you do." She handed me a flute filled with pale bubbly liquid. "Being first has its privileges. You get the first taste of champagne."

"Ooh, lucky me."

We clicked our glasses and I took a little sip. "Oh, that's good."

"Isn't it? Gus brought home a few bottles of the good stuff for us to enjoy tonight."

"What a great guy." I took another sip.

"Aye." Her smile was dreamy. "He's a keeper."

Emily and Gus had recently announced their engagement.

"I love to hear you say that." I held up my glass in a toast. "How are the wedding plans coming along?"

She made a face. "Slowly."

"Anything I can do to help?"

"Oh, you're a sweetheart, Shannon. But it's mainly my granny who's causing problems. She'd like us to come to Scotland, but only because she's afraid to fly."

"Scotland is always nice," I said.

"But Niall is here and all of our friends are here. Gus's whole family has been here for generations. I'd like my family to see our home." She sighed. "We'll work it out. My mother says not to worry. She'll give Granny a few shots of whiskey and get her on the plane."

I laughed. "Let me know if I can do anything."

"I will, and thank you, Shannon."

I glanced around. "The house looks great."

"We love it so much."

Emily had bought the old Rawley mansion a few years ago after the place had been sitting on the market for decades. The reason for this was that everyone in town knew the house was haunted by the ghost of Mrs. Rawley.

My crew and I had begun renovation shortly after Emily closed escrow. As soon as we walked into the house, the ghost made her presence known. Paint cans were thrown across the room, and chandeliers would begin to swing dangerously—until the afternoon when

Gus Peratti walked in. Suddenly Mrs. Rawley grew calm and behaved herself. But as soon as he left? Well, it was touch and go for a while.

Happily, Gus and Emily fell in love, and he moved in permanently, bringing peace to the house at long last. Later, we found out that Mrs. Rawley had been forced to marry a man her father chose instead of the man she was in love with. That beloved man was Gus Peratti's great-grandfather.

The doorbell rang.

"That must be the girls," Emily said, and dashed to the door.

I followed her and found Jane, Chloe, and Marigold standing on the front porch.

"Come in, come in," Emily cried.

Just as she was about to close the door, we heard someone shout from the street, "Wait for me!"

"It's Lizzie," I said, and watched as one of my oldest friends leaped over a rosemary bush like some kind of forest elf and scrambled up the front steps.

We hugged. "I'm so glad to be here," she said.

"Come on in." I pulled her into the house, where there were more hugs and kisses and compliments and laughs. The women tossed their jackets and sweaters on the bench in the foyer and then followed Emily through the wide hall and into the kitchen.

Chloe sidled up beside me. "I left my house at the exact same time as you did. How did you beat me here?"

I shrugged. "I'm always on time. I can't help it."

She frowned. "Well, I did stop to look at a pair of shoes, but that only took a few minutes."

I smiled. "There you go."

"And you've already got a glass of champagne." She pouted.

"That'll teach you," I said with a laugh.

"I have champagne for everyone," Emily called. "Come get a glass."

Jane cornered me alone in the hall. "Niall told me about Sarah Spindler. I knew her in high school."

"I didn't really know her, but Chloe did," I said.

"The newspapers didn't mention who found the body in the church, but Niall let me know. I'm so sorry."

I took a deep breath. "I am, too. It's awful. She was young and lovely and talented, and I have no idea why it happened."

"Eric will find out," she said. "The thing is, I worry about you."

"Thanks." I smiled. "To tell you the truth, I do, too."

Jane and I had been best friends since first grade, when we bonded over the fact that we were both taller than all the boys in class. These days, she was a few inches taller than me, but our friendship had stood the test of time—and height. Tonight she wore her long blond hair in a sophisticated twist, and her pin-striped navy suit and soft silk shirt looked impossibly chic.

"Please, please, take care of yourself," she said, hugging me once more before we walked into the kitchen.

"I love your kitchen," Chloe said, staring at the high ceiling and gorgeous crown molding, the huge island, and the double-sized farm sink.

It had once been a decent-sized kitchen with a large butler's pantry attached as well as a smaller room that Emily had termed a "winter pantry." We had removed the walls and turned the three rooms into one big fabulous space. The perfect kitchen for Emily, who made her living as a gourmet chef and baker.

"Your sister helped make it happen," Emily said. She had recently gotten a haircut, and it made her look even more like a young Audrey Hepburn than usual.

Marigold's thick auburn braid was tossed over her shoulder as she glanced around and lowered her voice. "And how's Mrs. Rawley behaving?"

I heard a rumbling sound coming from the dining room. We all stopped talking and stared at the lights that had begun to blink on and off.

Marigold's eyes widened. "I guess that answers my question."

"Gus will be home in a few hours," Emily said in a clear voice.

The rumbling and blinking stopped, and Emily smiled.

"That's just freaking weird," Lizzie muttered.

Jane shook her head. "I don't know how you live with that."

"She's a member of the family," Emily said. "And she loves Gus, which makes her my friend."

"It makes sense," I said. "He might've been her great-grandson. If things had worked out, I mean."

"You're crazy." Lizzie whispered the words in case the ghost was listening.

Emily chuckled and handed her a champagne flute. "Here, drink this."

"Thank you." Lizzie took the glass and gulped it down. "It's wonderful. I probably shouldn't have swilled it."

"Swill away, love," Emily said, giving her shoulder a little rub.

I grinned. "You're among friends."

Marigold studied Lizzie for a moment and said quietly, "You look harried. What's going on?"

Lizzie, usually upbeat and fun, was clearly stressed-out. She took another quick sip. "I've been traveling for the past few days, looking at colleges with Marisa. It's exhausting."

"Colleges?" I blinked in disbelief. "That's ridiculous. She's only twelve years old."

Lizzie held up a hand. "Oh please, don't you start. I'm having a hard enough time keeping Hal from a complete breakdown. He can't deal with the fact that our little girl is all grown up and about to move away from home."

"I don't think I can deal with it, either," I said, feeling gobsmacked.

"Speaking of weird," Marigold said. "Did you all hear about that poor woman who was found dead in the church?"

Lizzie was immediately on the alert. "What? What happened?" She stared at everyone around the table. "I haven't seen a newspaper in a week. I got home, and Hal had already left for the poker party. What's going on?"

Chloe's eyes widened and she looked at me for guidance.

Lizzie shook her finger at my sister. "I saw that look, Chloe."

My sister held up both hands. "I know nothing."

"Shannon?"

I winced. "I was hoping we wouldn't have to talk about it." Even though I'd already talked to Jane about it.

"Oh my God," Lizzie said. "You found another body?"

"Um, how about those Seahawks?" I said in a pathetic attempt to change the subject. My friends were well aware of my odd proclivity for finding dead bodies. Not that it made things any easier to explain.

Jane set down her glass and told the story. "Earlier this week, a woman was found dead in a chapel inside the Lighthouse Church."

"Inside the church?" Lizzie's eyes goggled. "Okay, I need details."

Chloe flashed me a look of alarm.

Jane had to take another sip of champagne before she could tell all. "Shannon found her."

Lizzie stared at me, then shook her head. "Girl, you are a force to be reckoned with."

"I'd rather not be."

"We understand," Marigold said. "But it does seem to be your role."

"There were a bunch of other people there at the same time," I said in my defense.

Lizzie cut to the chase. "Who was this woman? Do we know her?"

"Yes, we knew her." I grabbed Lizzie's hand instinctively.

"Now you're scaring me," she said. "Who was it?"

"I want you to take a deep breath," I said.

She frowned. "Oh God, it's bad."

"Please, Lizzie."

"All right, but you're scaring me."

"I'm sorry." I took a deep breath myself. "It was Sarah Spindler."

"No!" Lizzie shouted, and burst into tears.

I was still holding her hand, and she tightened her grip on me.

Emily looked on, helpless. "I'm so sorry."

Jane's eyes were filled with tears. "We all went to school with her."

Despite her tears, Lizzie managed to whisper, "She used to babysit Marisa and Taz. They both adored her. What will I tell them? How did it happen?"

I had to tell the truth. "She was . . . murdered."

"Nooo," Lizzie moaned, then sank down in the chair and buried her face in her hands.

Marigold scooted her chair closer, wrapped her arms around Lizzie, and just held her.

"I went to that church a few times when I first moved here," Emily said. "It was a lovely experience."

"I've been to concerts there," Jane said in a desperate attempt to lighten the mood. "The, um, acoustics are amazing."

Chloe nodded. "Because of the dome."

"Oh, yes," Jane said. "It's spectacular, isn't it?"

"Beautiful," Chloe agreed.

Emily sighed. "Can you tell us what happened, Shannon?"

"Yeah." I took in another deep breath and spent a moment wondering how many details to mention. I didn't want to say too much. "Someone hit her in the head. Bludgeoned her."

I wouldn't mention the blood or that someone had dragged her halfway across the church to hide her in the small chapel. Even though these were my dearest friends, I didn't want to burden them with the specifics. They shouldn't have to suffer with those images.

"But why would anyone want to kill her?" Lizzie cried.

"I don't know." I glanced around. "Maybe she saw someone doing something illegal. Or maybe she had come there with someone else, and they had a fight over something. Or maybe she surprised a thief who attacked her."

"In a church?" Marigold wondered.

I nodded. "I wish I could tell you more, but that's all I know."

Lizzie raised her head and looked straight at me. "But you'll find out more, won't you?"

I looked around at my friends and then back at Lizzie. "Yes, I'll find out more."

"And we'll help you," Marigold said. "You know we will. And speaking of which, I'm familiar with someone who works at that church. I can chat her up."

"Who do you know?" I asked.

"Her name is Flora."

"The flower lady?"

Marigold smiled. "Yes. She's a good friend of our store and belongs to our quilting bee. She does beautiful work."

"I've met her," I said. "She's been working at the church for years." I didn't bother mentioning her relationship to Buck. It wasn't important right now.

"Yes," Marigold said. "She brought the reverend's wife to our quilting sessions a few times, but she lost interest."

"Mrs. Patterson?" I said.

"Yes." Marigold smiled. "She seemed very kind and warm. But she just isn't a quilter."

"But Flora continues to come to the sessions?"

"Oh, yes. She's a great asset to our group."

"So maybe she knows something," Jane said. "Or she saw something odd."

"I'll ask her," Marigold said.

Lizzie said, "Just please be careful. We don't want anyone else to get hurt."

"I'll be careful," Marigold said, and patted Lizzie's shoulder. "And you know how people like to talk. The fact that a murder has just occurred is the perfect conversation starter."

Jane blinked. "Well, yes. I suppose it is."

I gazed at each of the women. "Do any of you know anyone else who might have a connection to the church? Maybe you could chat them up, ask them a question or two."

Lizzie sipped her champagne. "By now, everyone in town must know something about it. Word spreads fast around here."

"Like lightning," Marigold agreed.

"I just remembered," Jane exclaimed. "Uncle Jesse knew an old guy who worked there."

"You mean Mr. Brindley?" I asked. "He's still there. Mitch Brindley, the handyman."

"That's him. Uncle Jesse used to go to church in order to hang out with Mitch." She shook her head in amusement. "I think they played pinochle in the back room."

I had to smile. Jane's uncle Jesse had been my next-door neighbor from the time I was born. "You're probably right. I can't picture Uncle Jesse going to church to pray."

"Right?" Jane said, grinning. "But he liked Mitch. Of course, I can't ask Uncle Jesse about him now."

"No." I gave her a sympathetic smile. Her uncle Jesse had died a few years ago. "But if I mention Jesse's name, I might be able to get Mitch to talk to me."

"Just be careful," Marigold said.

"I will."

"I see Colleen fairly often," Emily said.

"The church secretary?" I said.

"Yes. She comes in at least once a week to pick up cookies or tarts or lemon bars. I think she takes them back to the church and shares them with everyone there. She's quite nice." But Emily's expression was troubled.

"Except?" I coaxed.

"Except she is a bit of a gossip. Always has something to say about the reverend and his wife."

"Good things?" Chloe said.

"Not always."

Interesting, I thought, remembering what Lavinia Patterson had said about Colleen. Maybe she was smart not to trust the woman.

Emily poured pasta from a large pot into a big serving bowl. "She's hinted that both of them have a wee problem with hoarding."

"I'm not surprised," I said. "They're still packing and cleaning up at the old church even though it's been several months since they moved to the new church. I guess it's understandable, though. They lived in the old place for more than thirty years."

Emily stirred the sauce one more time and then poured it carefully over the pasta. She used two large spoons to lightly toss it. Then she pulled another oversized wooden bowl from the refrigerator and began to pour her own homemade vinaigrette dressing over the salad. "The next time Colleen comes in, I'll ask her more about the people she works with."

"Okay, but please don't arouse her suspicions. I don't want her coming after you."

She waved my concerns away. "No worries, love. I'll be my usual sprightly self."

I had to smile. The word "sprightly" suited Emily to a T.

"Everything smells so good," Marigold said. "It's making me ravenous."

"Me too," I said. The tangy aroma of Emily's chunky pasta sauce was enhanced by the addition of freshly chopped basil, thyme, rosemary, and oregano. I could see the small pots of herbs sitting on the wide windowsill over her sink.

"Can you take this to the table?" Emily asked, handing me a large bowl filled with freshly grated Parmigiano-Reggiano that had my mouth watering.

"Sure," I said, taking hold of the bowl.

"I can take the salad bowl," Marigold said.

"It's heavy," Emily warned.

Marigold smiled. "I've got it."

"Shannon." I turned to look at Jane, who stared at me uneasily. "My mom went to that church."

I felt my mouth drop open. "She did?"

"Yes. This was a few years before she got sick and moved up to the Gables."

Jane's mother had suffered from depression and other mental illnesses, and spent many years off and on at the Gables. The place was formerly known as the Northern California Asylum for the Insane, a politically incorrect name if there ever was one.

"Did she ever take you with her?" I asked.

She nodded. "I know it's supposed to be an impressive space, very Gothic and intriguing. But, frankly, it gave me the willies."

"How so?" Emily asked.

Jane's shoulders hunched up and she shivered at the memory. "It probably sounds dumb, but the ceiling was so high, and the room itself was so dark, and there were gargoyles. It felt like they were staring at me, and I was scared." Jane's smile was self-effacing. "I was a weird kid."

"I've known you all my life, and you've never been weird," I said. "Unlike me."

"I can verify that," Chloe said.

Lizzie laughed, and that was when I knew she was okay with moving on from the sad subject of murder.

Chloe and Marigold carried several bottles of wine to the table. Jane jumped up and took one of the bottles, then began to pour the rich red wine into each of our glasses.

I followed Emily back to the stove. "What else can I do to help?"

She grabbed me in a tight hug and whispered, "You can find the blackheart who killed that lovely young lass and make sure he pays for his crime."

Chapter Nine

At the end of the evening, I made a list of each person my girlfriends hoped to contact during the week. Echoing Lizzie, I cautioned them to be careful. We all knew my warning wasn't necessary, but I still had to say it.

I had run into trouble—meaning *murder*—like this before, and my friends had always generously offered to help me solve the crime. The six of us knew practically every person in town, so why not use our contacts to figure it all out?

My friends knew how to deal with people, probably better than I did, since they all worked with the public much more closely than I. They were friendly and approachable, and they were all law-abiding citizens of Lighthouse Cove, so they knew better than to harass anyone. They would speak to people in a chatty, noncombative way.

"And we always get results," Lizzie reminded me.

"I know and I appreciate it," I said. "But somebody

out there was desperate enough to kill poor Sarah Spindler. I don't want any of you to take unnecessary chances."

"Because that person might be willing to kill again," Marigold said.

I gave a firm nod. "Exactly."

We decided to meet at Emily's tea shop for lunch sometime next week and report what we'd learned.

When I got home, Mac was just cleaning up from the poker game. I told him about my girlfriends' plan to talk to people connected to the church, and he was impressed.

"Your friends would be great at the Scooby-Doo game," he said with a grin.

"They just want to help," I explained. "Besides, among the six of us, we know just about everyone in town, so it's easy to talk to people."

"I realize that," he said, tossing a bowl of leftover peanuts into a baggie. "I remember comparing all of you to the Baker Street Irregulars a few months ago."

I laughed. "Except we're not exactly a ragtag band of ruffians."

"But because you've lived here for so many years, you can chat people up without worrying that they might think you're being nosy."

"Even though we *are* being nosy."

"True. But this is a small town, and people expect others to be friendly and, yeah, nosy."

"That's right," I said with a smile, pleased that he knew where I was going with this. But then I frowned. "Just please don't mention it to Eric."

"Not me, no way," he said, wrapping his arms around me. "It'll be our little secret."

The next morning, I met Wade, Niall, Billy, and Sean at the church steps. They had brought the backhoe and all the tools and equipment they would need to complete the work.

But before I did anything else, I called Eric, as requested. "My crew and I are here at the church."

"I'm home having breakfast with my beautiful fiancée."

"You're a lucky man," I said.

"Yes, I am."

I could tell he was smiling, and that made me happy.

"We'll be working along the north side of the church if you're looking for us," I said. "We'll be here most of today and tomorrow."

He made a sound of assent. "I'll be there in about an hour to meet up with Leo and Lilah. Some of my officers might get there sooner, but they won't bother you. I'll see you when I get there."

"Sounds good," I said.

"And Chloe says she'll swing by sometime this morning."

"We'll put her to work," I said, and signed off.

Niall pulled me aside and showed me the work his guys had already started, using the backhoe to excavate a two-foot trench along the foundation wall. Nearby was the pile of wet, muddy earth they had dug up.

I shook my head. "It sure looks like the drainage system has failed."

"Aye. We'll confirm it, but I think we'll need to replace the pipes and regrade the area." He pointed farther down. "Walk with me."

We walked another twenty feet along the church wall, and I saw that the ground was dry.

He was pointing toward the wet ground. "I believe we'll only need to fix this one twenty-foot section."

I walked back and forth, and studied the ground for another few minutes. "I trust your judgment."

"Thank you."

"What're you going to need?"

"I'll pick up the piping and get a half load of gravel and sand, and then we can start to regrade this area."

"Fine." We walked back to the steps. "Now what about all these pits and cracks?"

"All of them can be temporarily filled and smoothed over with quick-drying cement," Niall said, kneeling down on the second step. "That'll make it safer for everyone while we're working here. But as I told you, it won't be enough. There's really quite a bit of water damage. You can see the deterioration down here."

He pointed out where water had collected and caused cracks and separation along the edges of each level, especially along the base where it met the pavement. "And can you see these deeper cracks where the riser meets the tread? They can't be glossed over."

The tread was the horizontal surface of the step, and the riser was the vertical.

I bent down to study the damage and sighed. "The entire stairs need to go."

"Aye, they will," Niall said. "And we'll have to do what we can to fix the underlying cause before we pour the new steps."

I took another long look at the damage. "I thought some of these cracks were from earthquakes."

"Some of them may be," he said. "But my hunch is that water is the bigger enemy, causing more damage over time than almost anything else. We live by the ocean, Shannon, so of course it rains quite a bit, and then it often freezes over, putting more pressure on the surfaces. As you know all too well, when water seeps into places it doesn't belong and freezes, it expands and causes a good deal of damage."

"Of course." I stood up, appreciating that Niall was spelling it out in simple terms. "Okay. We'll have to figure out the water issues and eventually replace them completely, but not until we're finished with the entire project."

"You've the right of it," Niall said with a nod. "For now, we'll do what we can to smooth out the surfaces to keep us all from tripping over our feet."

"Thank you," I said with a smile.

Wade joined us and I asked, "Do we have all the materials we'll need to get it done?"

"Aye." Niall grinned at my foreman. "Wade is an expert shopper."

"That's why I keep him around," I said, chuckling.

Niall glanced over at the rest of the crew. "Everyone here has done this sort of work with me before. If it's all right with you, I'll get Billy started at the top of the staircase, and he can work his way down. I'll tackle repairing the cracks in the mortar around the stonework on the front of the church."

"Fine with me," I said. "Are we going to need more guys?"

Niall shook his head. "I think we're good for now."

* * *

An hour later, I took a break and Wade joined me. "I want to get Carla on the phone and finalize the arrangements she made to get the articulated boom lift over here."

Carla answered her phone on the first ring, and I asked her what the situation was. "I was just going to call you about that. Carter Construction can deliver it by flatbed truck to the church first thing Friday morning."

"That'll be perfect timing," I said.

"I thought so, too," she said.

As my father always said, the articulated boom lift was the snazziest piece of equipment we owned. We didn't use it all the time, so I was usually willing to loan it out to other construction firms in the area. Most of the companies around our town worked on Victorian homes that were often three stories high with extremely steep roofs. The boom lift was a godsend for many of us.

Despite the fact that it was an expensive piece of equipment, I only charged the other guys a nominal rental fee to cover maintenance and repairs. This was because everyone in town knew that my father had won the boom lift in a poker game years ago. So since it hadn't cost us any money to buy it, why would we charge an arm and a leg to rent it out?

Months ago, Carla had alerted the other contractors in town that we would need the exclusive use of the articulated boom lift for the next few months at least, though probably longer.

Maneuvering the piece of machinery into the church was something we had worked out months ago. We would be taking the lift into the church through the south transept door, where there were no steps to deal with. The side doorway was wide and tall enough to accommodate the chassis with the articulated arm in the horizontal position. Once we got it inside the church, the arm could be raised to a height of fifty-two feet, allowing my crew to work on the crossbeams and all the way up to that forty-eight-foot ceiling.

"By the way," I said, while we still had Carla on the phone, "I'm reminding you both that I want everyone to wear a safety harness if they're working on the beams or up on the roof, especially when they're using the lift."

"Of course," Carla said immediately.

Wade made a point of rolling his eyes. "Yes, boss."

I glared at him. "Are you trying to make me mad?"

He laughed. "Just kidding. Of course we'll all wear safety harnesses. Anyone who works on your crew is aware of that hard-and-fast rule."

"Okay," I said, mollified. "Thank you."

When I was younger and working for my father, I watched one of his crew fall from a pitched three-story roof. It was one of the most frightening things I'd ever seen. Nobody went on a roof or climbed the side of a building or went up in a boom lift without wearing a harness. It was the law.

I stared up at the roof of the church. I knew this building wasn't nearly as big as some churches in major cities, but dang, it was still pretty darn high. I wouldn't want anyone to fall from that height.

"While we're talking about it," Wade said, "we've never been up to the roof to inspect it."

"Madeline was assured by her architects that it was sound."

"I'm sure they're right, but I'd still like us to check it out for ourselves."

"I've got that on my list, too," Carla said.

"So have I," I said. "We might double-check with Mr. Brindley to see if he knows of any damage that's ever occurred up there."

"Good idea."

We finished the call to Carla, and Wade returned to help the guys working on the north side of the church. I walked around to the front to see if any headway was being made on the steps and the cracks in the masonry.

"Never had much time to get those cracks looked at."

I flinched at the sound and turned to find Mr. Brindley himself standing a few feet away from me. The guy moved like a wraith.

"Hey, Mr. Brindley. How are you?"

"I'm doing fine, young lady. Looks like you're making some progress."

"We are." I turned to face him. "I'm glad you're here. I was wondering if you knew when the roof was last inspected or if you're aware of any problems up there."

"It was inspected two years ago. I can get that report from Colleen."

"I would appreciate it. Thanks."

He nodded. "Someone told me I should talk to you about getting inside the church."

"I'm sorry, but nobody can get inside yet. That's by order of the chief of police. We might be able to get access on Friday."

He scowled. "But I've got to get in there. Just for a minute. It's important."

"I'm really sorry," I said, trying to sound sympathetic. "Maybe you can catch Chief Jensen when you see him, but I've got orders not to let anyone go inside until the crime scene investigation is completed."

"What's the big deal?" he said, staring at the tall double doors at the top of the steps.

I touched his arm to keep him from moving forward. "They're investigating a murder. We can't go inside until the chief says so."

He worked his jaw in frustration. "This is stupid."

"Maybe so, but you really don't want to cross Chief Jensen."

He snorted. "Huh."

"Is there anything I can do for you?"

He was still scowling. "No. It's personal."

"I understand and I'm sorry. You'll have to wait until Friday."

He gave an angry jerk of his chin. "I'll take care of it another way."

Ookay, I thought. The man had suddenly become overwrought. I wondered what he could possibly have left inside that was important enough to cause him so much turmoil. I tried to calm him down by changing the subject. "You know, I think my next-door neighbor was a good friend of yours. Jesse Hennessey?"

"Jesse." Mr. Brindley's only reaction was a half-hearted laugh that almost sounded like a cough. "He was a good friend."

"To me, too," I said. "And I'm a close friend of his niece, Jane."

"Huh." He wasn't being placated, but that didn't matter. I still couldn't let him go inside the church.

"Jesse was one of the good guys," I said conversationally. I didn't know this man, but I didn't want to see anyone getting angry around my construction site. It could cause trouble.

"Yeah," he finally said. "He was."

"Were you navy buddies?"

"No." He looked around as if he might find someone else to talk to who had more authority than little ol' me. "I gotta go."

"All right. See you later."

He walked purposefully across the town square, and I wondered what he meant when he said, *I'll take care of it another way.*

Was he going to try and sneak in some back door? I thought most of them were locked, but then, he was the handyman. He probably had keys to every door in the place.

And why was he in such a hurry to get in there?

I didn't believe he was dangerous, but I pulled out my phone and called Eric to report the conversation. Just in case.

For two days, we worked outside the building patching up cracks in the masonry, resurfacing the steps, repairing drainage, and regrading the north side of the church.

Then, Thursday afternoon, I got the call from Eric that we could go to work inside tomorrow.

"Swing by my place before you go to work," he said. "I'll give you the keys."

"Okay. It'll be pretty early," I warned.

"I'll be up. And do me a favor when you get there tomorrow."

"Sure."

"I'm fairly certain Leo and our team got everything

we needed, but if you happen to see anything suspicious or out of the ordinary, I want you to call me before you do anything else."

"All right." I was frankly surprised he didn't say, *Before you do anything* stupid.

"I mean it, Shannon. I don't want you investigating or sneaking around on your own. Someone committed cold-blooded murder inside that church. They killed a lovely young girl who had her whole life ahead of her. I don't want to see a repeat performance of that. You get me?"

His words gave me chills, and I was sure that was his intention. "I get you."

"Good."

I quickly changed the subject. "The prayer vigil for Sarah Spindler is tonight at the new church. Are you guys going?"

"I'm going," he said. "Not sure about Chloe."

"Then I guess I'll see you there."

The prayer vigil for Sarah that night was sad and somber, but joyful as well. Reverend Roy's words were very sweet, and Flora outdid herself with all the beautiful flowers. The music, a mix of soft rock and spiritual songs, was performed by a local band as well as the church organist.

A number of Sarah's friends shared wonderful stories about her, and there was plenty of laughter, along with a few tears. What came across more than anything else was the fact that she had been an upbeat, happy person who loved to have fun.

But it came as a surprise to some of her friends that Sarah had actually developed a real plan for her life. She had been the top salesperson in the cosmetic department at the local mall but decided to go back to school for a master's degree in art history after her parents took her to Paris, where she fell completely in love with the artwork at the Louvre.

Madeline talked about traveling with Sarah to New York and their visit to the Cloisters museum, where she hoped to give Sarah an idea of what they wanted to achieve at the Lighthouse Cove Museum.

"She was like a sponge," Madeline said, "soaking up the beauty of the artwork on display as well as the splendor of the building itself in all its medieval glory. Sarah was excited by the prospect of bringing that concept home, knowing we could accomplish something like that right here in Lighthouse Cove." She could no longer hold back the tears but still managed to add, "I will miss her so much. Her dedication, her energy, and oh God, that delightful little laugh of hers. I can still hear it. Can't you?"

I felt shivers up my arms as everyone in the room answered, "Yes."

After the vigil, we were all invited to the church hall for coffee and cake. I decided to attend in order to speak to Colleen, the church secretary. And also, there was cake.

I found Colleen talking with Reverend Roy in hushed tones, so I waited a few feet away until they were finished. Finally I approached her and reintroduced myself.

"Of course I remember you," she said. "How is the work coming along?"

"The church had to be closed up for the investigation, but we'll be starting back tomorrow, and I trust it'll go smoothly."

"Oh, the investigation." She grimaced. "Of course. I forgot they would have to do that."

I guess it didn't always enter into someone's consciousness, but considering that we'd just held a prayer vigil for the dead woman who was killed inside their church, maybe it should've. Colleen was a bit distracted, so I tried to bring her around to what still needed to be done at the old church. "I wonder if you know anything about the large cabinet in the sacristy."

"Of course I do. It's a beautiful piece of furniture and one of Reverend Roy's favorites. He was devastated when he realized that we couldn't bring it with us when we moved."

"I don't blame him. But I actually wanted to ask about the items inside the cabinets. The drawers and the cupboards and the armoire are still filled with clothing and silver and gold items that I assume were used by Reverend Roy. Will someone be coming to collect all of that?"

"Oh dear." She looked dismayed. "I thought Lavinia would've taken care of that."

I glanced around. "I would ask her about it, but I didn't see her here tonight."

"No, she couldn't attend the service," she said quickly. "I'll speak to her and I'll let you know."

"Thank you," I said. "It would really help if someone from the church would supervise, because I don't know what half the items are."

"Oh." Her eyes grew wider. "Oh, that won't do."

"Well, unless someone shows up to help me, it will have to do." I tried to temper my words with a smile. "Please don't worry. If you don't have anyone available, my crew and I will pack up everything very neatly and carefully. But I'm sure you'd agree that it would be better to have some guidance from one of you."

She was frowning even more deeply now. "I feel certain that Madeline must've told Lavinia about this plan."

"I'm sure she must've."

"But nobody told me," she lamented.

"Don't worry about it," I said cheerfully. "We'll be careful, but we've got to get it done. We're on a pretty tight schedule, and the cabinet has to be stripped of paint and sanded down before we can do anything else in the sacristy."

"Oh dear," she whispered, and she began to turn pale. Was she going to faint? "Lavinia must know that."

"I hope so," I said. "Maybe you can tell her that I'll be in the sacristy tomorrow morning and that I'll be emptying the drawers."

She shuddered but didn't say anything. What was she so nervous about? Was she afraid I would break something? Or was she afraid of Lavinia? Or Reverend Roy? I couldn't believe that. Maybe she was just afraid of something going wrong.

I ventured on. "One more quick question for you. Do you happen to have an inventory of the items that were left inside the cabinets?"

She took a deep breath and seemed to collect her wits. "No, we've never written up an inventory of anything in the sacristy." She coughed lightly to clear her throat. "I'll remind Lavinia of your plan to start clearing out the cabinet. I'm sure she'll want to visit you tomorrow to let you know what to do with everything."

"Good. I'll be there."

"Please be careful with anything you touch."

"Of course. Thanks, Colleen." I walked away, surprised that I actually felt some pity for her. The poor woman didn't know if she was coming or going. Did it have something to do with my announcement that I would be working in the sacristy?

I was now determined not to spend too much time alone in that room, and not just because Sarah had been killed in there. A lot of strong emotions seemed to be centered on the sacristy, and strong emotions could lead to dangerous actions. Even murder.

Early the next morning, after picking up the keys from Eric, I met my team at the bottom of the church steps. We had a quick meeting and reaffirmed everyone's assignments. I announced that I would begin working in the sacristy, and once it was completely empty, we would be able to deal with the excess layers of paint on that beautiful wood cabinet. Amanda would work with me.

Amanda nodded. "I'll take a look at it, but right now, I'm more concerned about all the sun-bleached timbers and beams I've seen. I want to check their viability and make sure they haven't rotted out or gone soft. We might have to replace some of them."

"That's critical," Wade said.

"Absolutely," I agreed. "We'll schedule things accordingly. Thanks, Amanda."

A horn honked, and I turned to see Carter Construction Company arrive with our articulated boom lift chained to the back of their flatbed truck, as promised.

Joe Carter waved to me. "I'll get this thing off the truck as soon as you're ready."

"We'll be taking it in through the side door, so I'm going to unlock everything first. Then we'll be ready to move it off the truck." I ran down the walkway and unlocked the doors, then jogged back to the front and waved at Joe. "We're ready whenever you are."

He gave me a thumbs-up, then flipped a switch inside the truck cab. Jumping out of the cab, he moved to the side of the truck, where a control panel was located, then pressed one of the levers to tilt the bed down until the end touched the ground.

I was relieved to know that the boom lift wasn't going anywhere yet. It was still securely chained, strapped, and belted to the truck bed.

Wade joined Joe on the truck bed, where they unstrapped the tires. Then they shifted the boom lift into neutral and slowly unspooled the winch cable until the lift was safely on flat ground. Only then, when the cable was slack, did Joe unlatch it from the chassis.

"Thanks, Joe," I said. "I appreciate you delivering it."

"You're the one who did us the favor, Shannon." He glanced up at the church. "Should be an interesting job."

"Oh yeah. It's been interesting so far."

He made a face. "I heard about the girl they found."

I nodded grimly. "I'd prefer things *not* be quite so interesting."

"Yeah," he scoffed. "Good luck with that."

I couldn't say much in response, so I watched him tighten the cable in order to keep it from dangling off the side of the truck. I knew for a fact that the cops would pull a tow truck over if they saw that cable swinging freely.

Finally, Joe gathered up the straps and hooks, and arranged everything neatly in a box behind the cab. Then he took off.

By ten o'clock, we had everyone working at whatever station Wade had assigned them, including him and me.

Amanda was focused on the double doors at the front of the church to determine what would be needed to bring back their original luster. She had thought they might just need to be oiled. She was the expert, but I had a feeling Madeline would prefer that they be sanded down and stained.

I had asked Sean to partner with Buck on the lighting issues, and I could see that they were already working well together.

I stood at the sacristy door with Wade, and he pointed at the massive piece of built-in cabinetry. "You sure you want to take this on?"

"You know me," I said. "I love this kind of job."

"I know you like to get into the nooks and crannies and clean it all up. And this looks like it's got a couple layers of paint on it."

"It's a gorgeous piece of cabinetry, but up close, it's kind of a mess. This will be the first time I've been able to check out what's actually inside all these drawers and cupboards, but from the very brief glimpse I got a few weeks ago, there's going to be a lot of stuff to go through. Once we've got that done, I'm going to remove the hardware and start stripping off the paint."

"That's not going to be easy," he said. "You'll need a ventilator. And probably some help."

"Probably. But for now, I've got it covered."

He grinned. "Of course you do. Just remember, if you need help, give us a shout."

"I will." I walked over to the cabinet and ran my hand along the row of tiny drawers at the far side. "All it needs is some TLC."

"That's what we're here for."

"Right?" I smiled. "What're you working on?"

He checked his wristwatch. "As soon as Madeline gets here, I'll grab Billy and Douglas, and we'll start unscrewing some of the pews from the stone floor."

"Sounds like fun." I lifted my hand in a wave. "I'm going to get to work on that cabinet."

The first thing I did—because that's how I roll—was count every drawer and cupboard and cubbyhole and closet contained within this cabinet. I found fourteen wide, thin drawers that looked like map drawers, one large armoire with accompanying hangers, eight cupboards of various sizes that were placed in different areas across the larger cabinet, and twelve normal-sized drawers that might hold stacks of undergarments and other clothing.

For my own personal reference, I had done a Google search for photographs of sacristies and found that this massive cabinet was not unusual at all. Many of the rooms I saw were spacious and comfortable and, along with their elegant cabinetry, often contained several well-padded armchairs, usually with a cushioned kneeler nearby, and a saintly statue or two. This room was missing a few of those items, and I imagined the statues and cushy furniture had been taken to the new church.

Next, I studied the layers of paint that covered the cabinet. I pulled out my Swiss Army knife and carefully dug away the layers in one small section. Since I planned to strip off the paint anyway, I wasn't concerned about leaving a mark. I just wanted to avoid nicking the wood itself.

I counted four layers of paint, which wasn't too bad for a piece of furniture that had been standing here for over 160 years. What baffled me was the mentality of someone who would want to cover a beautiful hardwood cabinet with paint in the first place.

Maybe it was just me.

The stripping of the paint would be difficult; Wade was right about that. But I wasn't too concerned, because I had done this kind of work before, most memorably in a beautiful butler's pantry I had worked on a few years ago. And I would have help if I needed it. Amanda, for one, had already assured me that I wouldn't be able to keep her away once we started in on the "messy stuff."

I stepped away from the cabinet and, for just a moment, surveyed the room. It was bigger than I'd originally thought, about twenty by twenty feet square. This cabinet took up one full wall. The wall facing this one had elaborately carved wood paneling that rose halfway up and was topped by wide crown molding, which created a wainscoting effect. Above the wainscoting were two large, well-preserved stained glass windows that allowed for a view of the town square and the ocean beyond.

The other two walls were covered floor to ceiling with the same wonderfully carved paneling. The room had a definite masculine vibe to it, and I thought my father would absolutely love it. Thinking of Dad, I made myself a mental note to call him tonight. I remembered that Flora the flower lady—and Buck's aunt—had gone to school with Dad. I would have to try and convince him to come for a visit while we were working here.

Finally, I began to open a few drawers. I was hoping most of them would be empty, but no such luck. In the first narrow drawer, I found a set of bright spring green vestments spread out neatly, along with several other matching pieces.

The fact that Reverend Patterson had left all of these behind was something I would have to deal with later. For now, I just wanted to know what I was looking at and why there were so many different items, so I pulled out my phone and googled "What does the priest wear?"

It worked. The large colorful piece that was worn over everything else was called a *chasuble*. This was worn over an *alb*, which looked like a long loose white linen dress. Another linen item was the *surplice*, which looked more like a loose tunic. It was shorter than the alb, which was full-length.

But back to the colorful pieces. Matching the chasuble were two different types of neckwear, like a scarf. One was narrower than the other, and they were both very fancy. These were a *maniple* and a *stole*. Each of the stoles I saw were at least eighty inches long. On Reverend Roy, they must've hung down to his knees. There were also a bunch of linen pieces that were worn around the waist or across the neck, depending on the celebration.

At this point, I was starting to get dizzy. How could one guy wear all this stuff at one time? I figured there were a bunch of meanings that went along with each piece.

This one drawer only held the colorful spring green pieces. I supposed the linen bits, like the alb and the surplice, must've been stored somewhere else. Or maybe they were in a pile of ironing that hadn't been done yet. Which made me wonder, who did all the ironing? A church lady like Flora? But I digress.

I pulled open another narrow drawer and found the exact same set of vestments as the green, except these were all purple with gold trim. The third drawer held all black vestments, again with gold trim. I wondered if those were for funerals.

In another drawer, I found yet another full set of green vestments, but these were emerald green. So spring green for spring and emerald green for fall? Just how many colors of vestments did one priest need? I wondered.

I walked to the other side and opened the large armoire. Hanging inside were a couple dozen different items, including several albs, each nicely ironed and hanging neatly in order. Why were they still here? Would someone be coming back for them? I wasn't about to throw anything away, of course, but still. Everything looked pretty pricey, and even if Reverend Patterson had bought all-new vestments and had no more use for these, they could always be given to a priest in need.

I closed the armoire and picked a cupboard to open at random. Inside were at least a dozen chalices. Most of them appeared to be solid gold or a mixture of gold and silver. They were all gorgeous and they had to be expensive. So why hadn't they been taken to the new church?

Maybe Reverend Patterson wanted to start fresh. Or maybe they just hadn't gotten around to packing this stuff up. I remembered the first time I'd peeked into this room, I had seen dozens of boxes stacked in here. Those boxes were gone, so I figured they must've been filled with other things. Even if the reverend and his wife didn't care about the money, there had to be some sentimental value attached to a number of the pieces. Many of them appeared to be quite old.

I held one up to the light, and despite some spots where it was tarnished, the chalice was beautiful. It was heavy, substantial, and unique. And once again, I wondered why they would leave behind so many valuable pieces.

Next I opened a random drawer and found piles of receipts. Literally hundreds of them in no particular order. I couldn't help myself; I riffled through the stack and realized very quickly that most of them were decades old. I pulled one out and skimmed the information. It was a receipt from a Mendocino linen shop. The name of the recipient was Bryant.

"Who's Bryant?" I wondered aloud. Maybe another church secretary? Or someone who ran errands for the reverend or his wife? I made a mental note to ask Flora or Colleen when I saw them again. And I would also ask why in the world they would hold on to a receipt that was forty years old.

After seeing all the items that had been left behind, I walked out to the nave and found Sean. "Who can we send to the store for packing boxes?"

"I'll take care of it," Sean said. "You want them in the sacristy, right?"

"Yes, thanks."

While I was out in the nave, I checked to see how my teams were progressing. Things seemed to be moving along nicely, so I went back to the sacristy to see what other odd treasures I could find.

A half hour later, a pallet of twenty brand-new boxes arrived, along with a roll of packing tape, and I was able to get started. I worked for another hour, first assembling the boxes, then carefully packing up ten sets of vestments.

It was fascinating to deal with such beautiful, expensive items that seemed to have been left by the wayside. For the moment, anyway.

At noon, I told everyone to take a lunch break, and I did the same. I walked out of the side door of the church and headed for the shops on the town square.

On a hunch, I pulled out my phone and, just for kicks, googled "Bryant Lighthouse Church."

I stopped walking to read the first entry. "Reverend Arthur Bryant, minister of Lighthouse Church, 1961–1992."

Good grief. I shouldn't have been shocked, but I was. Mainly because the previous minister had been gone for more than thirty years, and yet that cabinet in the sacristy contained receipts from his time at the church.

Why?

I wouldn't expect Reverend Patterson to clean out that cabinet, but what about his secretary? Or another underling? It didn't make sense.

I was a naturally tidy person, so I was trying really hard not to be judgmental, but I was starting to think Colleen had been right when she told Emily that the Pattersons had a wee problem with hoarding. Not that it mattered to me and my guys. Either way, we would pack all this stuff up, even if we privately thought some of it belonged in the trash. We didn't mind doing extra work. It was just weird, that's all.

Especially considering all these beautiful gold pieces.

I wished more than ever that Lavinia or Colleen were here to go through all of this stuff. It would be nice to find out if everything needed to be kept or if they intended to toss it all in the trash.

I put my phone away and continued walking to Paper Moon, my friend Lizzie's bookshop. Since I was working on the town square, we had decided to have lunch together at Emily's tea shop.

Lizzie was standing at the checkout counter, working on the computer. There were several customers browsing, but she was alone at the front.

I walked over to the counter. "Hi. Are you ready to go?"

"Oh, Shannon. Hi." She checked her watch. "I lost track of time." She glanced around and called, "Hal? I'm leaving for lunch with Shannon."

"Okay," Hal called from the back room. "Coming right out."

I looked around the shop. It was the cutest place on the square, with all sorts of books, of course, plus gift items and loads of paper goods. Note cards, invitations, cards for every occasion, along with clever scrapbooking kits for making your own cards and goodies. I could always find something fun to buy here.

Lizzie joined me at the front door and gave me a quick hug. "Thank you for rescuing me."

"We rescued each other," I said as she slipped her arm through mine.

"How's it going?" she asked. "I saw all those guys at the church yesterday, so I assume you're back at work."

"Yes. And it's going well."

"Good."

"Hey," I said, "since you work nearby, did you get to know Reverend Patterson and his wife when they were here at the church?"

"Lavinia? Sure. She's a pip."

"A pip," I said.

"Yeah. You know, she's cool, she's smart. She's fun. Interesting."

"A pip. Got it."

"And Reverend Roy is a doll," she continued. "They used to come in once in a while for birthday cards or whatever. Nice people."

"That's good to know."

We walked a dozen yards farther and turned into the adorable Scottish Rose Tea Shoppe owned by our friend Emily.

The soft chimes announced our arrival, and Emily walked out, looking impossibly chic in her black pants, white shirt, and black flats. "You're here. The others are in the back room, so go ahead."

I wondered who the others were. "Can you join us?" I asked.

"Yes, but I'll have to jump up now and again to help."

We walked into the charming back room, where Chloe, Marigold, and Jane sat at the big round table, already sipping tea.

"I didn't know you would all be here," I said. "This is a good surprise."

"I know," Jane said with a laugh. "We haven't seen each other in, what, three days?"

"Who keeps track?" I asked.

Chloe checked her watch. "And you're right on time."

"Always," I said, chuckling. "Of course, Lizzie and I only had to walk a half block."

"I'm starving," Jane said. "Let's order, then we'll talk."

"Sounds good," I agreed, and sat down between my sister and Marigold.

Emily bustled into the room with a young woman wearing a pink apron over black pants and a white shirt, a uniform of sorts, along with cheerful pink high-tops.

"Ginny will take your orders," Emily said. "And when she's finished and back at the front counter, I'll join you for a little while."

We all ordered the delicious coronation chicken—crustless chicken salad sandwiches, a pretty side salad, and chips—along with another pot of tea.

"We'll probably order dessert afterward," Jane said.

Lizzie was aghast. "Probably?"

"Absolutely," I said, laughing.

Ginny left to turn in the orders. We chatted about our families and the latest news, then gossiped about someone's wife, who had been seen last night with someone else's husband.

"That's terrible," Lizzie said.

"But not unusual," Jane said with a sad smile.

Emily sat down at the table to join us. "Well, I have news regarding our last conversation."

Lizzie sat up straight as if coming to attention. "What is it?"

"It's about Colleen, the church secretary."

"Do tell," Jane said.

"She came into the shop yesterday. I decided to ask her about Sarah, because why wouldn't I?"

"Exactly," Lizzie said. "So what did she say?"

"She thinks a stranger must've killed her," Emily said.

"Oh, come on," Jane said. "A stranger walked into

the church and killed this lovely young woman? Seriously?"

Emily's shoulders slumped. "I know, right? It was disappointing to hear her say it."

It wasn't just disappointing, I thought. It was *wrong.* Why would a stranger kill Sarah in the sacristy, then drag her lifeless body down the hall and dump her inside the small chapel? It had to have been someone familiar with the church layout. But I couldn't say that out loud. Nobody was supposed to know those kinds of details. Not yet, anyway.

"What did you say to Colleen?" I asked.

Emily gave a little cough to clear her throat. "I might've fibbed a bit."

"You lied?" I was amazed. "What did you say?"

"I said, 'All the news reports are saying that it was someone she knew.'"

There was silence. We weren't used to Emily telling lies.

"That was brilliant, Emily," Lizzie said. "I'm so proud of you."

"It really was amazing," she said shyly, "even though I was scared to death that lightning might strike me."

"You're just not a good liar," Chloe said, patting Emily's shoulder. "Not like me."

"Oh, Chloe," Marigold said charitably. "You don't lie."

She smiled. "Yes, I do."

"She does," I said. "She's really good at it."

Chloe grinned. "I really am."

"It's what makes you a brilliant television star," Marigold said in her defense.

Chloe laughed. "Yes, I'm always telling lies on the show."

"But you really have to," Lizzie said. "You can't walk into somebody's house and say, 'What a dump!' You've got to ease into it, right?"

"Absolutely right."

"It's admirable, how well you lie," I said, joining her in a laugh. Then I turned to Emily. "So about Colleen. What did she say in response to your lie?"

Emily sighed. "She said that if it was someone she knew, it must've been Madeline."

"Whoa."

Madeline killed Sarah? There was no way, I thought. But how interesting that Colleen would accuse her.

"That's harsh," Jane said. "Do you think she really believes that?"

"Honestly, I doubt it," Emily said. "I asked her if she had any evidence to back up her claim, and she confessed that she didn't."

"Well, that's too bad," Lizzie said.

I glanced around the table. "Anyone else have news?"

"I called Sarah's mother," Lizzie said. "Her name is Kara, and she and I got to know each other when Sarah was babysitting for us. She would drive Sarah over to our house, and usually, her father would pick her up." She took a quick sip of tea. "They would always come inside just to say hello and make sure everything had gone well that night."

"That's really smart," I said.

"They're wonderful people," Lizzie said, with a hitch in her voice. "I'm so sad for them. But anyway, Kara told me that Sarah was freaked out about something that happened at the church a few days before she was killed."

"Do you know what happened?" I asked.

"Yeah," Chloe said immediately. "What freaked her out?"

"Kara didn't have too many details, but she said that Sarah was determined to warn all the workers to stay out of the sacristy. She said there was something weird going on in there."

"Oh, great," I muttered.

"The sacristy." Chloe was clearly alarmed. "That's where you're working."

"I'm not in any danger," I said, trying to keep my voice calm and easy. But I flashed back to my conversation with Colleen the night before and felt a wave of fear wash over me.

"Apparently you are," she said, jabbing her finger at me. "And damn it, Shannon. If anything happens to you, I'll kill you myself."

Chapter Ten

I wrapped my hand around Chloe's extended finger. "I love you, too."

But instead of smiles, I caught Jane's glare. "Don't make light of Chloe's feelings or any of our feelings. We care about you, and we worry about you because, to be honest, you do have a tendency to . . ." She waved away the rest of that sentence. "Well, you know. We worry."

"A tendency to what?" I demanded.

Marigold jumped in, trying to be helpful. "To, you know, *find* people."

"*Dead* people," Lizzie finally clarified.

"That's right," Jane said. "So, do us all a favor and avoid the sacristy." She frowned and added, "Whatever that is."

"It's the priest's room," I explained. "It's where he gets dressed and prepares to say the mass or any other event he's officially participating in. It's got all his outfits and the chalices and gold plates and, you know, all those doohickeys in there. All those things he needs for conducting the church celebrations. It's right near the altar, so it's convenient, I guess."

"How do you know all that?" Lizzie asked. "You never really went to church much, did you?"

"Carla was raised a Catholic," I explained. "She gave me some info. And I can read. I know things."

"Maybe Carla should be the one helping you with those cabinets," Chloe said. "She'll know what's important or not."

"Not a bad idea," I mused.

"Really, Shannon," Marigold said, more softly than the others, as usual. "It sounds dangerous."

"I don't plan to spend my time in there alone," I insisted. "I'm within a few feet of all my other crew members, so I'm perfectly safe."

Chloe huffed out an irate breath. "I know you. You're in there with the door closed, right?"

"Well, sometimes. It gets noisy with everyone working." It was a flimsy excuse, but I wasn't ready to admit defeat. I frowned at each of them. "Look, I get it. I won't take chances. I'll have the door open. Are you okay with that?"

"You need a keeper," Chloe muttered. "That's the solution."

I knew she was afraid for me, so I leaned over and wrapped my arms around her. "I'm sorry I worried you. I'll get someone to come in and help me go through the cabinets."

"You bet your butt you will," she said resolutely. "And it's going to be me. I'll help you."

Lizzie giggled.

"What's so funny?" I asked.

"She said 'butt,'" Lizzie said, and snickered.

I stared in disbelief. "Lizzie, you sound like Taz. When he was seven."

Her son, Taz, short for Tasmanian Devil, was almost fifteen now.

Marigold covered her mouth, but I noticed her shoulders shaking.

Jane wasn't quite so subtle. She threw her head back and laughed out loud.

Emily let out a feminine snort.

I shook my head in disgust. "You're all so juvenile."

With that, every one of my dear friends exploded with laughter. At my expense, obviously.

I rolled my eyes, then straightened my shoulders and looked at Chloe. "Thank you for your offer to help. We start at eight o'clock every morning."

It was clearly the last thing she expected me to say. Her eyes widened with the realization that now she was stuck.

And finally it was my turn to laugh.

After I promised to work with a partner—I already knew it wouldn't always be Chloe—everyone calmed down, and we were able to continue with our reports on who had talked to whom around town. Nothing much had come of their investigations, but they assured me that they weren't ready to quit.

Meanwhile, lunch was awesome, as usual. I ordered the chocolate bread pudding with brandy sauce for dessert, and all I could say was, OMG.

As we were all about to leave, I remembered something.

"Have any of you ever heard of Arthur Bryant?" I

asked. "He was the reverend at Lighthouse Church until the early nineties."

Jane frowned. "Shannon, we were barely in first grade."

"And I was in kindergarten," Chloe said.

"I'm older than all of you," Emily said, "but I didn't live here in the nineties."

"I didn't, either," Marigold said. "I'm sorry, Shannon."

"I know it was a long shot, but I was hoping one of you might've heard the name somewhere or somehow."

"It's the kind of name that sounds familiar, but I've never actually heard it," Jane confessed. "And by the time my mother was going to the church, Reverend Patterson was in charge."

"Oh well, it was worth a try," I said. "Thanks anyway."

"We'll keep trying," Lizzie said firmly. "I'm not giving up on Sarah."

"Neither am I," I said.

The others agreed and there were hugs all around. After making a plan to meet again in a few days, we left the tea shop.

Chloe walked out with me and Lizzie. "I can't come back with you because I've got a bunch of errands to run, then tomorrow morning, I've got a lengthy Zoom call with my production team. But I've already arranged for one of Eric's team to stop by and help you. And I'll be able to swing by in the afternoon."

"There is no way I'm going to have a cop babysitting me," I said. "I have a full crew of big strong men and women. I'll ask one of them to help me."

"What exactly are you doing?" Lizzie asked. "Maybe Marisa could come by and stay with you for a few hours."

"I'm basically cleaning out drawers and cupboards to get this huge piece of furniture ready to be stripped and sanded and painted. But it's full of Reverend Roy's stuff."

"Why aren't his people taking care of that?" Chloe asked.

"They should be, especially if they want everything returned in good condition. Not that I would damage anything, but you know what I mean."

"Yeah. Why aren't they more concerned about their stuff?"

"I figure they're all just really busy. They have a small staff, and the rest of the people who help out are volunteers. Anyway, I'll get someone in there to help me out. It's not that big of a deal." I waved my hand, ready to end this conversation. Maybe it didn't make sense that I was doing the work, but I had to admit, it was kind of fascinating. Besides, we needed to get the cabinet cleared out, and since I really didn't want to assign any of my crew to do the job, I would simply continue on my own until the church sent someone over to take care of it.

"Okay," Chloe said. "I can make it over there tomorrow afternoon. Meanwhile, be careful."

"I will. You too."

She hugged me and murmured, "Love you."

"Love you more."

She gave Lizzie a hug, too, and then walked away. I strolled with Lizzie as far as Paper Moon, then continued on my own for another half block to the church. I stopped for a moment and gazed up at the building. From here, I could see the stained glass windows of the sacristy, where I would be working this afternoon.

There were four thin windows, two on each side of a stone buttress that slanted downward toward one of the thick masonry columns that supported the heavy wall.

Back inside the church, I sat down in one of the pews and took a moment to observe my people at work.

Forty feet above me, Buck was standing in the basket of the boom lift, studying one of the wooden beams. I checked to make sure that the safety strap was wrapped around his waist. I would've gone a little crazy if it wasn't.

Sean stood on the floor wearing a headset directly connected to Buck. They also had a video call set up between the two of them, and even from here, I could see Buck pointing to a spot on the beam where he intended to place one of the wireless remote-control motorized lighting units he had discussed with Madeline last week.

I was really happy with Buck's work. It was like we had all taken a giant step forward in applying electronic and tech knowledge to our everyday rehab jobs. I knew the guys were excited, and so was I.

On the other side of the church, Johnny stood at the top of a thirty-two-foot extension ladder, examining a stained glass window. Douglas, one of the biggest and strongest guys on my crew, was holding on to the ladder's base, keeping it steady for Johnny.

If we had been rehabbing an old house, we might've secured the ladder by laying a two-by-four across the feet at the bottom of the ladder and screwing it to the floor. But here, we didn't want to damage the marble and stone floors, so Douglas would have to do the job.

Having once fallen off an extension ladder, I appreciated their diligence.

Amanda and Wade were inspecting the nave's double doors, and they pointed out that one side was more worn and ragged than the other. I wondered if maybe some churchgoers had enjoyed giving it a harder shove on their way out of church than they did on their way in. Or maybe it had been attacked by rodents. Whatever the reason, the door would have to be patched up and sanded down, then Amanda would work her magic on the detailing. I wasn't worried. If anyone could restore it to its original beauty, Amanda could.

I thought with anticipation of all the good work we would be doing over the next eight to ten months.

And those positive thoughts morphed into the picture of Sarah Spindler as I'd last seen her. I slumped back in the pew. What could Sarah have possibly done that would cause someone to attack her so brutally? Did she catch someone doing something they shouldn't have been doing?

Something in that room had caused Sarah to freak out, according to her mother. Would I be able to figure out what had happened just by being in that space? Was I crazy to think that the room would give up its secrets? Maybe I was, but I would still try and solve this puzzle.

And even though this wasn't the kind of work I normally did, I was determined to keep at it until someone from the church came and took over.

Earlier this morning, I had called Lavinia again. I'd left her a message telling her I had spoken to Colleen last night and asked her to come by the old church when she had a few minutes to talk.

"I'll be working in the *sacristy*," I'd said, and ended the message. I didn't bother to add, *You know, the room where Sarah was murdered?* That might be putting too fine a point on things.

On the other hand, Lavinia might not have a clue that Sarah had been killed in this room. She might not even know about everything that was still being stored in the shelves and drawers and cubbyholes of the built-in cabinet. And if she didn't know, I would have to find out who did.

Twenty minutes later, I pulled another flattened cardboard box off the stack and folded it into shape. I sealed the seams with packing tape and repeated the action several more times. I had already stacked five boxes from earlier today. Five more boxes would get me through a few more drawers.

Even though I was more inclined to spend my workday hanging some drywall or framing a room, I found myself enjoying the job of sorting through these cabinet drawers. They were filled with the most intriguing stuff, not to mention beautiful and expensive pieces, and I seriously wondered all over again if we had a case of hoarding on our hands.

Again, I wasn't judging. Well, maybe I was, since nobody from the church had shown up yet to take the job off my hands. That meant I could giddily paw through hundreds of old receipts while I wondered why in the world someone would hold on to one from forty years ago for dinner at the Lobster Pot. It boggled the mind.

So, yeah, I was being judgy. And maybe a little nosy, too.

As soon as I had the thought, I laughed. There was no *maybe* about it.

I decided to put all of the receipts into one box and let someone at the church take it from there. Still, I found myself taking a little time to browse through them to see where they shopped and how they traveled and what they enjoyed. The Lobster Pot was a big hit, of course. That had to be true for a lot of families since it was one of the most popular restaurants on the North Coast.

I finished digging through all the receipts and moved to the next drawer down. This one contained dozens of composition books with the black-and-white speckled covers that I recognized from grammar school. The teacher would hand them out whenever we had to take written tests. It gave me a little twinge of nostalgia to see all of them stacked in the drawer.

I pulled one stack out and set them down neatly in the next box, then stared at them for a moment. If anyone thought I would let it go at that, they just didn't know me. Instead, I picked up one of the books at random and opened the cover.

The first thing I noticed was that the handwriting was excellent. There were three columns on each page, and it appeared to be some sort of calendar or schedule of daily events. At the top of each page was the date. One column indicated the time a meeting or event was to start. The next column was much wider because it was the full description of the event along with attendees and where it took place.

Skimming through, I saw that the descriptions were very elaborate, to the point that one meeting might take up the whole page. It didn't simply say, *Lunch meeting*. Instead, it listed the place, the weather, the view, where each person sat in the restaurant or the room, each person's mood and what they wore, who they spoke to, who their waiter was, the name of the maître d'.

On some pages, there was a dollar amount listed in the third column: *$225.00* was noted on one page, *$350.00* on another. I found one page that had *$1,000.00* written down.

I figured the dollar amounts indicated the price of the meal or the gasoline expended or gifts for the attendees. Although, I couldn't imagine a meal and a tank of gas cost a thousand dollars. But maybe there were other things going on.

I had a quick thought that maybe some of these expenditures had been made by Reverend Bryant, the previous guy in charge. But since most of the entries included the dates, it was clear that all of them had occurred after Reverend Roy had taken over the reins of the church. So it made sense to assume that these records had been kept by Colleen, the church secretary, for Reverend Roy's benefit. They would need these sorts of records for tax purposes. But they read more like a diary than a businesslike daily recording of an event.

I picked up a composition book from another pile and flipped through it. It was a few decades old and included some mildly interesting anecdotes of things happening around Lighthouse Cove. I started to close the book when something caught my eye. It was a description of a church event, and at the end, these words were underlined twice: "No one must ever know, not even MSB."

It sounded more like a melodramatic "Dear Diary" entry than an actual business notation such as those in the previous book that listed prices and details. I was almost disappointed that it didn't read more like a lover's secret entry. Something like:

Dear Diary,

No one must ever know, not even MSB. I will take the secret to my grave. And you know who I'm talking about, dearest Diary.

I imagined little hearts and flowers drawn all over the page and laughed at myself, then admitted that there wasn't anything to laugh about. For starters, who in the world was MSB? Someone who used to work at the church, maybe? I would have to ask Lavinia when—and if—she showed up. Or maybe I would ask Flora, because if this diary had been kept by Colleen, I didn't want to get the secretary in trouble with the reverend's wife, who had already mentioned that she didn't trust Colleen. I suddenly wondered if there were any books in the cabinet that belonged to Flora. After all, by her own account she kept the most accurate history of the church. And she was nicer than Colleen, who was usually all business—unless she was thoroughly flustered, as she'd been last night.

I wondered if Colleen knew that all of her diaries—or calendars or daily planners, whatever she called them—were still here in these drawers. Wouldn't she want to keep better track of them? Especially with so many details of church business, including cash amounts and names of people and places around town.

Maybe she didn't care. But of course she did. Not caring about something like that? It just didn't fit with her personality, which bordered on anal retentive with a touch of passive aggression and a great big scoop of *fear.* And who was Colleen afraid of? Lavinia Patterson? Reverend Roy? Or someone else?

It was almost three o'clock when Colleen walked into the sacristy. I was surprised to see her. She wore a long, flowing vest over a black leotard and black leggings and black flats. The outfit flattered her tall, willowy frame.

"I wanted to let you know," she said, jumping right to business, "I haven't had a chance to talk to Lavinia, but I've left her a message, and I hope she will be able to get over here sometime tomorrow."

"I appreciate it, thanks. As you can see, there's plenty more work to do."

"Yes, I can see that." She glanced at the boxes. "But you're doing a very good job."

"Thank you," I said, refraining from rolling my eyes. "But I would really appreciate having a member of your church here to help me."

She stared back at the boxes for a long moment, then frowned. "I'll let Lavinia know."

"Okay. But since you're here—"

"I really must go." She turned to leave, shocking me even more. "Have a good afternoon."

That was it? She wasn't even going to help a little? "Colleen, wait!"

She had the nerve to look at her wristwatch. "What is it?"

"I need to ask you something." I picked up the composition book and opened it to the marked page. "Do you know someone with the initials MSB?"

She blinked twice and then frowned again. She stared

up at the ceiling and ran her hand through her shaggy dark hair. I assumed she was trying to think of names. Maybe she was mentally reviewing the entire church roster. I wouldn't put it past her to have memorized it. Seconds later, she said, "Mr. Brindley, perhaps?"

"Mr. Brindley?" It was my turn to frown. "You mean, the janitor?"

She shrugged. "He prefers to be called the handyman. His is the only name that comes to mind with those initials."

Mr. Brindley, I thought. Mitch Brindley was so nondescript, so taciturn. But suddenly I recalled the day he was trying to get inside the church. He wasn't taciturn at all. He was insistent, demanding that he be let inside. Could he possibly have been the subject of that dramatic diary entry?

No one must ever know, not even MSB.

"And now I've really got to be going," Colleen said. And she dashed out of the room.

By the end of the day, I still hadn't heard from Lavinia. Every few minutes, I walked out to check on my crew and see if anyone needed my help. So far, they were all hard at work, performing their jobs like the well-oiled machine they were.

I sighed and returned to the sacristy to tackle another cubbyhole. This one was about two feet wide and had a pullout shelf that made it easy to see everything inside. And once again, I was blown away by what Reverend Patterson and his congregation had left behind. Would they come back and get all this stuff? I hoped so.

This space seemed to be where all the gold had been stashed, and it was a little like staring into a mini Aladdin's cave of treasures. I counted four chalices, and all of them appeared to be made of gold, or at least gold-plated. There were also twelve small bowls: six gold, three jewel-encrusted, and three silver. Additionally, there were six small, thin gold plates.

Maybe I hadn't spent much time going to church, but I'd seen enough TV shows and movies to know that these items were used by a priest when he said mass. I knew that the chalice held wine, the bowls held those little round wafers, and the thin plates held that one big wafer the priest held up during the mass.

Even though I had no idea what any of these things were actually called, it was easy to google the information. Of course, it would be even easier if there was actually a human being helping out.

I guess I needed to stop harping on that issue, because I really was having a pretty good time hunting down information about all these treasures. They had to be worth a small fortune, and I had to believe that the church would keep a record of everything, if only for insurance purposes. It was another question I would ask Lavinia, if I ever heard back from her.

I stood and stretched my back, then walked out of the sacristy and into the church to see how my crew was getting on.

"How are you all doing?" I said, loudly enough for the whole church to hear. "Does anyone need help?"

"We're good," Buck shouted from the ceiling, and Sean gave me a thumbs-up. They were still assessing the lighting situation, this time from one of the other wooden beams. I had to stretch back to get a look at Buck way up there.

"Okay, looks good," I said.

I turned and saw that Douglas and Johnny were more than halfway through their inspection of the stained glass windows.

Johnny waved and I winced. "Both hands on the ladder!"

He laughed but grabbed hold of the ladder. Douglas said, "No problems here, boss."

Wade and Amanda were just walking into the nave from the north transept. "The side door over here is going to need a lot of work. We were just talking about it."

"Do you need me?"

"Not right this minute," Wade said. "Maybe at the end of the day or first thing tomorrow, we can have a short meeting."

"Sounds good. Guess I'll get back to my assignment. I'll be in the sacristy if you need me."

I was halfway there when I saw Flora hurry over, open the door, and walk inside. I followed her into the room. "Hey, Flora. I'm glad to see you."

"Oh my goodness!" She patted her chest, something I'd seen her do more than once. "You nearly scared me to death."

"I'm sorry." I let her take a minute to calm down and watched as she slowly moved around the room, checking out all the boxes and the cabinet.

"Well, you certainly have packed up a lot of boxes."

"And sadly, I've barely put a dent in this thing." I patted one of the cabinet drawers. "I was hoping to see Lavinia by now, but maybe you can help me."

"I'll do what I can, dear. What's the problem?"

"It's all these drawers and cubbyholes and cupboards," I said, spreading my arms to take in the entire piece of furniture. "There are thirty-five of them, I think, and they're stuffed with things that belong to the church. Valuable things."

"Really?"

"Yes. I understood from Madeline that we could throw away anything that was left behind, but I know she didn't mean these kinds of items."

At random, I pulled open the narrow door of a cubby I hadn't been through yet. There was another set of vestments, this one rose-colored with gold brocade trim. It appeared to be new or, at least, lovingly cared for.

"Why, that's Reverend Roy's." Flora took a tentative step closer and lifted a corner of the cloth. "He wears it on the last Sunday in Lent as a way of gently shifting away from the dark purple of the season to the glorious white of Easter." She glanced up at me. "What is it doing here?"

"I have no idea. But wait, that's not all. There's plenty more to see." I opened the small cabinet and pulled out the shelf that held the gold chalices and other gold and silver paraphernalia.

"Good heavens." She actually took a step backward. I couldn't blame her. There was a lot of bling on that shelf. "This isn't right."

"I don't think so, either," I said. "And I don't think I should be the one going through everything, although I'm enjoying it. Lots of interesting things to see."

Her forehead was lined with concern, so I didn't say anything.

"Well," she said, and seemed to gather her courage. She walked over to one of the big drawers and opened it. And gasped.

"What's wrong?" I asked.

She didn't say another word, just stared into the drawer, so I joined her.

"Oh, good grief," I said. "I thought I packed all of those up. Now there's another drawerful."

"What did you say?" she said, still a little stunned.

I rolled my eyes. "I just finished packing at least forty of these little books. They're in one of those boxes."

"But . . . but . . . oh, dear lord." She reached for one of the books, and I noticed that her hand was shaking.

"Flora, what is it?"

She took a few long, slow breaths in and out. Then she opened to the first page and stared, looking completely puzzled. "What is this?"

"I think it's one of Colleen's calendars or her planner. Or whatever she calls it."

Her shoulders relaxed. "Of course it is. It's Colleen's." She breathed out a sigh of relief. "I now recall that she decided to start using these when she saw me writing in mine. They're relatively inexpensive, and the church purchases them in bulk for the children's religious classes."

"Ah," I said. "So you use these, too. To write up your church history entries."

"That's right."

I thought for a moment, then decided to go for it. "Since it's just you and me, can I ask you something?"

"Of course, dear."

I took the book from her and turned to a page in the middle. "What do you think these dollar amounts are here for?"

"Well, let me see." She took the book back and stared at the page for a few long seconds. "I don't actually know for sure, but if I had to guess, I would say that these are the amounts that a congregant might've promised to donate to Reverend Roy after they took part in whatever activity was described in the book."

"A congregant?" I asked.

"A member of the church," she explained.

"Huh." I thought about it. "That makes sense." I closed the book and handed it back to Flora. "Thanks."

Flora set the book down and left shortly after that. I realized a few minutes later that I hadn't even asked what she was doing here. I had a feeling maybe she was just curious to see what was going on around here. Or maybe she was hoping to talk to her nephew Buck. That made the most sense.

I had also forgotten to ask if she would tell Lavinia to come over here and help with all this packing. But I supposed I'd left enough messages on that subject already. And maybe Flora would pass the word to her anyway.

An hour later, I could hear my guys starting to pack up for the day, so I checked my watch. I had time to clean out one more niche, then I would leave, too.

I closed my eyes and randomly reached out to touch one of the many cubbyholes in the cabinet. I opened my eyes to see where I would be working next and had to grin at my silliness. It would definitely be time to go home after this one. I was starting to get loopy.

The cubbyhole I'd touched was one that had a decorative brass hook on the door that fitted into a brass latch. There were a few others with this design, but I hadn't opened any of them yet. I pulled out the hook and opened the little door to see what was inside. Miracle of miracles, inside I found . . . nothing.

Unlike every other drawer and cabinet in this behemoth piece of furniture, with all its nooks and crannies and cubbies, this one was empty. Weird.

"That just means I can pack up and leave now," I murmured. "Hooray for me."

I started to close the cubby door, but the last rays of sunlight filtering through the stained glass caught a glint of metal inside the little nook.

So it wasn't completely empty.

I would've missed it completely, except for that tiny flash.

The cubbyhole itself was too dark to see all the way inside, so I pulled out my phone and used the flashlight app to illuminate the small space. And at the very back, I saw two little cup hooks screwed into the side wall. Nothing was hanging from the hook closest to me, but on the one farthest away, I saw a small key dangling.

A key?

I had to stand sideways and crouch a bit to get my arm inside the space, then I reached all the way back to grab it. I pulled my arm out and stared at the key in my hand. It was a little one, about the size that would fit into a small lock or a jewelry box.

"Well," I whispered, "you can't go home yet." I had to find the keyhole that fit this key.

I closed the cubbyhole and slipped the outer brass hook into the latch. Then I took my time and studied every single drawer and space in the cabinet to see if one of them had a keyhole. It took me almost twenty minutes to check each and every one. And I didn't find one keyhole in the entire cabinet. Which was weird. You would think that a few of these drawers and cabinets would have a lock on them. But no.

I took a long look around the sacristy. Had there been another piece of furniture in here once upon a time? There wasn't anything else in the room now except this big built-in cabinet.

I checked out the two stained glass windows. Maybe they could be opened with a lock. But no. There were no keyholes to be found anywhere near the stained glass.

I wasn't ready to give up, but I was getting frustrated. It was late and I wanted to go home to Mac. I would just have to come back tomorrow and start the search all over again.

I slipped the key into my pocket for safekeeping, then checked that all the packing boxes were stacked neatly. I closed the sacristy door and walked around the central platform to the main aisle where, for some reason, I turned and gazed up at the dome. It really was a stunning bit of architecture. I stopped and listened, but I couldn't hear anything. And wasn't that a good thing? I laughed at myself again, but it wasn't really funny. The last thing I wanted was to hear voices in an empty church.

I hurried down the aisle and out the two sets of double doors, remembering to lock them as I left. Then I ran to my truck and drove home.

Chapter Eleven

I walked into the kitchen, where I was greeted by Robbie, who immediately demanded that I pay attention to him. I did as ordered. "Hello, sweetie." I reached down and scratched and petted his furry back. "Good boy."

"You talking to me?" Mac asked from where he stood in front of the stove.

I laughed. "Yes, you're a good boy, too."

My mouth was beginning to water from something tangy and delicious that he was cooking. I moved closer and watched him stirring together a gorgeous concoction of chicken, peppers, onions, and garlic.

"Are you making fajitas?" I stood behind him and wrapped my arms around his waist. "Smells incredible."

"I'm glad you're home."

"Me too." I laid my cheek against his strong muscular back and sighed with relief and happiness.

After a minute, he said, "Hey, you okay?"

"I'm fine," I said, and managed to pull away from him. "It's been a long day." I noticed his nearly full wineglass on the counter next to the stove. "I'm going to pour myself a glass of wine, and then you can tell me how your day was."

"That sounds like a plan." He gave the fajitas another thorough stirring, then put a top on the frying pan and turned to watch me. "I do have some news."

I carried my wineglass over to the kitchen table and sat down. "What's the news?"

"My agent called this morning."

"Everything okay?"

"Couldn't be better," he said, then grabbed his wineglass and sat down at the table facing me. "Are you ready?"

"Yes, yes! Tell me."

"Okay. The producers want to do a spin-off of the latest Jake Slater film, starring Siobhán O'Leary."

Siobhán O'Leary. The gorgeous redhead I'd met at the film premiere in Hollywood. The woman who had been cast because she looked exactly the way Mac had described her in the book. She looked like me. Curly red hair, green eyes. Beautiful. At least, that's how Mac had described her. I wanted to hate her but couldn't find it in me because she was just so darn nice. And so was her hunky husband, Terence.

"Wow." I sat back in my chair, feeling a bit gobsmacked. I didn't know which question to ask first. "What does that even mean?"

"It won't be based on any of my books, of course, but it's my character. My agency is insisting that I should write the screenplay."

"Absolutely, you should," I said. "Who would know the character better than you? And who could write the story better? No one but you."

He stood up and came around the table, then leaned over and kissed me so tenderly, so completely, that I felt a little dizzy. When I could catch my breath again, I stared up at him. "What was that for?"

"For having faith and confidence in me." He touched my cheek. "For believing that I can do it."

I frowned. "Well, of course you can. You're the best writer I know."

He laughed. "I love you."

I chuckled ruefully. "You know what I mean."

"I do."

"And I love you, too, Mac."

He kissed me again, then returned to his chair. He had to catch his breath, too, which made me smile all over again.

Finally, he said, "So, anyway, my agents want to meet with me to hash out the particulars. Then we'll all talk with the producers a day or so later and start the wrangling. Siobhán will be there, of course, so it'll be nice to see her again."

I nodded, then stood and crossed the room, then walked back. I was too nervous to sit. I hated that feeling of jealousy that bloomed unbidden when I heard the name Siobhán. "So, when will you have to leave?"

He stood and faced me, then ran his hands down my arms and pulled me close. "Tomorrow."

I pressed my forehead against his chest. "Oh no."

"Hey, what's wrong?"

"Nothing. I'll just . . . miss you." I mentally slapped myself, mentally shouted, *Get over it!* I'd rarely been dependent on anyone, but Mac had wormed his way into my heart, and I was really going to miss him, even if he was only gone a few days. I looked up at him and smiled as brightly as I could manage. "This is great news for you. Amazing news."

He touched my cheek. "I wish you were coming with me."

"Me too. But you know I've got this huge church rehab going on."

"I know. I wish things weren't so busy for you right now."

I gazed up at him. "You'll call me every minute?"

He laughed. "I might be able to call you every *other* minute."

"That'll have to do."

He pulled me close again. "I hate to leave with this thing hanging over you."

I looked up at the ceiling. "What thing hanging over me?"

"Very funny. You know what I mean."

"Yes, I know." I shook my head in disgust. "Another murder investigation. But, look, I'm not involved at all. Nothing's going to happen to me."

He stared at me. "That's not what I hear from Chloe."

I scowled. "That big mouth."

"Yeah." He crossed to the stove and pulled the top off the fajitas. An intoxicating aroma filled the room.

"That smells wonderful."

"I've got everything ready to go," he said. "All we have to do is heat up the tortillas."

"You already chopped up all the goodies?"

"Yes. They're in the fridge. The cheese is grated, too."

"You are incredible."

"I know." He grinned. "Let's put everything on the table and start eating."

I opened the refrigerator and pulled out all the small

bowls and put them on the table. There were chunky *queso fresco*, chopped cilantro, tomatoes, onions, lettuce, jalapeño peppers, three different kinds of salsa, and homemade guacamole.

"You went crazy," I said. "This looks so good."

I wrapped the tortillas in a clean dishcloth and stuck them in the microwave for thirty seconds.

"I wanted to make margaritas," he said, "but I'm only one man. I can't do it all."

I laughed. "You did just fine. And I'm always happy to drink wine."

"Yeah, me too."

We began to fill our plates with all the goodies. I took a deep breath and asked, "So what time do you leave in the morning?"

"They're sending a car at eight a.m."

"Are you flying out of Mendocino?"

"Yeah. They've arranged for a private jet to fly me directly to New York. Isn't that cool?"

I had to smile at the excitement in his voice. One of the best things about Mac was that he wasn't spoiled by his success. Taking a private jet across the country was an adventure to him, not an entitlement. And it made me love him even more.

"Yep," I said. "That's totally cool."

The next morning, I stood on the sidewalk and waved as the limousine whisked Mac away on the first leg of his trip to New York City. When the car finally disappeared around the corner, I felt a pang of loneliness so intense, I wanted to cry. Instead, I said out loud, right there on the sidewalk, "You're pathetic. Go to work." I followed my own advice and walked back into the house, cleaned up the kitchen, gave each of the pets a treat, and then drove over to the church.

I was about to park when I remembered that I had used up most of the boxes Sean had brought me yesterday. I put the truck back into drive and took off for the U-Rent Center just outside of town. I picked up twenty more boxes, and just to be safe, I grabbed another roll of packing tape.

Back at the church, I first checked on the progress that my teams had made yesterday. Everything was going smoothly so far. Niall and Wade wanted to check out the three small chapels to determine whether the stone flooring was deteriorating as badly as Madeline had thought on that first day we toured.

"Let's go," I said, and we walked around the central platform to the chapel.

Even though all traces of Sarah's broken body had been erased from the scene, my stomach still wavered a bit when I walked inside. And that was too bad, because this space was really very special, a precious little jewel box of a room. The statue of Mary with her ivory veil and sky blue shawl was the focal point, of course, and at its base was a wrought iron stand holding dozens of votive candles in small glass cups of different colors set on graduated tiers. Dark red, green, blue, clear. I could imagine all of them being lit at the same time and flickering colorfully as the air circulated in and out and around the room, stirring up the flames.

In front of the stand of candles was a kneeler where one would pray after lighting a candle for someone.

"The damage is minor," Niall was saying, and I had to concentrate to pick up the thread of the conversation. "But it's got to be dealt with soon." Niall stood by the stained glass window, pointing out the lead strip holding two pieces of stained glass together. "Right here, the calms got badly bent somehow, leaving a gap between the glass and the lead that allows rainwater to leak through."

"The calms?" Wade said.

"The *calms*, or the *cames*, as some say," he said, "are the lead strips with channels along each side that hold the glass and bind the different pieces together." He noticed my expression. "It's not as complicated as it sounds."

"Whatever you call it," I said, pointing at the bent section, "can you fix it?"

He looked at me, confused. "Of course."

I almost laughed. Why would I even ask? Niall could do anything. "That'd be great. Thanks."

With a glint in his eye, Niall murmured, "Did ya think I was just a pretty face?"

I couldn't help but burst out laughing. Then I smacked his arm, mainly because I couldn't think of a word to say.

Wade was chuckling, too, as he pointed down at the baseboard behind the statue. "Check this out, Shannon. Over the past dozen years or so, water has trickled from the window and down the wall to cause the baseboard to soften. You can feel it."

I stooped down to get a good look at the baseboard, then pressed the wood. "Oh, man. It feels like a sponge."

"Aye," Niall said. "We're lucky the rest of the floor is marble and unscathed by water."

"To be honest," Wade added, "we're also lucky that the baseboard can be replaced easily enough."

Niall straightened up. "What I fear is that there may

be further damage down below, but we can check on that when you have some time."

"The basement will answer a lot of our questions," I said. "Can we do it tomorrow morning, around nine o'clock? Today I want to finalize the cleanup in the sacristy, and I'm hoping I'll catch one of the church ladies over here at some point."

"Tomorrow's fine with me," Wade said. "Niall?"

"Aye, tomorrow's fine."

"Okay, good," I said. "Thank you, guys."

We walked down the hall, and I left them both in the nave while I ran out to my truck to get the folding chair I'd decided to bring in today.

I walked back into the church and headed for the sacristy, anxious to pick up where I'd left off yesterday.

I was relieved to see that everything was just as I'd left it. Call me paranoid, but after seeing all those exquisite items stuffed inside that cabinet, I wouldn't have been surprised to find out someone had sneaked in here late last night to steal something.

I set up the folding chair so I could sit down while I went through the lower half of the cabinet. I didn't need my back to go out while I bent over to check drawers and load up boxes all day. Yes, this was a relatively easy job, so, yes, my guys would laugh me off the site if I threw out my back.

I had transferred the little key I'd found last night to this pair of jeans, and now I double-checked that it was still in my front pocket. That was another thing I wanted to do today: find out where that key fit. It probably had nothing to do with anything, but it was a mystery and I wanted to solve it.

Before I did anything else, I put together five new

boxes, folding them into place and sealing them with long strips of packing tape. Then I sat down in front of the cabinet and went to work filling them up.

Sitting in this chair gave the room an interesting new perspective. I could pull out the lower drawers and go through them while sitting comfortably. This was good.

I pulled out the first of many drawers. Most of these long, narrow drawers held the fancy vestments that Reverend Roy wore, and this one was no different. The color of this chasuble—I remembered the name!—was red.

"You found my Palm Sunday vestments."

I jolted, then quickly turned around. "Reverend Roy."

"Hello." He smiled. "It's Shannon, isn't it?"

"Yes." I was surprised that he remembered my name and stood up to speak with him. "I didn't expect to see you here today."

"I was looking for my secretary, Colleen. Lavinia said she might be coming over here today."

"She came by yesterday for a few minutes, and I'm really hoping she stops by today, too. Flora was here earlier."

"Flora?" He frowned. "Our Flora? The pretty lady who does the flowers?"

"Yes." I smiled. "She's a lovely woman. She's been over here a few times to check on our progress. She's so nice."

"Yes, she is," he agreed. "And she comes by?"

"Yes." The way he was reacting, I hoped I wasn't getting Flora busted. "It turns out that her nephew is part of my crew. He's setting up the lighting for the museum."

"Flora has a nephew?" Now he looked flummoxed.

"Yes." It was my turn to frown. "Buck moved here from the Los Angeles area to work on this project."

"And he's Flora's nephew." He scratched his head, then grinned. "I've known Flora for more than thirty years, but I never knew she had a nephew in Los Angeles."

I chuckled. "I guess it's true what they say, that you learn something new every day."

"Isn't that the truth?" he said. "I'll have to track down that young man and say hello."

I smiled. "His name is Buck, and right now, he's working up in the rafters. But he's usually around here somewhere."

"Everyone is so hard at work. It's good to see."

"My crew and I do enjoy what we do," I said.

"I'm delighted to hear that." He continued strolling around the room, glancing at the boxes, studying the paneling. "Did you happen to see Madeline this morning?"

"I haven't seen her, either, but I certainly expect her to be here at some point. Would you like me to call her?"

"No, no, dear. Thank you. You're very kind, but I know you have work to do."

"It's no trouble. I like to have people around."

"So do I," he said jovially, and gazed at the mahogany cabinet. The massive piece of furniture suited him, I thought, since he was such a big, good-looking man.

"You know," he said, sighing, "this room used to be my sanctuary. I had everything I needed right here. These drawers and cupboards contained my whole life." He grinned. "It felt that way, anyway. And I had a big stuffed chair that stood right there against the wall." He slowly pointed at the opposite wall and seemed to be drifting through memories.

"It must've been very comfortable," I said.

"It was my refuge." He walked over to take a closer look at the stacks of boxes and appeared to be counting them. Then he moved to the wall and reached out to touch the heavy wood paneling, tracing his finger along the raised, grape-leaf-patterned onlays. Shaking himself out of his thoughts, he turned to face me. "Well then, Shannon. What exactly are you working on in here?"

"Right now I'm going through this entire cabinet and packing up everything that was left behind."

As I was explaining, he wandered over to the stained glass windows and stared out at the view of ocean and sky.

"Once I've got everything in boxes," I continued, "I'll have my guys take it over to your new church, where your people can go through and figure out what you want to do with all of it."

He turned and looked surprised. "That sounds like a job my people should be doing."

"I expect to see them at some point, and I'll be happy to turn it all over to them."

He laughed. "I'll bet you will." His laughter faded. "I thought Lavinia and Colleen had already taken care of this. They're always so busy, but I know someone in our congregation would be willing to help out."

"I don't mind doing it myself," I said. "But if anyone shows up to help, I'll happily share the burden."

He chuckled. Strolling over to me, he reached for the bright red brocade chasuble. "It's a beautiful color, isn't it?"

"Oh, yes. I'm amazed at all the stunning colors. Every one of them is more vivid and elegant than the last one."

He continued to gaze at the chasuble, and I wondered if he knew exactly what else was left in this room. I assumed that he realized how valuable all these items were. Maybe he just assumed that people took care of things when he wasn't looking. But when it came to this room, nobody was in charge. I didn't want to get anyone in trouble, but if someone had been assigned to take care of all this, they had fallen down on the job.

"It's really quite extraordinary," he said, and slipped the chasuble on over his head. "But when I'm dressed in all of this finery, I honestly feel like a true servant of my flock. I'd like to think it brings me closer to heaven."

I nodded, unsure of what to say to that.

He carefully took it off, but held on to it for a full minute, absently running his hands over the brocade. Suddenly, he looked at me and grinned shyly. "The ladies love to see me in my gold-and-white duds on Easter Sunday morning."

I bet they do, I thought and almost laughed. But didn't dare. I would imagine there were dozens of ladies in his congregation who hung on his every word.

"I've already packed up the gold-and-white set," I said, "and I certainly agree that it's very handsome. We'll make sure it gets to the new church as soon as possible."

"Roy? Are you in here?" Lavinia walked into the sacristy. "Here you are. Why, it's Shannon. Hello, dear." She glanced around at the stacks of boxes and the open drawers. "My goodness, you've been busy. But you shouldn't have to do all this work. I'll have someone come and help you tomorrow."

"I'll take all the help I can get," I said easily.

She patted my shoulder. "I'll make it happen."

"You can believe that," Reverend Roy assured me. "Lavinia makes things happen."

I smiled at both of them. "Thank you."

Lavinia grabbed Reverend Roy's arm and urged him toward the door. "Come along, dearest. We're going to be late."

At the door, he turned. "Goodbye, Shannon. It was delightful talking to you."

"Come back and visit anytime," I said.

He glanced around. "I can't seem to stay away."

Lavinia smiled and clutched his arm a little more tightly as the two of them walked away.

After they left, I realized that he had taken the red chasuble with him. I hadn't even noticed.

"So, that was odd," I muttered, and sat down to continue packing. "Odd but sweet." I had enjoyed spending a few minutes with Reverend Roy. He seemed like a thoughtful man and he had a good sense of humor. I could see why he was so well-liked by his congregation.

The light was beginning to change in the room, and I glanced up at the stained glass window. From where I was seated, I could only see the clear blue sky, but I was able to estimate that it was close to noon because the sun was directly overhead. If I walked outside, I imagined I wouldn't see any shadows. At least for another ten minutes, anyway.

"Shannon."

I looked at the doorway and was surprised to see Lavinia.

"Oh. Hi, Lavinia. What can I do for you?"

"Roy told me how kind you were to him just now,

showing him what you're doing with all the vestments and such. I wanted to thank you for that."

I was surprised but quickly responded, "You're welcome. He's a really nice man. You're both good people."

"Well, thank you." She took one step closer. "That's always nice to hear."

"It's true," I said with a smile.

"Look, I know you're doing a lot of work that I should probably be doing, or Colleen or one of the other ladies we work with. But since we've moved to this new facility, it's just been a whirlwind." She shook her head and laughed briefly. "I had no idea how hard it is to start over in a brand-new place. I've only lived here most of my life."

"I know a move like this can be hard physically, but it can also be an emotional time. I hope you're taking good care of yourself."

She shook her head and sniffled. "You are such a sweet girl. I'm so glad you're in charge of things around here."

"Oh, thank you." I grinned at her. "I do love my job."

"I'm glad." She leaned back and glanced down the hall. "Now I'd better go find that husband of mine. When I left him, he was showing off that red chasuble he picked up from you." She winked at me. "I tell you, seeing that man in his fancy vestments? He's like catnip for the ladies."

She giggled and hurried down the hall.

I was pretty sure my eyes goggled, and I had to sit down and contemplate her words. Catnip. Wow. I supposed it was a good thing that she considered her husband a handsome man. I'd just never heard it put quite that way before.

I seriously had to catch my breath. Then I had to laugh. People were funny, that was for sure.

I sat for another minute and thought about doing some more work before breaking for lunch. Glancing back at the stained glass windows, my eyes were drawn to the larger decorative paneling between two of the windows. I frowned as I suddenly noticed that there was something wrong with the grape-leaf onlay. I pulled out my tablet and made a quick note to have Amanda look at it. It looked crooked, but I thought it was probably just coming loose.

An *onlay* was a piece of wood that was designed and carved separately and then applied to a smooth wood surface, such as a panel like this one. It formed a grape-leaf pattern that wound up the walls and was quite beautiful.

The opposite of an onlay was an *inlay*, which was a design that was carved directly into the wood. Because onlays were made up of separate pieces of wood, they would occasionally come loose and hang at an odd angle.

This one might be as simple to fix as an extra application of glue.

I walked over to the panel and knelt down to get a good look at the onlay. I wanted to see how loose it actually was, because I could probably fix it myself without bothering Amanda. I touched it and was shocked when it swung farther away to reveal . . . a keyhole.

"Are you kidding me?" I gaped at the unexpected sight. I stood and reached into the tiny front pocket of my jeans and pulled out the key. Then I knelt back down, pushed the onlay out of the way, and slipped the key into the keyhole.

It fit.

I was ridiculously excited, and without thinking, I turned the key and heard it click.

"Now what?" I asked myself. I was half expecting the wall to shape-shift into a giant cave opening, but that was just my imagination running amok. With the key still turned in the lock, I tugged at it, and the entire piece of paneling opened toward me.

"What?" It was sort of like a cave opening, after all. Except it wasn't exactly gigantic. It was only about three feet tall by two feet wide. Still, that gave me plenty of room to crawl inside.

"Really?" I muttered. Was I actually going to crawl inside that pitch-black opening? The idea gave me a little twinge of fear, but how could I possibly pass up this adventure? I pulled out my phone and turned on the flashlight app—something I used with regularity these days—and aimed it into the abyss. I saw a short landing just inside the panel door, then stairs that led downward into more darkness.

"Here goes nothing." I crouched down and tentatively crawled through the door onto the landing. When I was all the way inside, the panel slammed shut.

"Oh no!"

I almost screamed but tried to just breathe instead. I attempted to push it open, but it must've locked automatically. I was thoroughly creeped out now, but it only took me a few more seconds to realize I wasn't in any danger—unless there were spiders with big ugly teeth. I shuddered at the thought and mumbled, "You're an idiot."

Well, I wasn't that big of an idiot, I told myself, because I still had my phone. With that in mind, I aimed the light at the steep stairs in front of me and wondered where they led to. Was this the rest of the large basement we had seen on the original blueprints? It had to be. But why had this part been cut off from the other part beneath the altar?

I aimed the light at the ceiling and saw that there might be enough room for me to stand up. The ceiling slanted downward dramatically, following the angle of the stairway.

That's when I realized that the slanted portion above me was the buttress I'd seen from the town square.

I aimed the light toward the bottom of the stairs. It looked like a tunnel and it ran in both directions. This space wasn't finished like a regular basement with drywall and a ceiling. As I had initially imagined, this was more like a cave, with the walls and ceiling made of solid rock. There was moisture down here, too, which made sense because we were a block away from the ocean.

I wasn't about to venture down the steps by myself. Not until I had a better idea of exactly where those tunnels led.

I noticed something piled on the landing and aimed my flashlight to figure out what it was. A large piece of cloth of some kind, bright green with various symbols on it: the cross, a stylized fish, Greek alpha and omega symbols, flowers.

I knew immediately that it was one of the priest's chasubles. But why had someone crumpled it up and tossed it in here? I started to lift it up and realized it was wrapped around something else. And it was smeared and crusted with something dark and rusty.

"Oh God," I said, and dropped it. And heard a

clunk sound. "Oh no. Damn it." The smears had to be blood. But what had made that sound?

A whole new set of goose bumps erupted on my arms, and I had to rub away the sudden chills. The dried blood had to belong to Sarah. And the green chasuble was probably what her killer had used to drag her down the hall and into the blue chapel, where he left her to die.

I swallowed hard and, with the tips of my fingers, slowly and carefully unwrapped the fabric. This was evidence, and I wanted to preserve it—but I also wanted to take a look. I just hoped Eric never found out about that.

Wrapped inside the material, I found something that looked like a scepter, the kind a king might hold, only smaller. Despite its size, it was heavy, at least a foot long with a wooden handle on one end. On the other end was a golden ball with holes and ridges on it. I'd never seen anything like it. Was it some kind of medieval weapon? I wanted to take a closer look, but I didn't want to touch it, so I set it down on the chasuble and shined the flashlight on it.

That's when I saw the blood caked on the ball end. And the chills returned with a vengeance. I remembered that Sarah had been hit with something round that had caused lines to form on her skin. I was pretty sure the ridges on this instrument had caused that pattern to appear.

Which meant, of course, that this had to be the murder weapon.

"Oh God." I had to suck in some air because I was suddenly breathless.

I had to get out of here. In case I hadn't made the

connection before, it was now obvious that someone else knew about these tunnels, and that someone was a killer. Did they plan to return to get rid of these blood-stained items once and for all?

I turned and pounded on the hidden panel and shouted, "Help! Get me out of here!"

It only took a few seconds for me to realize that I wasn't stuck in here. I had my phone, which I had been using as a flashlight. Duh! I swiped the screen to get my contact list.

I stared at Mac's name. *Call him,* I thought. Then I remembered he was out of town, and I was instantly depressed.

I was being an idiot again. *Snap out of it!*

I shook my head and pressed Police Chief Eric Jensen's private phone number instead.

He answered on the first ring. "What is it, Shannon?"

"Eric, you need to get over to the church, right now."

He must've heard something in my voice, because he didn't argue. "Where will I find you?"

I thought fast. "Okay, go to the sacristy and just . . . um, shout my name."

Eric paused briefly and I figured he was probably thinking, *What in the actual hell is she talking about?*

I was about to explain more, but then he said, "Give me five minutes."

Chapter Twelve

Rather than wait in this dank, dark space next to the bloodstained remnants of some killer's rage, I quickly phoned Wade. "Can you come to the sacristy right now?"

"Sure. Be there in a minute."

It wasn't more than thirty seconds before I heard heavy footsteps cross the room and then stop. "Shannon?"

I began to shout, "Wade!"

"Shannon? Where are you?"

I pounded on the door. "I'm in here."

"Uh, I can hear you, but I can't see you."

"Okay, do you see the decorative panel next to the stained glass window?"

"Yeah."

"It's actually a door, and there's a little keyhole under the loose onlay. The key is still in there. Just turn it and pull the panel out toward you."

"You're kidding me."

"Uh, no."

"Only you, Shannon," he said, and I could picture him shaking his head.

"Yeah, it's my thing." I rolled my eyes. "Please hurry."

"Okay. Sorry." I could hear him fumbling with the onlay.

"The onlay swings back and forth," I said. "See it?"

"Yeah, I got it," he shouted. "Found the key. Hold on one more second."

The door sprung open and I almost fell onto him. He grabbed me and pulled me across the threshold and into the room.

"Thank you," I said in an exhalation of breath.

"Are you okay? How did you get in there? What the—?"

He helped me get to my feet. Seconds later, there was a sudden pounding of footsteps, and Eric came rushing into the room. "Shannon! What's going on?"

"She's okay," Wade said.

Eric grabbed my shoulders. "What happened to you?"

"She was stuck behind that panel," Wade explained. "I just now got her out."

Eric glanced around. "What panel?"

"Okay, I wasn't exactly stuck," I said. "I'm fine." I didn't want them to worry about me, but I could already feel the bumps and bruises from being pulled out of there. I rolled my shoulders to work out the kinks and shook my head to steady myself, then looked up at Eric. "I found a secret panel that opens onto a set of stairs that leads down to an underground tunnel."

He gave me a long, steady look. "Seriously."

"Seriously," I said, and pointed to the panel.

"Look, just inside that door is the chasuble that the

killer must've used to drag Sarah down the hall to the blue chapel. There's dried blood on it. And there's some weird-looking instrument that's got to be the murder weapon."

"What's a chasuble?" he asked, then seemed to realize that it probably wasn't the most important question. "Where are these things? Show me."

"Wait," I said, holding him back. "You're not going to shut down the church again, are you?"

He gritted his teeth. "Just show me the damn tunnel."

"Okay, okay."

I turned the key, and once again, the panel flew open.

Eric got down on his hands and knees, and peered into the blackness. He pulled out a Mini Maglite and scanned the area.

"Did you touch the, uh, what'd you call it?"

"Chasuble," I said, then winced. "And, yes, I touched it. Sorry. I wasn't thinking."

"Don't worry about it."

"But I didn't touch the murder weapon," I hastened to add.

"Good to hear it." He snapped off the flashlight and backed up, then stood. Pulling out his phone, he called Stringer. "We may have found the murder weapon and the piece of cloth that the killer used to drag our victim through the church. Can you get over here right away?"

Eric paused to listen to Leo, then nodded and said, "As soon as you can get here." He ended the call and stared at me for a moment. "Did you go any farther into that cave? Or tunnel?" He frowned. "What is that space?"

"I think it's actually part of the basement that they

never finished. And no, I didn't go any farther. I stayed right on the landing."

"The door locked, and she had to call me to get her out of there," Wade added helpfully.

It was no use denying it. "That's right. As soon as I crawled in there, the door slammed shut. That freaked me out a little. And when I saw the blood on the chasuble and on that scepter-looking thing, I realized that the killer knew about the tunnel, so I wasn't about to go any farther."

"Good thinking," he said. "Do you know where this tunnel leads to?"

"Not a clue," I said.

He thought for a minute. "You've both seen the original blueprints?"

"Of course," I said.

Wade nodded. "Yeah."

"You think this is the entryway down to the basement?"

"It's a theory," I said. "But the basement they showed us when we did our first walk-through was much smaller than what we saw on the blueprints."

"Okay." He thought for a moment. "I want you both to come down there with me. We'll do a quick look around, and I want your thoughts."

"You got it," Wade said.

"I'll unlock the door." I turned the key and pulled the door open. "You want to go first?"

"Yeah." Eric crawled through the door.

"Careful you don't hit your head," I said quickly. "The ceiling's low."

"Thanks," Eric said from behind the panel, then added, "Yeah, this is a little low for me."

"Same goes for you," I said to Wade.

"Got it." Wade pulled his own Mini Maglite from his tool belt, then went in after Eric.

"And watch out for those stairs," I called. "They look really steep." It was probably a dumb thing to warn them about. With their flashlights, they could see for themselves.

While I waited for Wade to crawl through, I dashed over to the cabinet and pulled out a folded linen piece about the size of a handkerchief. It was the first thing I could think of, based on the little chapel veil I'd found stuffed in the door of the blue chapel. I'd be using it for a different purpose.

"I'm coming in feetfirst," I warned them, "so move away so I don't kick you." Then I followed Wade into the darkness. Before the door could shut, I folded the linen piece and slipped it between the latch and the strike plate. Then I pulled the door slowly until it appeared to be closed. If anyone entered the sacristy, they wouldn't notice that the panel was actually a door. That was what I hoped, anyway.

I switched on my flashlight app and looked around to see where Eric and Wade were.

"We're down here," Eric said.

The two of them had already gone down the stairs and stood on the ground below. I followed, being careful on the steep stairway. The last thing I wanted to do was miss a step and land on my head.

"Which way?" Eric asked.

"The altar is this way," I said, pointing to the right. "Which means the finished basement is this way, too."

"I remember," Wade said. "The door to the basement was back behind the altar."

"Right."

"Okay, so let's go this way," Eric said, and turned left.

The ground was hard compacted dirt. The wall was stone, and it looked as if it had always been here. *Wherever* here *is,* I thought. Had they meant to widen the church basement but never gotten around to it? Maybe the basement indicated on those old blueprints had been something they intended to add.

It was so dark and eerie down here, I suddenly wondered if they had ever used this old stone tunnel for catacombs. It was under an old church, after all, and that was what some churches used to do: bury people.

That possibility sent a wave of shivers down my back. Honestly, could they have buried people down here? No, I insisted to myself. But with every step I took, I expected to see bones half-buried in the depths of the cave.

We followed the tunnel for more than a hundred yards before there was a slight curve to the right. We followed it and suddenly saw someone coming toward us shining a flashlight.

"Whoa!" the person cried.

"What the hell?" Wade said.

Eric already had his weapon out and he shouted, "Police! Stop right there and identify yourself."

"Don't shoot!" The figure held up his hands and the flashlight pointed to the cave-like ceiling, causing the light to dance wildly on the surface.

"What's your name?" Eric demanded.

"My name's Buck Buckner. I didn't do anything." He aimed his flashlight right at me. "Shannon? Is that you? Hey, Wade."

"Buck," I said. "What're you doing down here?"

"Just getting back to work," he said.

Eric stepped forward. "Turn off that flashlight."

"Okay, okay." He turned it off.

"How did you get down here?" Eric asked.

"Oh, hey. Hi, Chief Jensen. What's going on? Is somebody missing?"

"Buck," I said. "You need to answer Chief Jensen's questions."

"Right. Jeez." He exhaled nervously. "Sorry. I took a lunch break, and I was just heading back to work."

"Through a tunnel?" Eric said in disbelief.

"I know, right?" He stuck out his thumb and pointed it toward the way he'd come. "There's a really cool opening under the pier that leads down to this tunnel."

"How in the world did you find it?" I asked.

"My aunt showed it to me."

There was a long moment of stunned silence. Finally I said, "Your aunt Flora knows about this tunnel?"

"Pretty cool, huh?" he said genially. "We were having lunch on the pier, and I realized it was getting late, so she said she'd show me a shortcut. Said it would take me right up to the basement of the church."

"Show us," Eric insisted.

He didn't move. "The thing is, my aunt asked me not to tell anyone about it."

"You've already told us," Eric said reasonably. "Now will you please show us?"

The question left Buck no opportunity to argue. He swallowed nervously. "Yes, sir."

In the dim glow of the flashlight, I saw Eric's expression and could almost read his mind. If Buck's aunt Flora knew about these tunnels and knew the way back to the basement, was she the one who'd left the priest's chasuble on the landing? The one with all the blood?

I cringed at the thought, but it made sense, unfortunately. Flora could be the killer. But why? What was her motive?

And then there was Buck. He seemed innocent and easygoing, but that could be an act. Could he have done it? But again, why?

He led us toward the pier, back the way he'd come. After another hundred yards or so, he stopped next to a barnacle-encrusted piling. He pointed to something a few feet farther under the pier. "If you take those steps up, you'll come out right by that fish restaurant."

"I can't see where you're pointing," I said, and walked in the direction he'd indicated. It was cleverly hidden behind several other pilings, and the opening was barely a foot wide.

We stared at it for a full minute. Eric slid between the pilings and disappeared for a moment, checking out Buck's story. He came right back, and he and Wade and I glanced at one another. We didn't say anything, but I could read their expressions of disbelief and astonishment. Wade and I had lived here our entire lives and had never known about these steps. And Eric had been chief of police for at least five or six years. I couldn't believe he wouldn't have known about this little secret passageway to a hidden tunnel. It sounded ludicrous, but it was real.

I had a sudden thought that Mac would kill to be in on all of this crazy intrigue. Imagine, tunnels under the pier that led to the old church! I would've loved to give him a call as soon as we got back, but he wasn't in town, and I knew he had a busy schedule. And, oh boy, I missed him more than I could say. I would just have to tell him all about it tonight when we talked.

"Okay, let's get back to the church," Eric said.

"Sure thing," Buck said.

We retraced our steps back into the tunnel, and the light quickly dimmed. Eric turned on his Maglite, and I got out my phone with the flashlight app. It was slow going, and that was okay with me because I didn't want to trip over something I couldn't see. And I wanted to study this bizarre tunnel. Some group of people had obviously constructed it, but how? And why? And when did they do it? It looked pretty old.

I shined my flashlight along the tunnel wall and examined it for a few seconds. Had they used pickaxes? It wasn't a smooth surface. In fact, it was badly pitted. I wondered if it was mentioned in any books on the history of our town. I had done quite a bit of reading on that subject, but I had never come across any reference to tunnels under the old church.

Maybe I would have a little talk with Flora when I saw her again.

Finally we made it to the stairs leading up to the sacristy.

"Aunt Flora said to ignore this first set of steps," Buck explained. "The basement is just a little farther down."

"Lead the way," Eric said.

About forty feet beyond the stairway to the sacristy was a large concrete structure that looked pretty solid.

"Here we go," Buck said cheerfully. "She said the door is always unlocked."

"It won't be after today," Eric muttered.

Three wide concrete steps led up to a heavy door.

Buck headed up the steps, but Eric stopped him. "Have you been through here before?"

"Never. But my aunt was right. It's pretty easy to get here if you've got a flashlight."

"Did she tell you how she found this tunnel?" I asked.

"She just said she's known about it for years."

"Are there many others who know about it?" Eric asked.

Buck shrugged, unsure of the answer. "I guess somebody must've told her."

Wade, Eric, and I exchanged another look. This was crazy.

"I can get the door for you," Buck offered.

"I'll get it." Eric pulled out his weapon. "Stay back."

Buck looked at me, his eyes widening. "Whoa."

"There's already been one murder," I said. "The chief needs to take precautions."

"I guess so," he said.

Eric turned the knob and pushed the heavy door open. I waited for him to give the okay, and then I followed him through the door.

He flipped a switch and the room filled with light. I walked in and nodded. "This is the basement we saw the first time we toured the church with Madeline. But the door leading to the tunnel was completely covered up by utility tables and stacks of chairs on pallets."

"I didn't even notice a door that first time we came here," Wade added.

It was a nicely finished basement and a reasonably good-sized space, but was much smaller than the blueprints had indicated.

The floor was a concrete slab, and the walls were covered in drywall and painted a pale yellow.

I remembered seeing several of the utility tables opened and lined along the wall. They'd held several industrial-sized coffee urns and other equipment that I assumed were used for after-church meetings with coffee and cookies.

The space was completely empty now.

The four of us climbed the basement stairs up to the back hallway directly across from the three small chapels. At the top, Eric turned to Buck and gave him a nod. "I appreciate your cooperation. You can go on back to work if you'd like."

"Guess I'd better."

I smiled warmly to make up for being suspicious earlier. "Thanks, Buck."

"No problem," he said with an easy grin.

"Wait," Eric said. "Before you go, I have a question."

"Yes?"

"You said your aunt swore you to secrecy about the tunnel."

"That's right."

"Did she happen to mention the names of anyone else who might be aware of the tunnels?"

Hearing Eric's question, I realized his strategy. He would ask the same thing in a variety of ways in hopes of getting a different response.

"No, but I got the feeling it was a church thing."

"How so?" Eric asked.

"She does all the flowers for the church services, you know. So she liked to put the flowers in buckets of water and set them down in the tunnel to keep them cool." He shrugged. "Said they'd last longer that way."

Eric nodded slowly. "Okay. One more thing, and this is for all of you." He gave each of us a look meant to intimidate, and it pretty much worked. "I don't want you to mention one word about this tunnel to anyone else. Not one word. Do you understand?"

"Yes, sir," Buck said immediately.

And suddenly, I understood perfectly. If the killer knew that I knew about the tunnel, I could be in danger. Same went for Buck and Wade.

And possibly Flora, I thought.

I met Wade's gaze and saw that he had made the connection as well.

"Got it, Chief," Wade said.

I looked at Eric. "I understand."

"Okay, you're all free to go. Thanks again for your help."

Buck gave us all a thumbs-up and then walked away, circling the wall behind the central platform on his way out to the nave.

Wade gave me a sideways glance. Was he suspicious of Buck? I was starting to lean that way, too. From day one, there had been so many coincidences surrounding him and his aunt Flora. And I knew what Mac thought of coincidences.

"I'd better get back to it, too," Wade said to Eric. "Unless you need me for anything else."

"Not right now," Eric said. "But thanks."

"It was enlightening." Wade looked at me. "I'm going to go check on everyone. See who needs what."

"Text me if anything comes up," I said. "By the way, while I was perusing the basement walls for hidden doors and such, I did notice some water damage in a couple of spots."

"Yeah, I saw that, too."

"It may be superficial, but I doubt it."

"Me too," he said. "We'll check it out with Niall tomorrow."

"Nine a.m.?"

"I'll be there. And I'll remind Niall when I see him."

"Good. Thank you." I watched Wade take off and turned to Eric. "I don't suppose I can go back to work in the sacristy."

He was checking his phone. "Leo just texted. He'll be here in a minute."

"You're going to close down my room, aren't you?"

"Sorry, kiddo. Just for a day or so. Leo needs time to process the scene."

"I understand. But I've still got my tool belt and a jacket in there, so I'd like to grab them before Leo gets started."

"I'll walk you over there."

"Okay." We approached the door to the sacristy, and I reached for the handle.

He held up his hand. "Wait."

Then I heard it. Someone was inside the room. There were sounds of a drawer opening and shutting abruptly. Then another cupboard was opened. I knew which one it was, because its top hinge always squeaked loudly. The cupboard slammed shut.

I looked up at Eric. "Do you think it's Leo?"

"No."

Of course not, I thought. As an experienced crime scene investigator, Leo Springer wouldn't be rifling through that big cabinet without some guidance from Eric.

I had half expected to find Leo standing out here in the hall until Eric showed up.

"Stand back," Eric murmured to me, and for the

third time today—or was it the fourth?—he pulled out his weapon.

He twisted the doorknob and pushed the door open quickly, took one step into the room, and shouted, "Freeze!"

The woman standing by the open cabinet drawer whirled around and screamed.

I took one peek inside the room and was seriously shocked. "Madeline?"

Chapter Thirteen

"Oh, Shannon. Thank goodness it's you." She clutched her neck with both hands, obviously frightened. But what had she been doing in here? Was she frightened by Eric? Or was there something else going on?

I hesitated, then said, "It's good to see you, Madeline. Everybody's been looking for you. We weren't sure when you'd be back."

"I wasn't sure, either. I . . . I just needed to take a few days away. It was so . . . so horrible losing poor Sarah like that."

Out of the corner of my eye, I noticed that Eric had taken a few extra seconds before he holstered his gun.

"It's been hard on everyone," I said. "I thought I'd have a chance to talk to you at the prayer vigil the other night."

"I left as soon as it was over," she said. "I was just a mess, so I decided to take a break and go visit my family." She looked at Eric. "I called your department to let them know I was leaving town for a few days."

Eric nodded. "I got the message."

She could've taken a few more days off, I thought, because she still looked completely wiped out. Usually, she was at the top of her game, beautifully dressed and coiffed, but today she wore funky old jeans and a stretched-out sweatshirt. Her skin was pale and her hair was mussed. I was surprised she had even shown up today.

She looked from Eric back to me. "What's going on?"

"Let's step out into the hall, shall we?" Eric said.

Madeline looked surprised. "Oh. All right."

I quickly grabbed my tool belt and jacket and followed them out to the hall.

Eric closed the door behind me. "I'm afraid this room is off-limits for a few days."

She tried to smile. "I hope I wasn't breaking any rules by going in there."

"May I ask what you were doing?" he said cordially.

"Oh. Well. I, that is, I just wanted to make sure the cabinet drawers had been cleaned out."

"And were they?" he asked.

"Uh, no. There are still dozens of church items filling the drawers. It looks like someone started going through them and packing things, but they still have a long way to go."

Eric's smile was downright charming. "And may I ask why that's a concern of yours?"

Unfortunately, his charm didn't work on her, because she was clearly insulted by the question. "I'm in charge of everything that's going on here." She spread her arms to take in the whole church. "This entire renovation is my responsibility. If something as seemingly insignificant as that cabinet isn't cleaned out, it interrupts our timeline. It slows everything down. Do you understand?"

Madeline sounded so defensive that it made me wonder if she was telling the truth. Was I being unfair? Maybe, but I had a sneaking suspicion that she'd had a completely different reason for rifling through that cabinet. Was she looking for something? Maybe she'd hidden something inside one of the drawers. Did she know about the secret panel that led to the tunnel underneath the church?

I was reminded of the Scooby-Doo session I'd played with Mac a few nights ago. Good grief, was it only a few nights ago? I shook my head at the realization. Anyway, I recalled that Mac had come up with a frighteningly feasible reason why Madeline might've killed Sarah: her basic jealousy of Sarah, the younger, prettier woman, and the fact that once the project was finished, the town council would fire Madeline and bring Sarah on as a cheaper replacement.

But that wasn't fair, was it? I hadn't gone along with Mac's theory that night, and I still had a problem believing Madeline could've killed her assistant. But fair or not, I was certain that, right now, the woman wasn't being truthful. Now I'd have to figure out what her real story was.

Despite what I considered highly suspicious behavior, Eric wished Madeline a good day and thanked her for speaking with him.

As soon as she disappeared down the hall, I turned

on him. "Why did you let her go? Don't you think she's hiding something?"

"Without a doubt," he said, his eyes narrowing in on a theory of his own. Sadly, he wasn't inclined to share it with me. "But, Shannon, I prefer to wait for Leo Stringer's findings before I draw any conclusions."

Despite Mac's theory, I hadn't actually considered Madeline a possible suspect until I saw her in the sacristy just now digging through drawers and looking and acting as guilty as could be. And then, to see her so outraged by the chief of police daring to ask her questions. As if he didn't have the right to do it during a murder investigation. It made me wonder.

It seemed as if she might be protesting too much.

An hour later, Madeline had calmed down, and she was busily showing Buck and Sean where the artwork would be placed along the south wall of the nave so they could get a good idea of where to install the lighting fixtures for optimal illumination.

"I think that's going to be perfect," she said. "You guys are doing a great job."

"Thanks, Madeline," Sean said from forty-five feet above the floor.

I was standing by Madeline and watched her interact with my crew. "Do you feel like things are starting to take shape for you?" I asked.

"It's going really well," she said with a grateful smile.

"We've got a good crew," I said, then brought up a sensitive subject. "I wanted to let you know that I was making pretty good progress with the sacristy cabinet until the police turned it into a crime scene."

Madeline gasped. "A crime scene? The sacristy?"

"Yes."

"I saw all those boxes stacked in there," she said. "You're the one packing everything?"

"Yes," I said, and smiled ruefully. "And you're right. I've barely made a dent."

She sighed. "Didn't Colleen send someone over to help you?"

"No. She and Lavinia have promised to send help, but I guess they got wrapped up in something else. Or maybe it's just not a priority for them like it is for us. That's why I decided to start emptying those drawers and packing things up myself."

Madeline considered this. "Colleen wouldn't have the time to help you. She's busier than anyone, always making appointments and meeting with church members. I'm not sure how they would survive without her."

"She does seem very efficient," I said, nodding.

"I wish I had been here to help you," she said. "I really love to do that kind of work. But with poor Sarah gone, I was feeling so befuddled. I had to take a few days off to be with my family and just sit and think about life. And death. Sarah was . . . important. She was like Colleen in that way. She took care of so many details." She shook her head, looking bereft. "I'm lost without her."

"I'm sorry," I said. "If there's anything any of us can do to help you, please let me know."

Her eyes teared up. "You're all doing so much. I'm very grateful."

"I was thinking, since I can't get into the sacristy for a day or two, I might help Billy and the guys who are working on these pews. I'm not sure how far along they are, but I could help remove the kneelers from some of them. What do you think? Does that work for your schedule?"

"I'm so glad you asked me about my schedule, because I do have one." She smiled brightly. "In fact, I have a master plan for all of the pews, and I can go over it with you."

"A master plan?"

"Yes." She laughed lightly. "I call it my pew plan."

I grinned. "That's hilarious."

"I have my moments," she said, and managed another smile.

The old Madeline was coming around, and I was glad to see her.

We sat down in one of the pews and went over her plan. It was elaborate, with diagrams and charts included. Every single pew was given a number and an assignment, listing where it would be going and the time frame involved. For instance, Madeline wanted to put several pews along the walls of the narthex in case people wanted to sit while waiting for friends or for a ride. But those pews couldn't be moved into the narthex until we had reconfigured that space to include a ticket counter as well as a gift shop at one end.

"We have twenty-five rows with two pews in each row. That's fifty pews. That's a lot. I really do have a plan for all of them, but I wanted to wait and see how they'd fit in with the final art installations."

"That makes sense," I said.

"I was also thinking about selling some of them. It would make a statement to see a church pew in someone's living room, don't you think?"

"Honestly, I do." I thought for a moment. "Whatever

you want to keep for the museum, my crew and I would be happy to strip and refinish them for exterior use."

"That's excellent, thank you," she said, and tapped something into her tablet. "In the meantime, you're free to remove the kneelers from the first twelve rows."

"That works for me." I lifted my power drill out of my toolbox and set it down on the seat of the pew.

"Wow, you're ready to go," she said.

I grinned. "Always."

We were interrupted by the sound of frantic footsteps *tip-tip-tapping* on the marble floor. I looked up in time to see Whitney Reid Gallagher dashing down the aisle right toward me.

I groaned. "Oh hell." I gave Madeline a quick smile and said, "I've got to go check on something, but thanks so much for helping me out with this."

"No problem," she said, then saw Whitney and smiled. "Oh, hi, Whitney."

Madeline had no idea how much Whitney annoyed me, and I wasn't about to tell her. Not while she was still basking in the glow of Whitney love. No doubt it would turn sour one of these days.

I rushed down the aisle toward the central platform.

"Stop right there, missy," Whitney said with an arrogant sniff. "I want to talk to you."

"You'll have to make an appointment." I kept walking.

"Hold it!" she cried out. "I'm going to report you."

I laughed out loud, then turned. "Report me to whom?"

"I happen to be the newest member of the Lighthouse Cove Historical Society, so everything you do in here is subject to my approval."

The Historical Society was a lovely organization,

and the few people who worked there were always helpful.

"Oh, Whitney, that's wonderful," Madeline said.

Whitney didn't bother to acknowledge the compliment, just hurried to catch up to me.

"You realize you're being ridiculous," I said. "You will never have approval power over my work."

She thrust her shoulder angrily. "Well, somebody should."

"Nice try. The Historical Society does a lot of good work, but interfering with *my* work isn't one of their aims. So you're just lying." I turned and walked away. It was for her own good since, whenever I got this close to her, I had the biggest urge to smack her. And she'd love to have me arrested for assault and battery.

More than anything else, I didn't want to have a knock-down, drag-out fight in front of Madeline, who didn't know our history.

"You can run, but you can't hide," Whitney taunted me.

"You're a twit," I said under my breath.

"I heard that!" she shouted.

Ears like a bat, I thought as I headed for the hallway. I began to run, knowing I could lose her around the back. Her stiletto heels wouldn't be able to keep up with me. It wasn't that I couldn't handle a fight. But I was just so tired of her crap.

How had she and Madeline become friends? Madeline had exquisite taste in so many things, while Whitney was just tacky. She was proof positive that all the money in the world couldn't buy good taste.

I couldn't spend time worrying about it, though. I just had to get away. I got to the other side of the church, then snuck out through the north transept.

Once outside, I walked to my truck and climbed into the cab. Pulling out my phone, I called Wade.

"I saw you make your escape," he said, chuckling.

"I'm not proud," I said. "I just had to get away from her."

"She's a piece of work, all right." He lowered his voice. "She just started berating Sean for moving the boom lift a couple of inches and scaring her out of her wits."

"Thankfully, she has no wits, so it's no great loss."

"Ooh, snap," he said.

I winced. "Sorry, that was harsh, but seriously? She's yelling at Sean?"

"Yeah. It's still going on." He held up the phone. "Can you hear her?"

"I can hear her." I shook my head. "What does she want? Why is she here?"

"She just said something about 'pulling the plug on Shannon's project.'"

"She's lost it," I said. "It's Madeline's project and they're supposed to be friends."

"I think she believes you're still in the building, so she's deliberately yelling loud enough for you to hear her."

"Oh, brother." I shook my head. "Look, I'll come back and get her out of there."

"No way," he said. "This is the most entertainment we've had all day."

I chuckled. "You sure?"

"Yeah. I'll give her another five minutes and then call the police."

I laughed. "I love you, Wade."

"I'm a lovable guy."

As everyone in town knew, Whitney was married to

Tommy Gallagher, the assistant chief of police. And he could usually be counted on to show up and escort his wife home, like he'd done on that first day, right after Sarah was killed.

I checked my wristwatch. "Okay, if you think you can handle her, I'm going to head on home."

"Sounds like a plan," he said. "We'll see you in the morning."

"Nine a.m. in the basement."

"Right. Have a good one."

After tossing Robbie's crocheted fish toy across the living room for him to catch and return, I paid some bills and then spent time going over crew schedules and an updated rundown of work to be done on a daily basis. Finally, I closed my tablet and walked away from my job.

The sun was still out, so I went to my garden and began clearing the weeds and checking on the water lines. Then I harvested some veggies for a salad.

I felt so virtuous after putting my salad together that I called Bella Rossa and ordered a pizza to go with it.

The restaurant was two blocks away, so rather than waiting for the delivery guy, I walked there. I needed to move, needed to get out of the house, if only for twenty minutes. I had things on my mind and I wanted to talk to Mac.

I expected to hear from him at some point tonight, but I knew it would be late when he got back to his hotel room. It was only nine o'clock in New York City, and he would invariably be going out to dinner with his agent or editor or a few of his city friends. He always stayed out late because he liked to walk around the city and take in the scenes and the views. He would call me when he got back to his hotel.

But darn it, I really needed to talk to him, especially after discovering that hidden door and finding the tunnel underneath the church. I couldn't wait to tell him about it. He loved that kind of stuff, and I figured that once he saw it for himself, he would probably put it into a book.

After all, it would be the perfect spot to hide a bomb.

I marveled at how close we'd gotten over the last year, ever since he moved in with me. We had been close before, but living together was something altogether different. Neither of us had ever lived with anyone before—besides our families, of course—so this was something new for both of us. And we knew we had something pretty great together. But whenever he left town, I always got a little anxious, wondering if this would be the moment he realized that he wanted something more exciting than small-town life in Lighthouse Cove. And me.

I hated feeling so needy. I really wasn't, not usually. I told myself to get over it. Maybe I would call Chloe and give her the chance to tell me the same thing. It sounded a lot better when Chloe or one of my girlfriends berated me for being so dumb rather than privately moaning and groaning over it. But that still didn't stop me from doing it.

At Bella Rossa, the hostess greeted me by name, and each of the waitresses I saw waved to me. I knew them all, not only because I came in here at least once a week but also because my uncle Pete owned the place.

I walked over to the bar to order a glass of wine while I waited.

"You want a glass of wine while you wait for your pizza, Shannon?" the bartender asked, as though he'd read my mind.

"Sure. Thanks, Ray."

"I just got a case of Pete's private reserve Pinot Noir. I think it's his best yet."

He poured a glass and set it in front of me.

I took a sip, then grinned. "Wow. I think you're right."

"Enjoy," Ray said, and moved down the bar to serve another customer.

Besides owning the Bella Rossa restaurant and wine bar, Uncle Pete also owned a vineyard and winery in nearby Anderson Valley. It was nice to have it all in the family.

"Why, it's Shannon. Hello, dear."

I turned at the greeting. "Flora. Hello. How are you?"

The flower lady wore a pretty pink sweater over black wool pants. This might've been a special occasion.

"Oh, I'm just dandy, dear. How are you doing?"

"I'm fine. Do you eat here often?"

"Oh, yes," she said, her eyes gleaming. "It's the best. I especially enjoy it because I went to school with your uncle Pete."

"That's right." I nodded, remembering. "You went to school with my dad, so you must know my uncle Pete, too."

"I do. They're both such nice men."

"I'd have to agree with you," I said, smiling. I reached for my wineglass and glanced around. "Is Buck with you?"

"Oh, yes. He's parking the car."

I scanned the bar area, then leaned a little closer. "Can I ask you something?"

"Of course."

"How long have you known about the tunnel under the church?"

"Oh dear." She glanced around as well. "Buck told me about his run-in with you and Chief Jensen. I believe he was more frightened than he let on, but we'll keep that between the two of us." She paused and gazed out the front window for a moment. "I've known about that tunnel for more years than I can count. We always kept it a secret because of Lavinia."

"Lavinia?" I was surprised. "She wouldn't let you tell anyone?"

"Oh, no, it's not that." She waved a hand in frustration. "I'm not explaining it very well. You see, back when I first started working for the church, Reverend Bryant was the head of the congregation. He was Lavinia's father."

I blinked. "Wait. Her father was the reverend here? And then she married the next reverend?"

"Yes. The problem was, Reverend Bryant, her father, was a stickler for propriety. A lovely man to his congregation, but I must confess, he showed little tolerance when it came to Lavinia. He considered her incorrigible and punished her regularly."

My eyes narrowed. "Punished her?"

She sighed. "If it were just spankings, that wouldn't be so bad. But he liked to use his belt." She paused, then added, "And occasionally, his fists."

"But that's terrible."

"Yes, it was. He used to grab her arms and shake her. She always wore long sleeves, even on the hottest days of summer."

"Because he hit her? Bruised her?"

She gave a vigorous nod. "To get away from him, she would hide out in the tunnel under the church. She loved to read romance novels, and she'd hide them, along with a flashlight, in a hole near the basement door."

"Oh." It all made sense now. "Did she tell you about the tunnel?"

"No." Flora looked slightly abashed. "One day I followed her."

"Was she angry?"

"I think she was relieved that someone else finally knew. She swore me to secrecy and I kept my promise. Until recently."

"With Buck."

"Yes." She sighed. "Maybe I shouldn't have told him, because now it seems that several more people know."

I couldn't help that. "So that's why you never talk about the tunnel."

"We didn't want Reverend Bryant to get wind of it."

"Are you sure he didn't know about the tunnel?" I asked.

"Absolutely sure," she insisted. "If he had known, he would've done something really awful to Lavinia."

"Like what? Kill her?"

"Maybe." She scrunched up her face in revulsion. "I wouldn't have put it past him. Once, he hit her so badly, she lost consciousness. She wound up in the hospital."

"And they didn't report it to the authorities?"

"Lavinia was very good at covering up the truth."

"Where was her mother?" I asked.

"According to Lavinia, her mother had died years earlier."

"You sound skeptical," I said.

She made a *tsk-tsk* sound, then said, "I'm sure Lavinia wouldn't lie about such a thing. But I never met the woman, so I can't really say."

"And nobody else came to her rescue?"

"I don't think so. You have to understand, Reverend Bryant was the beloved leader of the local church. Who would believe he'd do something like that to his own daughter?"

"Who indeed?" I murmured. "Is he still around?"

"No," Flora said, looking troubled. "He developed dementia and died almost twenty years ago."

It probably wasn't charitable of me, but I couldn't be sorry he was gone. "And Reverend Patterson took his place. And met Lavinia. They fell in love and were married soon after."

"A happy ending," I said lightly.

"And he is a lovely man," she said, smiling.

"I'm glad." I took a sip of my wine. "Does he know about the tunnel?"

Her eyes widened. "Oh, no, dear. Nobody knows about the tunnel but a select few. We would like to keep it that way."

"All right." I frowned at her. "But Chief Jensen knows. And now so do I."

"Yes, I know." She exhaled heavily. "I suppose it won't stay a secret much longer. But Lavinia will be very upset if she finds out that everyone knows. It has always been her refuge."

"I understand." I wasn't about to get Flora busted if I could help it.

"Here's your pizza, Shannon," Ray said, placing the square box on the bar.

"Thanks, Ray." I turned to Flora. "I won't say anything."

She smiled and patted my arm. "I would be very grateful if you wouldn't."

"I appreciate you telling me the story." I took the last sip of wine, then stood and reached for my pizza box. "I hope you enjoy your dinner."

Buck walked into the bar. "Hey, Shannon. You joining us for dinner?"

"Hi, Buck." I smiled as I noticed once again what a big, good-looking guy he was. "I can't do it tonight. I'm taking my pizza and heading on home."

"Okay." He grinned. "Enjoy."

"You too. See you tomorrow."

I walked home with my pizza, contemplating everything I'd learned tonight.

I couldn't believe that those two reverends didn't know about the tunnel, especially since the secret panel was right there in the sacristy. The sacristy was their special room, filled with everything they wanted or needed. It was where they changed into their vestments and prepared themselves for mass. And where they spent time meditating and praying.

And I couldn't quite believe that for the last forty years or so, a couple of women had been sneaking into the sacristy when they weren't looking and had been skulking over to that secret panel to go into that tunnel. It was crazy.

Maybe the women hadn't always used the sacristy panel for access. Maybe they had used the door in the basement. That would be a more straightforward way to go. But that begged the question, Didn't the reverends ever go into the basement? Did they not see that door? Weren't they curious about it?

Maybe not, I thought with a shrug. Maybe they stayed away from that room and left it all for the flower ladies and the handyman.

The *handyman*. Mr. Brindley. Was he in on the secret of the hidden tunnel? Would he do anything to keep it from being revealed? He seemed to be very devoted to Lavinia. Maybe he'd seen Sarah sneaking into the tunnel and killed her to keep Lavinia's secret.

I rolled my eyes at that ridiculous scenario.

But I wondered if Mr. Brindley knew about Reverend Bryant's nasty habit of beating his daughter. I guessed I would have to ask him tomorrow.

"No," I said aloud. The first person I would talk to tomorrow would be Eric. I had to tell him what I'd found out.

I grimaced. I really hated the idea of betraying Flora's trust in me. And what could Eric do about a dead reverend, anyway? Even if he was a monster, and it sounded like he was, there was nothing Eric or the courts could do to punish him now.

Maybe I would just mind my own business and stick to the work I needed to get done.

I picked up my pace and walked faster. I was anxious to get home, have some pizza, and wait for Mac's call. He'd been gone less than twelve hours, and I had already gathered new information and was starting to consider several viable suspects. We were way beyond the Scooby-Doo game now.

Chapter Fourteen

Mac never called.

I fell asleep waiting to hear from him, and the next thing I knew, it was six thirty in the morning and the alarm was going off. I stumbled out of bed and took a quick shower, then dried my hair and dressed for the day.

He should've called. I didn't care about the reasons why he hadn't. I just wanted to know that he was safe and, you know, alive. And also, why didn't he call? Did I sound needy? Okay, I *needed* him to call me so I wouldn't picture him hurt.

So I texted him. "Just checking that you're safe. Talk soon." I added a red heart and hit send.

In the kitchen, I made coffee, then played with Robbie, Tiger, and Luke for a few minutes. I prepared their food and water for the day and placed their bowls on each of their individual mats.

Then I cut up some strawberries, tossed them into a carton of yogurt, and added some granola. I'd taken a few bites when Mac called. I answered on the first ring. "Mac."

"I'm sorry I worried you, babe. I was out really late last night and didn't want to call and wake you up."

"You know you can always wake me up. Or just send a text. I was kind of worried. But you sound fine."

"I am," he said. "Just a little tired."

"So, were you out with Eleanor?" His agent loved to wine and dine him whenever he went to New York City.

"Yeah. There were a few of us. Fabulous restaurant. It was sort of a celebration because this deal is going to happen, and I'm going to be writing the screenplay."

"Oh, Mac, that's wonderful."

"Yeah, it is. I'm actually pretty excited about it. The deal is fantastic, but I don't want to say too much about it right now. Don't want to jinx it."

I smiled. Mac wasn't superstitious except when it came to money deals. I couldn't blame him. "You'll tell me more when you get home?"

"I will. Promise." He paused, then said, "After dinner, Siobhán and I stopped for a drink in the hotel bar. We ended up talking for a few hours."

"Oh. That's nice. I hope she's doing well." Did my words sound as hollow and phony as I felt?

I hope she's doing well? Seriously? No! Actually, I hope she choked on her whiskey and soda!

Ugh. I had just morphed into the girlfriend from hell.

But really, they talked for hours? And he couldn't call? Or send a damn text?

Just breathe, I thought, *and count to ten.*

"Was Terence with you?" I asked, hoping my voice

sounded pleasant and not like the jealous girlfriend I had suddenly turned into.

"No, he wasn't," Mac said. "That's why we stayed up talking for so long. They're breaking up."

"Oh no. That's too bad. He seemed like such a nice guy."

"Well, he was a nice guy, sort of," Mac said, "until Siobhán was offered this new picture deal. Apparently, Terence can't handle having a wife who's more successful than he is."

"What? Does he live in a cave?" I said, then realized I'd said it out loud. "Oops. That was rude. Sorry."

"Don't be. Turns out, he might as well live in a cave. Not a nice guy after all. More like a knuckle-dragging troglodyte."

"Oh dear." And automatically, I felt bad for wishing Siobhán would choke. Except . . . why did she have to stay up all night talking to *my* guy?

One, two, three, breathe. Four, five . . .

"But wait, it gets better," Mac said.

"What do you mean?" I was going to have to take a yoga class or something. I couldn't stand this emotional roller-coaster sensation. I dropped down onto a kitchen chair and propped both elbows on the table. "What happened?"

"Terence showed up at the hotel last night," he said. "He found us talking in the bar and made quite a scene."

"Are you all right?"

He hesitated.

I felt my heart plummet down to my stomach. "Mac?"

"I'm okay," he said, then admitted, "I have a few bruises. Nothing serious."

"Oh my God, he hit you?"

"Well, he was aiming for Siobhán. I just happened to block his fist."

"He was going to hit his wife?" I might've shouted it. "Oh my God, that's horrible! Seriously, are you all right? Is Siobhán all right?"

"Siobhán is fine, love. But it seems Terence has a problem with alcohol and anger. It wasn't the first time he tried to attack his wife."

"That poor woman," I said.

"Yeah. But she'll be all right. She's strong and smart. And she's got a good team backing her up now. She's going to stay in New York for a while. And apparently Terence starts back to work on his show next week."

"She's not going to press charges?"

"Not right now. It's enough that they'll be separated by an ocean. He'll be in Ireland and she'll stay here, at least for a month or two. Eleanor has that summer house on Nantucket, so she might stay there."

"That sounds perfect," I said. "And hopefully he'll get some help."

"I'm pretty sure the court will order him to get help."

"I hope so."

"I'm just sorry I didn't connect with you last night," Mac said. "I knew you'd be worried."

"I was." I swept my hair away from my face and straightened up. "So, tell me what happened after he hit you."

My stomach clenched. It hurt just to say those words.

"Believe it or not, the bartender took care of me. He's got a whole supply of those instant cold packs and bandages and homeopathic gels and ointments behind the bar."

"So, you were hurt!" I cried. "You're the one who should press charges."

"No, no. I'm okay, I swear," he said. "Anyway, the bartender should be given a medal. Apparently, it's not the first time a fight has broken out in there. And by the way, this hotel is one of the most refined, elegant places to stay in the city. So, go figure."

"Wow" was about all I could manage to say.

"So, then the police were called. Terence was arrested. Siobhán cried all night. I haven't been to bed yet."

I was exhausted just listening to him. I took a few more breaths in and out. "So he was arrested, after all. Good."

"Yeah, it's good. Siobhán realized that he needs to get his comeuppance."

I breathed out a sigh. What a night he'd had. "Are you going to try and get some sleep?"

"No." And now he sounded really tired. "I have a lunch meeting in two hours with more bigwigs who'll pin down more details. After that, I'm getting on a plane and coming home."

"Oh, thank goodness."

"So, what's happening there?" he asked, clearly ready to change the subject. "Tell me what you've been doing."

Where to start? I thought. Finally I said, "It would take me too long to explain. Just come home and I'll tell you everything."

"That doesn't sound good."

No, it wasn't good, but I wasn't about to get into it right now. "It's mostly just weird stuff," I said.

He laughed. "Okay, I can handle weird. In fact, I thrive on weird."

"Then you're going to love this."

"I love you, Red," he said softly.

"I love you, too, Mac. And I miss you."

He chuckled. "I've barely been gone twenty-four hours."

"Feels longer than that."

"For me, too. Look, I know you're probably heading out to work, so I'll call you after the meeting when I'm on my way to the airport."

"I can't wait."

It was too bad the church was only a few blocks from my house, because I daydreamed about Mac as I drove. I needed more time to think about him and all the horrible—and wonderful—things that had happened to him in New York.

I didn't want to think too much about Siobhán. She was so beautiful and very sweet and charming and funny, and she and Mac were really good friends. Now that the movie deal was about to happen, they would probably be seeing each other regularly. I would have to learn to deal with it.

I parked my truck a half block down from the church and got out to open the tailgate. I jumped up into the truck bed, picked up my heavy toolbox, and set it down on the tailgate. Then I jumped down to the ground, pulled the toolbox out, and slammed the tailgate shut.

I walked along the north side of the church, checking on the trench that we'd dug up last week. Niall and his men had done a brilliant job. Before they'd excavated the area to find the broken pipe, Niall, always thinking of the overall aesthetic, had instructed his guys to carefully remove squares of sod prior to the digging.

When the job was done and all the dirt had been replaced, they had very neatly arranged the squares back in place and watered them well. In a few weeks, the grass would be thick and healthy, and we would barely be able to tell that any work had been done at all.

I walked into the church and saw Niall standing in the narthex sipping from a thermos that I knew held a few cups of strong black tea.

"Good mornin' to ye, Shannon," he said.

"Hey, Niall." I joined him. "I wanted to tell you what a great job you did fixing the broken pipe out on the north side of the church. It looks beautiful. I can barely tell that you dug it all up."

"I appreciate that," he said. "I must credit my crew. Those two fellows make me look good."

He always looked good, I thought. Especially when he walked around town wearing his kilt. But never mind that.

"Please pass along my thanks to them," I said.

"Will do." He took another sip of tea. "Are we ready to tackle the basement?"

"I'm ready."

The door swung open and Wade walked in. "Good morning."

"Morning," I said. "You're just in time. Do you need to take care of anything before we get to work?"

He checked his watch. "Nope. I'm ready to go."

"Good." We walked into the nave, and I said good morning to all of my guys as we strolled down the aisle. We headed to the hallway, and as we hit the curve behind the central platform, Lavinia walked up the stairs from the basement.

"Lavinia," I said, trying not to sound too judgmental. She still hadn't managed to send over any help with packing and cleaning up the sacristy. "How are you? Can I help you with anything?"

"You're a sweet girl, Shannon." She frowned at the two men, then said, "I was hoping to see Madeline, but I couldn't find her. I guess she'll be in later."

She was looking for Madeline down in the basement? *Hmm.* "She should be here in a little while. I can ask her to call you."

"Never mind, dear. I'll give her a call. Or maybe I'll come back." She fisted both hands on her hips and gave me a look that almost felt like a confrontation. But then, some people just liked to stand with their hands on their hips. I had heard that it gave a person the illusion of power by taking up more space.

I didn't think Lavinia had that issue, but then again, she was a powerful woman in her own world. She was also one of the most positive people I had ever met, so I would be nice and cut her some slack. "Is there something else I can help you with?"

She leaned in closer. "Yes. Do you know why there's crime scene tape across the sacristy door?"

"Yes." I lowered my voice. "The police found something that may be linked to Sarah Spindler's death."

Her eyes widened. "They did? Oh my glory, do you know what they found?"

I did, but I wasn't about to tell her or anyone else what it was. Eric would kill me.

Wade looked at Lavinia, then pointed toward the basement stairs. "Sorry to interrupt. We'll see you down there, Shannon."

"Okay." I watched the two men disappear down the steps, then turned and smiled at Lavinia. "I'm afraid I don't know what the police found, but I can let you know when it's safe to get back into the sacristy. Did you leave something in there?"

"Well, yes," she said. "All of our precious church items and Reverend Roy's brocade vestments are there. I would love to collect everything as soon as possible."

I had lost track of how many times I'd already told her this, but I tried to be patient. Maybe she had retention issues because of the way her father had treated her. Who knew?

"Yes," I said, "I imagine you would. And I would love some help, so anytime you can send some people over, I've got boxes ready to be packed, and we can finish up the job in no time."

"Well then, I'll make it happen," she said cheerily. "I'll be sure to send Colleen over as soon as the sacristy is open again."

Colleen? According to Madeline, Colleen was the busiest person there. But I would take anyone Lavinia wanted to send me. "That'll be a big help. According to the police chief, we should be able to get back in there by tomorrow morning at the latest."

"That's good to know. Thank you, Shannon." She glanced over my shoulder. "I think I'll just cruise around and see how you're progressing."

"Cruise all you want," I said. "And Madeline may show up anytime now."

She looked puzzled, then smiled. "Oh, yes. Good. I'll be looking out for her. And if you happen to see Colleen, please ask her to call the office."

"Sure will." But now I was really confused. Or maybe it wasn't me. Maybe it was Lavinia.

I watched her head for the nave, and I went in the opposite direction toward the basement stairs. I found it interesting that Lavinia was momentarily clueless when I mentioned Madeline. Did she forget that she'd used the artistic director as her excuse for being here? And then she asked about Colleen. She couldn't seem to keep track of her people.

Maybe I was being too hard on her. Her mind had to be so full of details that she might've forgotten why she was here.

But I didn't really believe that.

As I reached the stairs, I heard someone running toward me, and it freaked me out for a nanosecond. Whitney again? I stared at my surroundings and wondered if there was somewhere I could hide.

"Hey! I want to help!"

I whipped around and grinned with delight at my sister. "You're hired."

Chloe grabbed me in a hug, and I held on a little longer than normal.

"What's wrong?" she said immediately.

"Not here," I murmured, then said more loudly, "We're working in the basement today. Got some water damage to repair."

"Exciting," she said.

"Oh yeah. Never a dull moment around here." I turned and looked at her. "You're still going to join us for lunch today, aren't you?"

"Of course. That's actually why I decided to come work with you today."

"I'm glad. We can walk together."

"And we'll talk," she said, determination in her tone.

By the time we got to the basement, Niall and Wade had identified the four most substantive cracks in the walls, along with several smaller veins that we would deal with as well.

Foundation cracks were something we had all dealt with, especially with old houses. And it was normal when you lived near the ocean, like we did. Water damage was a fact of life.

"Oh no, I didn't bring my tools with me," Chloe said dramatically.

I laughed. "You can use our tools. But that was a nice try."

She flashed a saucy grin. "Thank you."

The first thing we did was sweep away as much of the dirt and dust along the cracks as we could. For this, we each used a stiff brush. Niall had several and handed one to Chloe.

"This one has a smaller handle, just your size," he said.

This time her smile was full of gratitude. "Thank you, Niall."

I loaned her a pair of work gloves, and we all got down to business. We needed a clean surface around each crack in order to allow the epoxy to bond with the concrete wall.

Along each crack, we inserted small, round access ports that would be used to inject waterproof epoxy deep into the cracks. We would also be applying a clear epoxy to the surface of the crack itself, then smoothing it out so that nobody would be able to tell that it had ever been damaged in the first place.

Chloe was helpful, but I knew that her real plan was

to take some videos and photos for her television show. And she got some good ones. I was okay with that because, frankly, Niall could've done the entire job by himself with one hand tied behind his back. The man was amazing.

As Niall prepared a batch of the epoxy resin, we each picked one of the cracks to work on. Then, using a caulking gun, we began injecting the prepared resin into the cracks through the ports we had inserted. We started with the port closest to the bottom of the wall and continued to inject until we saw the substance starting to come out of the next port up. That signaled that the interior of the crack had filled up to that level. Then we capped the bottom port and moved to the next one up. We continued this process all the way up the wall.

It was a process we had all gone through countless times, but I had to admit, there was a kind of simple joy and satisfaction in knowing that the bonding agent was filling up all those cracks and slowly hardening, allowing the venerable old building to stand strong for another hundred years or more.

We finished the basement job right before noon, and Chloe and I broke for lunch. We left the church and walked through the town square to pick up Lizzie on the way.

Lizzie's outfit was monochrome, as usual. She was short, barely five foot one, and had always believed that if her entire outfit was one color—today it was red—it made her look taller.

"Have you talked to any of the girls?" I asked her. "Do we have any other suspects?"

"I talked to Emily yesterday," Lizzie said. "She thinks Lavinia is stretched to the breaking point, and she doesn't know why."

"I agree with her," I said. "But that doesn't mean she's guilty of anything."

"Maybe she's working extra hard to get the new church in shape," Chloe said.

"Maybe," I said. "And she might simply be stressed-out that they moved."

"Why would that stress her out?" Lizzie asked. "I should think she would love to be in nice, new, clean surroundings."

I thought about it. "But it must be hard getting used to a new place when she's lived her entire life in the old place."

"Her entire life?" Lizzie said.

"She's married to the current head of the Lighthouse Church, and she was the daughter of the previous head. So that pretty much covers her entire life."

"Why didn't I know that?"

"Because we weren't around when her father was in charge."

"I guess not," she said. "So how do you know?"

"I hear things," I said with a shrug.

We arrived at Emily's tea shop, and Ginny escorted us into the back room, where Jane and Marigold already sat at the round table sipping their tea.

We all greeted one another, and Lizzie and Chloe sat down.

I turned to Ginny. "Isn't Emily here?"

"She said I should apologize for her, but she had to run to the post office. She'll be back any second."

The post office was at the end of the town square, only a block away.

"Okay," I said. "We'll just get jacked up on tea while we wait for her."

Ginny laughed. "We made it pretty strong today."

"That's the way we love it," Lizzie said.

"Thanks, Ginny." I sat down and poured myself a cup of tea.

"How are you, Shannon?" Marigold asked. I could see the concern in her eyes.

"I'm fine. I have some news to share, so I'll wait for Emily before getting into it."

Jane clapped her hands. "Goody."

Lizzie talked about her ongoing search for the perfect college for Marisa and how she might not survive. Then Jane revealed that her new restaurant at the Gables had received another fantastic review, this time from a *New York Times* food critic.

"That is huge," I said. "Congratulations."

"Yes, congrats, Jane," Chloe said. "We should be toasting you with champagne, but Shannon's working with power tools today, and that could get dangerous."

"Let's get together for dinner next week," Marigold suggested. "Then we can toast you in style."

Emily walked in. "I'm sorry I'm late. You all have tea. Have you ordered?"

"We waited for you," I said. "Not that our order will be a big surprise. We always get the same things."

"Coronation chicken sandwiches, salad, and chips," Lizzie said.

"And scones and jam for dessert," Chloe added.

"I had your bread pudding last week," I said. "It was

so good, I wanted to curl up and take a nap. So I'll stick with scones this time."

Emily laughed. "Good thing, because I already put in the order."

"We're so predictable," Jane said, shaking her head.

"I prefer to think we're dependable," Marigold said with a resolute nod.

"That's a much better way to put it," Jane agreed.

I turned to Emily. "Before we go any further, Lizzie said that you've seen Lavinia?"

"I told her what you told me," Lizzie confessed.

"That's fine," Emily said.

"So, do share," Jane said. "What's Lavinia up to?"

Emily looked concerned. "Well, the thing is, she's been in three times this week to pick up scones and pastries."

"That doesn't sound so bad."

"But she hasn't been here in almost a year, at least. It's always Colleen."

"Maybe she just wanted to shake things up a little," Lizzie said. "Get out of the church. Take a walk, breathe the fresh air."

"Nothing wrong with that," I said.

"So, was she acting strange?" Marigold asked.

Emily grimaced but said, "Yes, just a bit strange, or maybe *tweaked* is a better description for her behavior. She didn't seem to be all there."

"*Hyper*, maybe?" Jane suggested.

"Crazy?" Lizzie said.

Emily winced at the term but said, "A little bit."

"So, where is Colleen?" Chloe asked. "What could be keeping her from picking up the goodies?"

"I have no idea," Emily said. "I assumed they had her working on some big project for the new church."

"Maybe so," I said. "But I just ran into Lavinia at the church, and she asked if I had seen Colleen."

"I don't understand," Lizzie said.

I shrugged. "Neither do I."

Jane narrowed her eyes. "Weird."

"I know, right?" I said.

"She might just be busy, like you said." Chloe raised her eyebrows and took a sip of tea.

"Maybe," I said, "but Lavinia would know that."

Chloe nodded. "Good point."

I gazed around the table. "So, Colleen has disappeared and Lavinia is tweaked. Any other oddities occurring that you've heard about?"

Chloe grinned. "You have a way with words."

At that moment, Ginny wheeled in a cart that held our lunches. We settled into eating and enjoying and chitchatting about other topics.

After a few minutes, Marigold looked around the table. "So, I just realized that except for Lizzie, who's the old married lady, every one of us is either engaged to be married or in a serious relationship. Has anyone set a wedding date yet?"

"Good question," Jane said, grinning. "And I'm happy to give liberal discounts to anyone who wants to use the Gables to celebrate their wedding or as their honeymoon destination."

"Nice," Chloe said.

"Chloe, what about you?" Lizzie asked. "Have you and Eric set a date yet?"

Chloe's eyes widened and she gave a subtle shake of her head.

Instantly, I was worried. "What's wrong? Is everything okay with you and Eric? You're not fighting, are you?"

"No. Everything's super. We're just sort of . . . waiting."

"For what?" I asked. "You're both stupid in love. Let's have a wedding." Then I looked at the rest of my friends. "I guess I could say the same for all of you. Let's have a wedding."

Nobody said anything. I looked back at Chloe, who wouldn't meet my gaze. "What is it? What am I missing?"

She gave Jane a sideways glance. And now the others wouldn't make eye contact. It was like they were all in on the same joke, and I didn't know the punch line.

I stared at each of their faces, then studied Chloe's expression. And that's when it hit me. "Oh my God, Chloe. Are you waiting for Mac to propose to me?"

She looked at the others and then turned back to me. After taking a deep breath and letting it go, she said, "I just don't want to be a cliché."

"What the hell does that mean?" I asked.

She shrugged. "You know, the beautiful younger sister who gets married before her older spinster sister. It's such a tacky stereotype."

"Hold on a minute," I said, putting my hand up in the universal gesture for *Stop*. "Did you just say the words 'older spinster sister'?"

She took a deep breath. "Maybe."

While my dearest friends laughed uproariously, I bared my teeth at Chloe. "I'm really going to smack you."

"You'll have to catch me first," she goaded. "I'm younger and faster than you."

"And I'm stronger than you. It might take me a while to catch you because I'm old. But when I do, I'm going to hurt you."

I took a big gulp of strong tea, then said, "And by the way, that tacky stereotype of yours has been used for centuries. *Sense and Sensibility*, anyone?"

The other girls were in hysterics by now, and I scowled at each of them. "I just don't know you people anymore."

By the time we were walking back to the church, we were buddies again. Still, I had to admit it was weird to realize that besides Lizzie, every one of my friends was engaged to be married—except me. And even though we'd joked about it, I couldn't help but wonder if Chloe really was waiting for me to get married first.

If she was, then that was just dumb. And my sister wasn't dumb. Most of the time, anyway.

As Chloe and I walked into the church, Eric came toward us, his long stride making the distance seem shorter than it really was. "Shannon, I was looking for you. You've got your room back."

"Really? That was fast."

"That was all the time Leo needed."

"Great. Thank you."

He turned to Chloe. "Hey, babe."

"Hi, you." She reached up and kissed him because she knew it made him blush.

"I'm going back to work," I said, and on a whim, leaned over and gave Chloe a kiss on her cheek. "See ya."

"Hasta la vista, Sista," she said.

When I was halfway down the aisle, Eric said, "You might have company in there."

"Okay," I said, and kept walking.

If Chloe wanted to help, that was fine with me.

I walked into the sacristy and was shocked to see Lavinia in there going through the drawers. She let out a little shriek when she saw me.

"Sorry if I scared you," I said. "How's it going?"

"Great. I was just going through things, seeing what we're up against."

I noticed that the cupboard in which I'd found the key to the hidden panel wasn't closed all the way. I wondered if she realized that I was the culprit who had taken it.

Of course she did, I thought. I'd been the only one working in here for the past few days. But she didn't look angry or suspicious. And it wouldn't matter anyway, because the key was now safely in the hands of the chief of police.

"Well then," I said, "everything in those boxes should go to the new church, and we have a whole stack of boxes left for you if you want them."

She grabbed my arm affectionately. "Thank you so much for getting all those boxes. They're a godsend."

"I was glad to do it," I said, smiling. "So, I'll leave you to it. Unless you'd like help or you have any questions for me."

"Not right now, but if I think of anything, I'll call or text you."

"Sure." I gave her my phone number and she programmed it into her phone. Then I left the sacristy and went out to check on my crew. And wondered the whole time if Lavinia was simply packing things up or trying to find something specific. Like that key. I could always walk in there and find out.

But I let it go for now, because I recalled that Lavinia wasn't the only one who had been rifling through those drawers. We had caught Madeline doing the same thing the day before.

What was up with that? Was she looking for the key, too?

I was determined to keep busy, so I spent the rest of the afternoon unscrewing the kneelers from the pews in rows one through twelve. My power drill got a nice little workout, which always made me happy. Of course, the only way I could get the job done was to kneel down on the hard stone floor without the benefit of those comfy velvet-lined kneelers. But as Mac sometimes said, irony is not dead.

Speaking of Mac, he had called to let me know he was on his way to the airport, where he expected to board the private jet and be home by six o'clock that evening.

I was ridiculously happy to hear his voice and couldn't wait to see his handsome face, even if half of it was black and blue and swollen from his run-in with a very angry man who apparently enjoyed using his fists to settle his problems.

I shivered at the thought and couldn't help but draw a comparison to Lavinia's father. How much psychological damage had he inflicted on his daughter? Was it enough to turn her into a killer?

And what about Madeline? What had she been looking for in the sacristy the other day? Whatever it was, she had lied to me and Eric when we walked in on her.

And then there was Flora the flower lady, who freaked out the other day over that pile of old composition notebooks. I couldn't imagine her killing someone, but I had been wrong before.

And where was Colleen?

Good grief. That made four church ladies behaving oddly. Had one of them been driven to kill? Why? What secrets were they really hiding? I only hoped we would find out and the killer would be brought to justice before someone else had to die.

Chapter Fifteen

I wanted to get home early in order to clean up before Mac arrived. But as I packed up my toolbox, Buck called to me from high up on the boom lift. "Yo, Shannon. Have you seen Madeline today?"

Someone else wants to see Madeline?

"No," I said, "but she'll probably be here tomorrow." And if she wasn't, I planned to call her. We needed her guidance on some of these repairs and additions.

"Good," he said. "Hey, check out this new pin spot. Pretend you're the sculpture."

"Okay." I struck a silly pose and waited for it. It took Buck a few seconds, and then a light flashed on, and I turned to look at the wall next to me. It was subtle; the play of light and dark was used to great effect.

"There's not a lot of spill," I said. "You've got it laser focused."

"I know!" He was excited. "You're softly lit, but it's still dark enough around you to create this cool kind of dramatic tension."

"I like it," I said, grinning up at him. "Great work."

"Thanks. I'll show it to Madeline tomorrow."

"I'll be here. See you then."

I stood on the front steps and watched the limousine pull up in front of the house. The driver got out and opened the back door, and Mac stepped out, carrying his overnight bag over his shoulder.

I waited at the top of the steps while he thanked the driver and then climbed up to the porch.

He tried to smile, but I could tell he was in pain. The area all around his eye looked tender and swollen. I was pretty sure it was turning purple. "Hey, Red. You look beautiful."

"And you must be exhausted." I gave him a quick kiss and we walked together into the house.

"I'm pretty wiped out," Mac admitted. Just inside the front door, he dropped his carry-on. "But man, am I glad to see you."

"I'm glad to see you, too."

He enveloped me in his arms and just held on. After a while he said, "Do me a favor?"

My arms were wrapped around him. "Anything."

"Don't ever make me go there by myself again."

I had to smile. "I'm not sure I made you do it this time, but I'm happy to prohibit you from ever doing it again."

"That would be for the best." He rested his chin on the top of my head. "I've got to sit down."

"Would you like a pain reliever?"

"Oh yeah. Thanks."

"You sit down and I'll bring it to you."

He collapsed on the sofa, and I went into the kitchen cabinet to get two ibuprofen and a glass of water.

His eyes were closed when I returned, and I nudged him in case he'd fallen asleep. "Here you go, Mac."

He took the pills and the water and popped them into his mouth. After swallowing, he gazed at me. "I look pretty bad."

"You look like a hero to me."

"Sit with me?" He patted the cushion and tried to smile, but he was obviously hurting. I sat down and he laid his head on my shoulder. "Tell me what's been going on around here."

I figured he would fall asleep any minute, but still, I slowly began to relate everything that had happened since he left yesterday morning. Including the suspicious behavior of Lavinia and Madeline.

"What about Flora?" he asked. "There are way too many coincidences surrounding her."

"Yeah, she's on my list. And Madeline, too. I found her rifling through the cabinet drawers, then a couple of people were looking for her, but nobody could find her."

"And what about the church secretary?"

"Colleen. I saw her a few days ago, and since then, several people from the church have been looking for her. So, where is she?"

"She's missing, too?"

"I doubt she's really missing. She just hasn't come around lately."

"Has Reverend Roy made an appearance?"

"Yes," I said. "He was nice. Sort of rambled around the sacristy and talked and reminisced about the room. I think he misses it."

"Sounds like you've interacted with a whole boatload of suspects. I'm proud of you."

I smiled. "You'll be even prouder when I tell you about the hidden tunnel."

He lifted his head a few inches. "Hidden tunnel?"

"That's right. I found a little key inside one of the cubbyholes of the big cabinet in the sacristy. I kept looking around the room for a keyhole, and I finally noticed that one of the wooden onlays was loose, so I checked it out, hoping I could fix it with some wood glue. But it wasn't loose. It swung back and forth, and behind it was a—"

"A keyhole?" Now he sat all the way up. "Wait. You found a freaking keyhole?"

I laughed. "Yes. So I slipped the key in the hole and turned it, and the big wooden panel swung open."

"Whoa," he said. "Hold on, now. You . . . found . . . a . . . hidden . . . tunnel?"

I started laughing. "I did. And then I crawled inside to check it out."

"Oh my God." He sat forward and turned to look at me. "You are my hero."

"But wait." I held up my hand. "As soon as I slid into the space, the panel slammed shut."

His eyes widened. "You were stuck in a tunnel? Was it dark?"

"It was pitch-black." I smiled. "But I had my phone."

"That's my girl." He leaned back against me. "Wow."

I told him about finding the bloody vestment and the weird scepter-looking thing, also coated in blood, on the landing just inside the hidden panel.

"Hold on," he said. "Can you describe that scepter thing? What did it look like?"

"It honestly looked like a smaller version of a royal scepter, only one end was big and round like a ball. It looked gold-plated. The other end was smooth wood. I'm pretty sure that end was the handle, and someone struck Sarah with the heavy rounded gold end."

"Did the gold ball have little holes in it?"

My eyes widened. "Yes. Little holes and ridges. How did you know?"

"I know what it is."

"Seriously?" I stared at him. "What do you think it is?"

He sat forward on the couch and turned toward me. "Okay, during certain religious ceremonies, the priest will sprinkle holy water on the congregation, and they do it using the kind of instrument you described. It's called an aspergillum."

"Asper–what?"

He grinned. "Aspergillum. And it's used with an aspersorium, which is a big bowl, also often gold-plated, that holds the holy water. So the priest dips the aspergillum into the bowl and fills the gold ball with water, then flings the water over the crowd, then dips it back in the bowl to refill it."

"How in the world do you know all this?"

"I used it in a book. There was an evil sect of bishops plotting to take over the Vatican."

"Of course there was." I rolled my eyes.

"It happens," he said with a happy shrug. "Anyway, murder and mayhem ensued."

"They always do," I admitted. "So what's it called again?"

"An aspergillum."

"Aspergillum," I repeated.

"Exactly." He stretched, then relaxed back against

the cushion. "So, back to the tunnel. You were on the landing where you found the bloody murder weapon."

"Right." I described the stairs leading down into the tunnel and where it led to and how we ran into Buck in the tunnel and how Flora was the one who told him about it.

"What the—?" He shook his head in disbelief. "Holy moly, Shannon. That's incredible. I should've been here."

I smiled and nodded. "You absolutely should've been here."

He blew out a breath and pulled himself up from the sofa. "I want to see that tunnel."

"Now?"

"Yes, right now."

"But you're exhausted. Wouldn't you rather get some sleep first and then check it out tomorrow?"

He grinned. "Do you even know me?"

I had to laugh. "Okay, let's go."

He reached down to help me up from the sofa. His hand was big and strong and warm, and I loved the feeling of his skin against mine. "Let's go."

We threw on jackets and found two small flashlights that we each slipped into our pockets. We held hands as we walked to the town square and up to the church. I had the keys to the main door, so we stepped inside and followed the hallway around to the sacristy.

"It's a little creepy in here at night," I said, glancing at the shadows made by the ambient outside light being filtered through the stained glass windows. Muted shades of blue, red, yellow, and green were cast across the floor all the way to the opposite wall.

"Do you want to turn on a light?" he asked.

"I'd rather not call attention to our presence." Even though I had every right to be here, I didn't want some concerned citizen alerting the police. I knew exactly what Eric's expression of disapproval would look like, and I didn't want to see it tonight.

We made it to the sacristy, and once we were inside, I turned to Mac. "I gave my key to Eric, but I don't think I'll need it."

I knelt down and stared at the razor-thin space between the doorjamb and the panel itself.

Mac bent down to take a closer look. "This is the panel you're talking about?"

"Yeah." I pulled out my pocketknife and slid the blade into the narrow space. After a few seconds of maneuvering, the knife caught on the edge of the thin piece of linen I'd placed in there yesterday.

"What is that?" Mac asked.

"I slipped this in here yesterday to keep the panel from slamming shut. It worked."

He knelt beside me. "That was pretty smart."

"Yeah, but now I've got to slide the linen out while I try to get a hold of the panel at the same time. Otherwise, it'll slam shut again."

"Can I help?" he asked.

I smiled at him. "You can aim the flashlight for me."

"Okay. Anything else?"

"I'm pretty sure I've got this," I murmured, carefully easing the cloth out bit by bit.

"I'm thinking good thoughts."

I laughed lightly. "Very helpful." With my knife, I managed to press against the door with enough pressure to force it to open just wide enough for me to slip a couple of fingers inside. "Got it."

"Whew." He sat back on his heels. "You're good."

I pushed the panel open all the way. "And there it is."

"Freaking awesome," he whispered, and kissed my cheek.

"Ready to check it out?"

"Yeah. But we need to make sure the door stays open." He pulled off his jacket and wedged it under the panel to keep it from shutting.

"Wait," I said. "It's dark and damp down there. You might get cold."

"I'll be fine."

"No, really." I knew he was in pain, so I didn't want him catching a cold or worse. I walked over to the cabinet and opened a drawer at random, and pulled out one of the older vestments. "Use this."

"You sure? It looks pretty valuable."

"Then they should've packed it up and taken it with them." I knew I sounded cranky, but what the heck? It had been a long week. Before I returned to Mac, I locked the sacristy door. "Just in case."

"Probably a good idea," he said as he picked up his jacket and replaced it with the chasuble, which I had folded neatly. Slipping the jacket on, he said, "Okay. We're good to go."

"It's a little awkward getting in there," I said. "You've got to crawl through the doorway."

I demonstrated and he followed right behind me, arriving next to me on the landing.

"Is this where you found the bloody evidence?"

"Yeah, right here," I said, pointing to the spot. Then

I aimed my flashlight at the ceiling. "We can stand up, but the ceiling is really low, so please be careful not to hit your head."

"Yeah, I don't need to do that." He followed my advice and we walked down the steps. At the bottom, he slowly shined the flashlight in every direction. "This is fantastic. There's actually a hidden tunnel under the church. You grew up here and you never knew about it?"

"Never. Isn't that crazy?"

"Yeah." He swept the light toward the tunnel wall. "It looks like stone, but it's rounded. Did they use a pickax?"

"That's what I thought."

He stepped right up to the wall and touched it. "It's got to have been here for a hundred years or more."

"They might've done it when the church was first built, which was over 160 years ago."

He ran his hand across the surface. "How cool is that?" He moved a few more feet and suddenly tripped. "What the hell?"

I reached out and grabbed his arm. "Are you all right?"

"Yeah. Almost fell over something." He pointed his flashlight toward the bottom of the wall, then quickly backed away. "Holy crap."

"Oh my God!" I gasped, then had to press my hands over my mouth to keep from screaming.

The darkness and the cold and the horror shut us up for a full minute. Maybe we were in shock, because it took a while before Mac demanded, "Who is that?"

I had to brace myself, then finally managed to stare down at the body.

"Do you recognize her?" he asked.

I held up my hand, then looked away and tried to breathe.

He took hold of my arms and gave me a gentle little shake. "Shannon. Who is it?"

I stared at him and gulped in some more air. My throat was dry, but I managed to whisper, "It's Colleen Sayles."

"The church secretary."

"Yes."

We both looked down at her. Wrapped tightly around her neck and fashioned into a big bright bow was the spring green brocade stole that matched the chasuble that had been used to drag Sarah Spindler to her death. Reverend Roy would've worn this stole on those days that the church deemed Ordinary Time.

But he would never wear it again, and nothing about this scene was ordinary.

An hour later, it was bright as daylight in the tunnel, thanks to a half dozen light trees that had been placed in various spots, with several positioned close to the body.

Leo Springer was kneeling down next to Colleen and quietly running his tests, checking for signs of whatever he needed to know. Time of death. Cause of death. Temperature of the body. Had she been turned over? Dragged to this spot? Was there a murder weapon?

Eric knelt down next to Leo and whispered something. All I overheard from Leo were the words "petechial hemorrhage."

As someone who'd received her criminal justice degree from *CSI: Miami*, I'd heard the term before and was pretty sure that Colleen had been strangled.

One look at Mac, and I could tell he knew what the words meant, too.

Leo would have to determine all of those things and more, all while staring at the body in this foreboding tunnel. The crime scene specialist had the look of a muscular monk. His thinning hair was cut in the style of Julius Caesar as depicted on a Roman coin. I had a feeling he got those big muscles from carrying around his two heavy metallic cases all the time. They each had to weigh twenty pounds, at the very least. Despite the muscles and the haircut, he was the kindest, funniest man I knew.

Leo's assistant, Officer Lilah O'Neil, was busy taking pictures from every possible angle. She was also making a bunch of phone calls, although I couldn't hear what she was saying from where we stood. I knew that one of those phone calls would be to the county medical examiner, letting them know that a body would be delivered sometime late in the night.

Mac and I had been shuttled away from the body, and now we stood near the stairway at the edge of the lights while Eric questioned us. We were the ones who had found her, and even though we had no idea how Colleen had wound up here, Eric needed to know what we knew.

"When did you last see her?" he asked.

"She came into the sacristy on Friday," I said. "We had a brief conversation about the items remaining in the cabinet. Before that, I saw her at the prayer vigil Thursday night."

"What was her frame of mind that last time?" he asked.

"She was fine," I said, but shook my head, knowing

it wasn't really accurate. "I mean, she was in a hurry and very businesslike, not overly friendly. She answered a question about something I'd found in the sacristy cabinet. And then she rushed off. That was the last time I saw her."

He wrote it down in his notepad, then asked, "What was the question you asked her?"

I was afraid he would ask me that. "I was going through some of her old calendars, and I asked her about some initials I found."

He just gazed at me patiently.

"The initials are MSB. She guessed that it probably referred to Mr. Brindley, the handyman."

"Brindley, the handyman." He puzzled over that one for a few seconds, then asked, "So, what were those initials in reference to?"

"There was a short description of a church event, a festival, I think. And at the end of the paragraph there were a few words that were underlined. Twice."

"And the words?" he asked, his pen poised over the pad.

"The words were, *No one must ever know, not even MSB*."

"Not even MSB," Eric repeated. "And Colleen thought it referred to Mr. Brindley."

"I think she was guessing."

"Was there something she knew about him?"

"No. Just his initials. His name is Mitch Brindley. I don't know his middle name. Maybe Colleen knew it. She was very efficient. I wouldn't be surprised to hear that she'd memorized the entire church directory. But anyway, that's the name she just came up with."

"What do you think?" he asked.

"You mean, do I think Mr. Brindley is the guy they're talking about in the diary?" I had wondered about this for a while, but still. "I'm not sure."

"Why not?"

I cleared my throat and hoped I would make sense. "Because if you've met him, you would think he's a pretty stolid fellow. You know, kind of impassive. Not the type of man who'd be written about in a woman's diary. Or a daily planner. Or whatever. But that day you closed down the church and he wanted to get inside, he was persistent and determined to get by me. So who knows? Does that make him the kind of man who might've been a rake back in the day?"

"A rake?" Mac started laughing. "Talk about dramatic."

I gave his arm a light smack. "You know what I mean."

"I do." He flashed his best smile.

"Anyway," I said, "even with that momentary show of determination, I don't think Mr. Brindley was the kind of man to appeal to the church ladies around here."

Eric nodded and slipped his pen and the notepad into his jacket pocket.

"Are you going to close us down again?" I asked.

"First, I'm going to have Tom escort you home."

I frowned. "Which way?"

"I'm not letting you crawl back into the sacristy, if that's what you mean. He'll take you through the basement door. And once you're inside the basement, he'll have to take both of your shoes to eliminate your footprints."

"Okay," I said, giving in to the inevitable. "But again, are you going to close us down?"

"What do you think?"

"I think you should close off the sacristy and the basement because those both lead into the tunnel. But we could still work in the main area of the church. You know my people would never trespass on your crime scene."

He glared at me through narrowed eyes, then finally shrugged. "Sounds reasonable."

I grinned and gave him a quick hug. "Thank you."

"All right, all right. You two should go home. And put something on that eye, Mac. It looks painful."

"Oh, it is. But you should see the other guy."

Once we got home, Mac used another one of the instant cold packs he'd brought from the New York hotel, and I gave him more ibuprofen. He slept with his arms around me all night long, as if he were afraid I would leave his side sometime in the night. He should've known better.

The next morning, he woke up with less pain, but now the skin around his eye was turning yellow and purple.

"I look worse than bad," he said staring at himself in the mirror. "But I feel a hundred percent better, thanks to you."

He kissed me and held on to me for a long while. It wasn't like him to cling to me so much, but I wasn't going to complain. I loved having his arms around me, no matter the reason.

And, yes, I briefly considered that his behavior

might've been a sign of a guilty mind, but that just wasn't Mac. He wasn't a devious guy. In fact, he was honest to a fault. Besides, he had told me all about his evening with Siobhán crying on his shoulder, along with the fight with Terence that ensued.

I trusted him completely and considered that matter closed.

Before I left for the church, he said he had a few phone calls to make, but as soon as he was finished, he would walk over and hang out with me.

"I can't stay away," he said softly.

My heart began to melt. "That's so sweet."

He began to laugh. "I love you, Red. But what I really can't stay away from is that creepy old church and that hair-raising tunnel underneath. It's given me a million new ideas for some truly gruesome scenes."

I had to laugh, too, even as he was kissing me.

He pressed his forehead to mine and closed his eyes. "I don't mean to be flippant about the murder of that woman." He opened his eyes and gazed at me. "It's a defense mechanism, you know. Because the thought of you being the one to find both of those victims? It seriously turns my blood cold."

"It's been pretty awful," I admitted. "You'd think I'd be used to it by now, but how do you ever get used to something like that? Well, unless you're a cop. And I'm not."

"No. And I hope you never have to get used to anything like that again." He thought about it for a moment. "But if I can be honest, those victims couldn't be in better hands than yours."

I stared at him. "What in the world does that mean?"

"You notice things, Red," he said. "Maybe it's because you're creative and your job is to bring order and beauty to the projects you work on. So when something is wrong or off or broken or destroyed, you take notice. You look around and see what the problem is, and you seek solutions. You pay attention to the small things. Like the way the dust on the floor was swept up. Or like the, um, what'd you call it? That onlay? On the wood paneling? The way it was hanging just slightly wrong?" He grinned now. "And you found the keyhole. Pretty clever of you."

I waved away his compliment. "That's just my job."

"And a hundred other people with that same job wouldn't have noticed. But you did." He kissed me again. "Because you pay attention. And that's how you'll find justice for those women."

I walked into the nave and was pleased to see everyone working their jobs as if nothing bad had happened the night before. Did they even know about Colleen? Had someone made the announcement?

I found Wade midway among the pews along the main aisle. He was staring up at the stained glass windows.

"What're you looking at?" I asked.

"Oh, hey, good morning, Shannon. I'm just watching how the light comes in at this time of day. Buck suggested that we track the natural light every hour so he can program the lighting accordingly."

"That's smart. I'm glad we hired him."

He stared at me. "Something's wrong. What is it?"

I took a big deep breath and exhaled slowly. Wade had known me too long and could tell when something was off. So I told him exactly what had happened last night.

"Are you kidding me?" he said, keeping his voice down so as not to alert everyone else. "This is insane. I noticed the crime scene tape, but I figured after everything that's been going on these last few weeks, that was normal operating procedure."

I had to admit he had a point. "This time it means we really did find a body in the tunnel last night."

"Come on!" He gaped at me. "In the tunnel? For real? How? I mean, who? I mean, what happened? And who's 'we'?" He took a deep breath in and let it out to slow himself down. "Tell me."

"The 'we' is Mac and me. He got home from New York City, and I told him about the tunnel, and he wanted to see it. So we came over here, and we crawled through the panel in the sacristy and walked down the stairs and into the tunnel. He wanted to get the total experience, you know? He was psyched."

"Oh, I can believe that," Wade said. "That scene would be right up his alley."

"Absolutely. So we were looking around, and he was examining the surface of the tunnel wall, and he practically tripped over the body."

"Whose body?" Wade demanded.

"Didn't I say? Sorry. It was Colleen Sayles, the church secretary."

"What?" He paced away from me, alternately shaking his head and staring up at the ceiling. Then he turned and walked back, still shaking his head. "I can't believe it, Shannon. She was so nice. I mean, all those church ladies are nice. Why would someone kill her?"

"I haven't a clue. I'm only guessing, but I suppose she must've seen something. Or overheard something.

Or walked in on someone doing something. The same thing we wondered about Sarah Spindler. And in both cases, it doesn't make sense."

"Oh God. I'm really sorry. And I'm sorry that you had to be the one to find her. That's got to suck."

"It does," I admitted. "It truly sucks."

He was still frowning as he scanned the room to check out our crew. Everyone was doing their thing, working hard. "Nobody has said anything, so I don't think word has gotten around yet."

"Good," I said. "They'll all hear about it soon enough, but maybe we can have an hour of normalcy before we all have to freak out again."

He watched me for a moment without saying anything.

"What is it?" I asked.

He scowled. "You've really had a lot to deal with on this job, and it's barely even started."

"I'm okay." I shrugged. What else could I say?

"Yeah, sure you are," he said, rolling his eyes. He seemed to consider his words, then said, "Look, I don't even want to ask, and I know it's morbid, but how did she die?"

I leaned in close and murmured, "She was strangled." The sudden image of Colleen with that garish bow around her neck made my stomach clench. I wasn't ready to share that fact with anyone else.

"Oh, jeez. I'm sorry I asked." He closed his eyes and shook his head. He put his arms around me and gave me a hug. "I'm so sorry."

"Thanks." I was ready to cry now.

"Hey, Shannon," Buck called. He entered the nave

from the north transept and jogged over to me, looking excited. "I wanted to show you one of our new lights. It's so cool."

"Great," I said, relieved that he had interrupted a sudden onslaught of tears. "Let's see it."

He held the light in his hand and aimed it at the nearest wall and began to click buttons. We watched it narrow down to a pin spot, then slowly widen. "And you can set it to strobe, in case there's an exhibit that calls for something wild. Watch."

The light began to flash and pulsate, and he turned it off quickly, knowing some people had a bad reaction to strobe lights.

"I've actually seen things like that in a museum or two," I said.

"Yeah. It can be really effective in some exhibits."

"Get your stupid buckets out of here," a woman said, her voice low and insistent.

Wade, Buck, and I looked around, then stared at one another.

"Did you say something?" I asked.

"No," Buck said. "I thought you did."

Wade glanced behind him. "What was that?"

"I'm sick of cleaning up your mess," the woman whispered harshly. She kept her voice low so she wouldn't be overheard. But we could hear her.

"If anyone is guilty of leaving a mess, it's you." It was a different woman. She whispered, too, but her tone was lighter.

"You want to talk about guilt?" the first woman said.

That's when I realized the voices were coming from in front of the altar, under that beautiful dome. No wonder we could hear them! It made me think that Madeline might want to start calling it the "Whispering Dome."

I nudged the two guys, then pointed in that direction.

"Oh hell," Buck said, frowning as he observed the women near the altar. "That's my aunt."

"And that's Lavinia," I said.

"You can actually hear them," Wade said. I remembered that he had been talking with Madeline under the dome when we all heard the conversation. So this was the first time he was hearing someone else's voice project from under the dome.

Lavinia whipped something out of her shoulder bag and waved it in Flora's face. It was one of the black-and-white composition books I'd packed away last week. "Here's proof of your guilt!"

"Where did you get that?" Flora quietly demanded.

"Where do you think?" Lavinia hissed. "I've been going through these for the last month. They were all left inside the sacristy. That was careless of you."

"I thought I had all of mine. Maybe you're reading Colleen's."

"Nope. This one is yours. And by the way, who is MSB?"

My mouth fell open. *Are they talking about Mr. Brindley?*

Flora reacted similarly and tried to grab the book. "Give that back to me right now."

They can't possibly be talking about Mr. Brindley. Can they?

"There's too many people around here," Lavinia hissed. "We're taking this downstairs."

Lavinia grabbed hold of Flora's arm and dragged

her off the platform. It was really no contest. Lavinia was so much bigger and stronger than Flora, who was petite. The two disappeared behind the wall.

Buck looked at Wade and me. "I've got to help my aunt!" he shouted, and took off after the two women.

Wade ran after Buck, and I was about to follow when Mac strolled up. He knew in a flash that something was going on and took my hand. "What's wrong?"

"Come with me" was all I said, and we both ran after Wade.

When we reached the stairs to the basement, I stopped and pulled out my phone. "I've got to call Eric."

"I just saw him," Mac said. "He was on his way to the tunnel with Tommy."

"Good. He's close by." I pressed his number and he answered on the first ring.

"Get to the church basement," I said. "Lavinia and Flora are there. I think one of them is your killer."

I hung up the phone and stared at Mac, who grabbed my hand. "Let's get down there."

We jogged down the stairs. When we got to the basement, I saw Buck holding Lavinia back from attacking Flora. Struggling to get loose, Lavinia screamed at Buck. "Who the hell are you?"

"Language, Lavinia!" Flora cried. "What would Reverend Roy say?"

"Oh, shut up, you prissy little thing," Lavinia said. "And you keep his name out of your mouth!"

"Whoa," Mac said. "This is out of control."

"Who is MSB?" Lavinia demanded.

Flora scowled. "None of your damn business!"

"Language, Flora," Lavinia said sarcastically.

"You read my journals!" Flora cried.

"That's right," Lavinia admitted. "I wanted to prove that you slept with my husband!"

"You don't know what you're saying."

The other woman cut her off. "You did! I knew it! You harlot!"

Flora glanced around and realized they had an audience. "Lavinia! You're embarrassing yourself. Stop!"

"How dare you scold me? You're the one who slept with my husband!"

Flora cast an uncomfortable glance at Buck. "This is crazy."

Lavinia huffed. "He would never have slept with you if you hadn't thrown yourself at him."

"I didn't!"

"I suppose I can't blame you," Lavinia said, then smoothed her hands down her sweater in a preening move. "After all, the man is the closest thing to God on Earth."

I glanced at Mac, who looked as horrified as I was by the woman's abrupt attitude switch. First she was livid, and now she was coy. It was weird.

At that comment, Flora appeared to have lost her ability to speak. The rest of us were too shocked to say a word.

Lavinia continued her diatribe. "He never would've betrayed his vows if not for you!" She broke away from Buck and grabbed Flora's throat.

In an instant, the basement door was flung open, and Eric and Tommy stormed in.

Flora was trying to push Lavinia away, but Lavinia was stronger and still had her hands around Flora's throat.

Buck thought fast. He pulled the high-powered

strobe light out of his pocket and aimed it at Lavinia. The room was suddenly filled with intensely pulsating light, and I had to shut my eyes.

Lavinia screamed with rage and had to cover her eyes from the blinding strobe. Eric took advantage of the moment and snapped handcuffs onto her wrists.

Flora threw herself into Buck's arms, and he held her tightly. "It's okay," he murmured. "It's going to be okay."

"Oh, Mickey," she sobbed. "I'm sorry you had to hear all that. But thank you for saving my life."

"Mickey," I repeated slowly.

Buck looked at me with a sheepish smile. "I told you she's the only one who ever calls me that."

"Mickey Buckner," I murmured.

"It's Michael," he said.

"Michael Stephen Buckner," Flora whispered.

I imagine my eyes were as round as saucers. "MSB."

"Yes," Flora whispered, as tears stung her eyes. "I used to be a big romance reader, so I pretended it stood for My Secret Baby."

Eric had pulled Lavinia halfway to the stairs when she turned and screamed, "Your baby!" She broke away from Eric and ran straight at Flora. Even handcuffed, she managed to plow into Flora and knock her over.

Eric swore as he yanked Lavinia back again, but that still didn't stop the woman from spewing her hateful words. "You whore!"

I was frankly shocked and had to shake my head, remembering how I'd thought she was such a lovely woman. Clearly, I was wrong.

Tommy rushed across the room to help Eric control Lavinia.

"You shameless floozy!" she screamed at Flora. Then she looked at Buck. "And you! You bastard!"

"How dare you!" Flora cried, finally fighting back as she moved in and slapped Lavinia. "Don't you dare say one more word to him, or I won't be responsible for my actions."

Tommy quickly grabbed Flora and pulled her away from Lavinia. That didn't stop Lavinia from continuing her tirade against the flower lady.

Finally, Buck took his aunt's hand in his. "Aunt Flora, is there something you want to tell me?"

"Oh, sweetie," Flora said, and the tears began to flow. "I was such a young, impressionable girl when I met Reverend Roy. I didn't think I would ever fall in love with someone like him, but I did. I'm sorry I couldn't tell you the truth."

"He's a man of God!" Lavinia intoned. "He would never love you!"

Flora managed to ignore the woman and concentrated on Buck. "When I realized I was pregnant, I didn't know the kind of danger I was in until a very good friend warned me."

"What was the warning?" Buck asked.

"My friend told me to go somewhere far away and have the baby there and never come back. She said that you'd never be safe if she found out about you. So I went to my sister's home in Fillmore, and we decided it would be the best place for you to live. I knew my sister and her husband would be wonderful parents to you."

"They were," Buck said, then added, "They *are*."

"I know, and I'm so glad." She was wiping away tears now. "All I wanted was for you to be safe and happy, and I knew they would provide all of that and would love you as much as I did. I wanted to get you away from that woman so she could never hurt you."

Buck nodded slowly, at a loss for words. I couldn't blame him.

"But you came back here," I said.

"I did. This is the only home I've ever known, and I always loved working for the church." She looked at Buck. "And I wanted to give my sister and her husband and you a chance to be a family without me interfering."

Mac nodded. "That was thoughtful of you."

"Was your good friend also a member of the church?" Eric asked.

"Yes, of course," Flora said.

"Colleen?" I guessed.

"That's right," Flora said.

"She was the one who warned you?" I asked.

"Yes. She was much more aware of things than I was. She knew what Lavinia was like, and she also knew some of her secrets." Flora stared at Lavinia and said, "She made you pay."

Lavinia fumed. "She betrayed me!"

I glanced from Lavinia to Flora. "Are you saying Colleen blackmailed her?"

Flora smiled. "I would never call it that. But remember those numbers you asked me to explain?"

"Yes."

"Reverend Roy enjoyed having Colleen around. She was sophisticated and beautiful and smart. So whenever there was an event with donors and wealthy congregants in attendance, he insisted that Colleen be there to impress everyone with her knowledge of finances and history and, oh, everything else."

"Was Lavinia there, too?"

"Oh, of course. And that's how Colleen found out that Lavinia was cheating on her husband with a visiting bishop."

"What?" I might've shouted the word, but I wasn't alone. Everyone in the room was staring at Lavinia in shock.

Lavinia screamed. "Liar!"

"Somehow I think she's telling the truth," I said.

She bared her teeth. "No! All of you women are liars and whores!"

"Oh, shut up!" Flora said. "Hypocrite."

Lavinia was stunned into silence. I was pretty sure it wouldn't last.

"So, Colleen found a way to get back at Lavinia for betraying Reverend Roy," Mac said.

"Exactly." Flora nodded. "The payments to Colleen were worth it to Lavinia because she never wanted Reverend Roy to find out."

It was weird to see Lavinia standing there taking it all in. For the moment, she was quiet, but her expression told me that she was clearly seething with fury.

Mac kept an eye on her as well, as he asked Flora more questions. "Why would Lavinia cheat on her husband?"

"He cheated on me!" Lavinia shouted.

Ignoring her, I asked Flora, "But why did Roy stay with Lavinia?"

"The church forbids divorce," Flora explained. "He would never leave his wife, no matter how much he wanted to."

"He didn't want to," Lavinia cried. "He loves me!"

I stared at the woman and took an educated guess. "And that's why you killed Colleen?"

"She deserved it." Then she clamped her lips together, and I wondered if she would say anything more about it.

I hesitated, then asked, "But why did you kill Sarah?"

Her eyes sparked with anger and something darker. Madness? Maybe. All her sins were being exposed, and now her wrath seemed to have enveloped her. Had she ever really been completely sane? I wondered if her father's abuse had driven her over the edge long ago.

"Little busybody. She was always sneaking around here." She tossed her hair back, righteously indignant. "And she happened to overhear a conversation I was having with my husband."

"About what?" I asked.

"About the fact that I was sick of him being so nice to that strumpet!" She pointed at Flora, and Buck instinctively moved to shield his aunt.

"Reverend Roy was nice to everyone," Flora insisted.

"Especially when you strutted around like a hooker," Lavinia snarled. She shook her head in disgust. "That young woman was always looking at me, judging me. I knew she would try to go after him. She's just like you. Another hussy."

"You thought she would come after your husband," I reiterated. "So you killed her."

"You killed that innocent young woman," Flora said, her eyes wide with horror. "Oh, Lavinia."

"And you were next!" Lavinia cried.

"Oh," Flora gasped.

"Did you lure Colleen into the tunnel?" I asked, trying to get her to talk some more. "Or did you kill her upstairs and drag her down there?"

"It's *my* tunnel!" Lavinia screamed. "You stay out!"

I took a deep breath and exhaled slowly. Lavinia had completely lost it, and I didn't have the heart to keep questioning her.

"That's enough." Eric stepped forward, clearly feeling the same way. "Lavinia Patterson, you're under arrest for the murders of Sarah Spindler and Colleen Sayles."

"I'll kill you all!" She tried to jerk her arm away from Eric, but he held fast.

"You really don't want to threaten the chief of police, ma'am," Tommy said, taking hold of her other arm.

The two men flanked Lavinia and led her kicking and screaming up the stairs and out of the church.

The silence was suddenly deafening.

"Wow," Wade said. "My head is spinning."

"Mine too," Buck admitted. He walked over and took his aunt's hands in his. "Aunt Flora, are you all right?"

"I've been better," she said, her voice a little shaky. And now she looked up at Buck and said, "I'm so sorry. I never wanted you to hear the truth, not like this. I just hope, someday, you'll be able to forgive me."

Buck wrapped her in his arms. "I've known the truth for a while now."

I thought Flora might faint right then and there, but Buck held her tightly. "When my father was dying," he said, "he told my mother to finally tell me. And once we had buried him, she sat me down and revealed the truth: that you are my biological mother and that Reverend Roy was my father."

Flora was sobbing now. "I'm so sorry, dear." She had to take a few breaths to calm down. "But honestly, I'm glad they told you. I pray that someday you'll be able to forget what happened here and simply think of me as your aunt who loves you very much."

Buck grinned. "I have always thought of you as my absolute, most favorite, most beloved aunt in the world. I don't see why that should ever change."

"Oh, sweetie," she murmured, reaching up to pat his cheek. "You are such a joy to me."

His smile was brilliant. "I love you, Aunt Flora."

"I love you, too, Mickey."

He smiled. "Let's go home."

"Please wait," a man said.

We all turned and saw Reverend Roy walk down the last two stairs and step into the room.

Did he hear all that?

I gauged the timing and realized that he'd probably passed his wife upstairs as she was hauled off to jail by Eric and Tommy. Did he know his wife was homicidal? Had he overheard Flora's exchange with Buck just now?

Obviously uncomfortable, Reverend Roy cleared his throat. "The police just took Lavinia away. When I asked what was happening, she told me I would find out by going down to the basement. Can someone explain what she meant?"

"Ooh, boy," Mac whispered, slipping his arm through mine.

"Oh dear," Flora said. "I'm afraid it's a long story."

"Let me start," Reverend Roy said, and coughed nervously to clear his throat. "I'm not innocent in all of this. I knew Lavinia could be volatile, but I never thought . . . well, I never thought it would come to this."

"You mustn't blame yourself, Roy," Flora said stoutly.

He smiled at her. "Still my champion after all these years?"

Her lips thinned stubbornly. "You're a good man."

"You of all people, Flora, know my sins. I wasn't always a good husband to Lavinia. I strayed once."

"Just once?" Mac asked.

Roy glanced at him and nodded. "Yes, just once. Sometimes that's all it takes to realize that the wrath of God is real, and we are wise to fear it."

The wrath of God? I wondered. *Or the wrath of Lavinia?*

The reverend looked around the room and met each of our gazes. "I apologize to all of you for the pain and fear you've had to endure these past few days." He gave Flora a smile of remorse, then studied the young man standing next to her. Tall, muscular, blond, blue-eyed. "Flora, I think it's time I met your nephew. Would you introduce us?"

"Oh my," she whispered, and had to take a moment. "Yes, of course, Reverend Roy. This is my nephew, Michael Stephen Buckner. We call him Buck."

Then she turned to Buck. "Sweetie, this is Reverend Roy Patterson, a good man and a kind man. Very much like yourself."

Buck hesitated, then extended his arm, and the two men shook hands.

"We could go upstairs and talk some more," Reverend Roy suggested. "Over lunch, perhaps?"

Buck glanced at me, as if asking permission. I nodded. "Enjoy your lunch."

As the three of them walked up the stairs, I began to feel some real hope for this place. Not right away, but maybe someday.

There was utter silence until they reached the top of the stairs and disappeared around the corner. Even then, it took me, Mac, and Wade another minute to absorb what we'd just seen and heard.

Finally, Mac said, "Never a dull moment with you, Irish."

"I try to make it fun."

We walked up the stairs, around the hall, and into the nave. I was still shaking from Lavinia's palpable rage as well as feeling a little weepy after the tender moment between Flora and Buck. I didn't know what to think about Reverend Roy's sudden appearance, but I hoped it meant something good for all of them.

As Mac and I walked around the altar, my phone buzzed and I checked my texts.

"It's from Chloe," I explained, and read the text out loud. "She says, 'Don't go anywhere. I'll be there in one minute.'"

"Sounds important," Mac said.

I gazed up at him. "You might as well go on home and rescue Jake Slater from some fate worse than death."

"His Ferrari is about to go over a cliff, but that's not important. I want to see what's up with Chloe."

That's when we heard the *tip-tip-tapping* stilettos on the stone floor of the narthex.

"Oh no," I groaned. "Now you're stuck. I'm so sorry."

On cue, Whitney sashayed through the open door of the narthex and entered the main section of the church. And I wondered, not for the first time, why there weren't more lightning strikes whenever she walked inside.

"Just who I was looking for," she said saucily, her shoulders flexing back and forth for Mac's benefit. Today she wore her usual stiletto heels with pleather leggings in a shade of fuchsia never before seen in nature. A shimmery pink crop top completed the outfit. Stunning, in a retina-burning sort of way.

"We were just leaving," I said, and tried to go around her.

"Not so fast, little missy," she snapped, and stepped in my way. "I have something I think you'll be very interested in."

"I doubt it." I grabbed Mac's hand and we started to walk away.

She raised her voice. "You might just change your mind when you see this photo featuring a certain MacKintyre Sullivan."

In that moment, I pictured my head swelling up like a Macy's Thanksgiving Day Parade float about to explode. I felt my eyes bulging out, and I believed I might begin to breathe fire.

I turned, shook my finger, and said in a gruff voice I hardly recognized, "Don't you even whisper Mac's name. In fact, don't even *think* his name, or I will squish you like the creepy little bug that you are."

Mac touched my back. "Shannon, come on. Let's go."

That's when I heard rapid footsteps approaching from somewhere behind us. I couldn't turn and see who it was, though. I had to keep my eye on Whitney in case of a sneak attack.

Chloe moved right in front of Whitney and held up her hand like a traffic cop. "Stop right there."

"Get out of my way," Whitney said.

I stared at Chloe. "What's going on?"

"So, she told Tommy," Chloe began, "who told Eric, who told me that someone took a photograph of Mac in New York and tried to turn it into some sleazy story on the Internet. So, naturally, Whitney couldn't wait to run over here and rub your nose in it."

"But why?" I asked.

Chloe snorted. "Because she's a horrible person with no class."

"I have class!" Whitney insisted.

Chloe chuckled. "But you don't deny that you're a horrible person."

Whitney stamped her foot like a spoiled child. "Just shut up."

Mac stepped forward. "What's this all about?"

Chloe pulled out her cell phone and swept the screen. "That bleach-blond sleaze-monger Celeste Simmons was apparently following Siobhán O'Leary all around New York City until she hit pay dirt when Siobhán met Mac for a drink." She held up the phone so we could see the photo and the headline.

"Celeste Simmons," Mac muttered. "The woman smells dirt anywhere she goes."

"Looks like she found some," Whitney said snidely.

Siobhán was barely in the picture, just some of her red hair cascading in the background. Whoever had taken the picture had been more interested in catching her husband, Terence, at the very moment when he swung his fist at Mac. The headline read, "Sexy Siobhán Has a New Protector."

I cringed at the photograph. "This is terrible."

"Shannon, you can't possibly think—" Mac began.

"Of course not," I said quickly, handing the phone

back to Chloe. "But it hurts my stomach to see him attack you."

Mac blinked at me, then blew out a breath. He touched my cheek and kissed me. "I love you very much."

His voice was so gentle, so sincere, I felt my eyes water. He kissed me again and pulled me into his arms. I wrapped my arms around him and held on.

"Thank you for that," he whispered.

"You told me what happened," I said. "I believe you."

Whitney was scowling. "You should at least read the story."

"Why?" I asked. "If Celeste Simmons wrote it, it's a bunch of baloney for sure."

Whitney stared at me as though I was speaking another language. After a moment, she let loose a frustrated little scream and stormed out of the church.

Chloe started to laugh. "I love ya, Sis."

"And I love you back." Then I gazed at Mac. "I have to ask you something."

"Ask me anything."

"Did you ever date Celeste Simmons?"

"God no." He looked horrified. "On my last movie, she tried to sneak into my hotel room. I had her arrested."

"Ooh." I winced. "That had to leave a mark."

He grinned. "I love you, Red."

"And I love you back."

Of course, Reverend Roy, despite cheating on his wife and fathering a child he didn't know about, was adamant about defending his wife, Lavinia.

Flora still supported and admired him, and she

assured us that she would continue to serve the church as the flower lady and unofficial historian. She made it clear that she and the reverend had never rekindled anything upon her return to Lighthouse Cove.

I wondered if Buck would move up here permanently. Selfishly, I hoped so. He had great skills when it came to lighting and electrical issues. Plus, he was simply a good guy, and he seemed happy working with all of us. We could always use more of that on our crew, especially with the new Homefront project. I was already looking forward to planning that and other new projects.

That afternoon, my crew and I joined Madeline and took a few minutes to talk about Sarah Spindler and our memories of her. It felt right to keep it casual and just chat about her. I told the group about Lizzie's connection to Sarah as her kids' babysitter, and Chloe shared her experience with Sarah on the volleyball team. Madeline was laughing and crying as Chloe talked about Sarah's vicious serve, and she managed to share her own thoughts with the group as we all shed a few tears along with her.

Just before we ended the session, Madeline said a few words about Colleen. Looking at me, she said, "Remember I told you how Colleen and Sarah were so similar?"

"I remember," I said. "You said they were both important in their jobs. They each took care of the details."

"That's right," she said. "I could add so much more. Sarah was funny and sweet and smart. And honestly? I'm still feeling lost without her."

Wade reached for her hand and squeezed it lightly. "That's a pretty nice way to remember her."

She looked at him, her eyes filled with tears, then glanced around. "I'm feeling lighter today than I have in a while. I'm glad you're all here with me, talking about Sarah. I'd like to dedicate a room in the museum to her."

"That's such a good idea," I said, and leaned over to give her a hug.

"Then it shall be done," she said, and punctuated the decision with a sniffle and a laugh.

Epilogue

After everyone went back to work, I gazed up at Mac. "I'm really glad you were here to see everything that happened today, especially down in the basement. Mainly because it would be so grueling to have to repeat the whole tortured scene all over again."

He slung his arm across my shoulders. "You would never be able to reenact the level of rage that enveloped Lavinia."

"And I'd never want to," I assured him. "That was chilling."

"So, after all that, are you actually going back to work?"

"I'm afraid I have to," I said. "We've got to make up some of the time we've lost. What about you?"

"Same goes," he said. "I left Jake and his Ferrari at the edge of that cliff."

"You've got to fix that."

His laugh had a sinister note to it. "Oh yeah. I'll fix it."

I studied him. "You have an evil streak."

He chuckled. "I do enjoy torturing my people."

I took a closer look, then reached up and touched his cheek. "How are you feeling?"

"I'm okay. I'll pop a couple more ibuprofen when I get home, then try to get a few pages done and maybe take a nap."

"That's a very good idea. I'll be home early. Maybe we can go for pizza?"

"Didn't you just have pizza last night?"

I gazed up at him. "Yes. But can you ever really have enough pizza?"

"Nope. Never." With a laugh, he pulled me into his arms and kissed me thoroughly. When he finally stepped back, there was applause throughout the church.

I scowled at my crew. "Cut that out."

But Mac took a bow. "Thank you very much."

I had to laugh. "You nut."

"Come home early," he whispered, then quickly kissed me again and walked out of the church.

Mac called two hours later. "Hi."

I was forty feet up on the lift checking out a bad case of termites in one of the timbers. I called down to Amanda. "You're right. It's got to be replaced."

Amanda nodded and made a note on her tablet.

I answered the phone. "Hi."

"Hi," Mac said. "Listen. I've got a problem over at the lighthouse."

"What's wrong?"

"I heard from Frank. Looks like part of the railing around the main gallery is broken. I'm on my way over there, but I'm hoping you'll take a look at it with me."

Frank and his wife, Irma, were the caretakers of the

lighthouse mansion. Mac had lived there until recently, when he'd moved in with me and turned his beautiful oceanfront home into a writers' retreat.

"Of course," I said. "I was about to finish for the day anyway. I'll drive up and meet you there. Give me twenty minutes."

"Thanks, Red. I'll see you there."

I turned onto Old Lighthouse Road and tried to avoid the potholes and cracks that Mac had never bothered to repair. His attitude was that if he repaired the road, then more people would show up. I couldn't argue with that.

I parked in front of the lighthouse. Mac's SUV wasn't around yet, but I noticed the two SUVs parked behind the mansion. I assumed they belonged to the writers who had come to the retreat for a week of intensive writing, along with the joy of waking up each morning and hearing the sounds of the ocean waves and the seabirds chirping.

I walked into the base of the lighthouse and headed for the circular staircase that would take me up to the main gallery. I stopped and pulled out my phone to send Mac a text. "I'm at the lighthouse and heading up to the gallery. See you soon."

The climb to the top of the lighthouse was not a carefree walk in the park. It was over one hundred feet straight up, and the spiral effect could be tricky, depending on where you placed your feet on each step. At intervals there was a bench for resting and a window to look out at the ocean. I found it helped to stop at every window and take a look at the beauty before me.

The good news was that my crew and I had recently

refurbished this entire structure, inside and out. We had reinforced the main gallery and the stairs so that it was as safe as possible. But that just made it more troubling to hear that something up there had broken.

I made it to the main gallery level and took a minute to catch my breath from the grueling climb before I opened the door to walk outside.

And gasped.

It wasn't because of the strenuous exercise but because Mac was standing there waiting and watching me.

"I didn't see your car," I said.

"I wanted to surprise you."

"You succeeded."

That's when I noticed the small table and two chairs that had been set up along the railing. The table was covered with a white linen tablecloth, and there were two place settings and two crystal champagne flutes.

"Oh, Mac, this is lovely. But what's going on?"

He started to laugh. "You brought your toolbox."

"Well, you said something was broken."

He was still laughing but managed to say, "I love you, Red."

"I love you, too." I walked over and kissed him, all the while thinking, *Did I forget a special date?*

He grinned as if he could read my thoughts. "I just wanted to surprise you with something different."

"You succeeded. Trust me, this is a whole new level of different."

"Good. How about some champagne?"

"You know I love champagne."

"I do." He lifted the bottle and set it on the table, then proceeded to tear off the foil, wrap a clean cloth around the bottle, and pop the cork. Then he poured the golden bubbly liquid into our glasses and raised his in a toast. I joined him.

"To my Shannon," he said. "The most beautiful, clever, loving, smart, funny woman I have ever known. Thank you for letting me be a part of your life. Mine is a thousand times richer and fuller because of you."

"My goodness, you're going to make me cry."

"Don't cry, love. Be happy."

"I am, Mac. I truly am. And everything you just said?"

"Yeah?"

"Back at you."

He laughed again and I thought, *What a wonderful sound.*

We clinked our glasses and sipped.

"This is delicious," I said.

"Let's sit down," he said, and pulled out my chair. He sat down, too, and sipped his champagne.

"This is heavenly. Much better than pizza." I took another sip of champagne. "This view is spectacular."

"I ordered it just for you."

The air was cooling and the sky was beginning to turn pink as the sun headed toward the horizon.

"The sunset is going to be amazing," I said.

His smile was roguish. "Yeah, I did that, too."

I beamed at him. "You do it all."

He took my hand. "You inspire me."

We took a few more sips of champagne and watched the sky change colors.

After a few minutes he said, "I have something else for you."

"You do?"

"Yeah. I hope you like it." He reached under the

table and pulled out a large square insulated bag. He opened the bag and removed the box of Bella Rossa pizza.

"Oh, my hero! You remembered the pizza!" My laughter wafted out over the ocean. "You are crazy. And you're also the man of my dreams."

He stood, leaned over the table, and kissed me. "You are crazy, too. And also the woman of my dreams."

Then he sat back down and placed a piece of pizza on each of our plates—which he'd also pulled out of the insulated warming bag—and handed me one.

"It's probably not very hot."

"It's always delicious any way you serve it."

We each folded our pizza slice in half and took a bite.

"Pretty darn good," he admitted.

As we dined on pizza and champagne, we laughed and talked about everything that was going on. By some unspoken rule, though, we avoided mentioning the murders or the creepiness or the fistfight or any of the other disturbing parts of the last few days.

We finished our first piece of pizza, and Mac poured more champagne.

"There's one more thing," he said.

I wondered if there would be ice cream. "What's that?"

He moved his chair to be closer to me. "I know you love me, Shannon, and I love you."

I smiled. "It's true."

"And I know you are a strong, smart, capable, self-sufficient woman who can handle anything. But I'm still sorry I wasn't here for you when you ventured into that dark, disturbing tunnel alone. I want to be here for you, Shannon. I want us to venture into the future together. More than anything else, I want to marry you and love you forever."

He pulled a small box out of his pocket and opened it for me. "Will you marry me, Shannon?"

My heart was so full, I had to take a moment and breathe, slowly, in and out. In and out. I wanted to remember everything in this moment. The champagne, the pizza, the ripples on the ocean, the colors of the sunset, this man.

I stared at the big, sparkling diamond in the little velvet box, then gazed into Mac's dark blue eyes, and touched his handsome bruised face. "I love you so much, Mac, and I always will. And, yes, I will absolutely marry you."

He stood and pulled me into his arms. He lifted me up and slowly twirled me around, then kissed me as I floated on air around him. It would've been the most romantic moment ever, if only I hadn't been wearing my steel-toed work boots. Which, come to think of it, made it absolutely perfect in every possible way.

Keep reading for an excerpt from
Kate Carlisle's next Bibliophile Mystery

THE TWELVE BOOKS OF CHRISTMAS

I stared out the wide kitchen window as a black stretch limousine pulled to a stop in front of our new second home. A few moments later, another limo arrived and I had to take a few bracing breaths. "Have we done the right thing?"

My darkly handsome husband, Derek, quirked an eyebrow. "Regrets already, Brooklyn, darling?"

"God, yes." I tried to laugh, but the sound bordered on hysterical. "We couldn't settle for a cozy dinner for four, could we? No way. We had to invite thirty-four people for dinner on Christmas Eve. Thirty-four people! Or is it thirty-five?" Did it really matter? Either way, we were about to be besieged in our brand-new house. With family and friends, but still. "Are we crazy?"

"Of course not," he said, his British accent lending extra credibility to the statement. "It's a perfectly respectable thing to invite favorite friends and family members over for Christmas Eve dinner."

"Is it?" I wondered. "We're likely to cause a frenzy."

He laughed. "Would that be so bad?"

I gaped at him.

"Maybe they won't all show up," he said, but he was still laughing.

"Oh, please," I said. "You know they'll all be here."

He gently rubbed my shoulders. "All the people we love best."

His kind words calmed me down a smidge, as they usually did. It would all work out and we would have a good time. After all, this was the reason we'd built our second home in Dharma, the small town in the Sonoma wine country where I'd grown up. We wanted to be close to family, so now we were about to welcome my parents, two brothers, three sisters, various spouses, and lots of children to spend Christmas Eve with us. Derek's parents were coming too, along with several of his brothers, their wives, and more children. We were also expecting our good friends Gabriel and Alex, along with my parents' guru, Robson Benedict, and his aunt Trudy. It was going to be an interesting evening.

"It'll be lovely," Derek insisted.

"It'll be chaos."

He chuckled and rubbed his hands up and down my arms. "As it should be, darling. After all, it's Christmas."

I tried to remember to breathe. "Christmas. Right." I watched another limo drive up and park. It sounded extravagant, but we had gone ahead and ordered a number of limousines so our friends wouldn't have to drive through the hills after a long night of good food and lots of wine. It just made sense.

Derek kissed my forehead, then slowly let me go and gazed out the window. "Look on the bright side. At least you don't have to cook."

"Good point." I was the absolute worst cook in the world, and everybody knew it. Happily, the entire evening was being catered by my sister Savannah's fabulous restaurant in downtown Dharma. Most of her staff had been here all day, prepping and cooking a huge feast, using our brand-new, clean garage as their backstage area. Across the living and dining rooms, tables had been beautifully set for dinner. Tasting stations had been arranged outside on the terrace, where Savannah's staff would serve cocktails, wine, and a number of yummy hors d'oeuvres and munchies before the dinner began.

The entire house looked festive and smelled wonderful. Our Christmas tree was magical with flickering fairy lights and at least a hundred handmade ornaments covering its boughs. I had to admit I'd gotten carried away with crafting dozens of tiny three-dimensional books—with tiny first-chapter pages included!—that we would be giving to our guests as takeaways. As a bookbinder specializing in rare book restoration, I considered it my duty to always give books as gifts, and I tried to be creative about it.

Scattered under the tree and spreading nearly halfway across the living room were oodles of beautifully wrapped gifts. Most were for the children. And, yes, we had gone overboard, but why not? This was our first time hosting Christmas Eve, and we wanted it to be special.

When the front doorbell finally rang, I took a few more seconds to silently freak out, then rested my head on Derek's strong shoulder. Smiling bravely, I said, "I'll get it."

He reached for my hand. "We'll go together."

An hour later, the chaos that I'd warned Derek about was upon us. But, okay, it wasn't quite as horrifying as I'd imagined. People were chatting and laughing while enjoying the wine and appetizers. Christmas carols were playing in the background, and the children were sneaking peeks at all the goodies under the tree. For the most part everyone was having a lovely time.

My oldest friend, Robin, held court on the living room couch with baby Jamie, my darling new nephew. There was some minor controversy brewing since Jamie's dad—my brother Austin—had taken to calling the little guy Jake. But whatever they decided to call him, the wee one was constantly being whisked away by anyone with an urge to cuddle an adorable baby boy. And who didn't have that urge once in a while? He was such a good baby and just one more reason why Derek and I had decided to build a second home here in Dharma. I loved all my brothers and sisters and their kids, but I'd especially wanted to be near Robin when she had her first child. Derek and I both wanted to be a part of their lives, and that wasn't always easy to do while living and working in San Francisco. This way, we could have the best of both worlds.

A few years ago, Derek's parents had surprised us all by buying their own second home in Dharma after we'd introduced them to my parents before our wedding. Now the four of them were best friends and part-time neighbors, too.

My sister China, who was seven months pregnant with her second child, sat down next to Robin, and the two began exchanging childbirth horror stories. Anyone was welcome to join in, but seriously? I loved them both, but I tended to steer clear. Mainly because I'd heard the worst of the stories before, but also because yuck. Am I right?

From across the room, I met Robin's gaze, and her eyes gleamed with mischief. She knew all that childbirth talk made me a little queasy. I was pretty sure she did it on purpose, but I loved her anyway. Even when she regularly warned me that "you're next," often followed by a spine-chilling, bloodcurdling laugh.

I regularly assured her that I *wasn't* next, but she still enjoyed taunting me with all the grisly details of her labor pains as though that might be some kind of temptation. I personally thought she spiced up the stories just for me. We had been besties from day one when my family and I arrived in Dharma and I first saw her, a skinny little eight-year-old, clutching her bald Barbie doll. Even at that early age, I recognized a fellow misfit when I saw one.

I smiled at the memory, took a sip of champagne, and nibbled on a melted-Brie mini quesadilla as I made my way across the room, checking that everyone was enjoying themselves. I savored the Brie as well as the eclectic bits of conversation I overheard as I moved through the crowd. I couldn't wait for everyone to open their presents, especially the ones I'd made. In the past, my sisters had given me some grief for always giving books as gifts. But what did they expect? Books were my life. I made my living by restoring rare books. What else would I give as a special gift to the people I loved?

I was happy to hear that this was the year that everyone wanted books again, especially the parents of the youngsters who were just learning to read. Both Derek's and my family members were voracious readers, so they had made it clear that books as gifts were once again in vogue.

Still, I had decided to venture a bit farther afield with my gift giving, especially for the adults in the family. It had taken me months to complete everything, but I had managed to make every gift by hand, mostly using recycled books, and I was excited to see the reactions they got.

I stopped at one of the food mini stations, and a waiter poured me another glass of champagne. I took a sip and happened to glance at the front door, which was wide open to let in the cool evening breeze. I saw my mother standing on the front porch talking to her friend Ginny Morrison. I'd only met her twice. A little girl with curly blond hair was huddled against Ginny's legs as though she was frightened to venture any farther.

"Oh, Brooklyn," Mom said, waving me over. "You remember my friend Ginny?"

"Of course." I walked out to the porch and gave the woman a brief hug. "Merry Christmas, Ginny. And who is this?"

The three of us stared at the little girl clutching Ginny's legs. "This is my daughter, Charlotte," she said, stroking the child's hair.

"Hi, Charlotte," Mom and I said in unison.

She gazed up at both of us. "Yesterday was my birthday."

"My goodness," Mom said. "Happy birthday, sweetie."

"Happy birthday, Charlotte," I said. "How old are you?"

"I'm five years old." She held up five fingers.

"Isn't that wonderful?" Mom said softly.

"Would you both like to come inside and sit by the Christmas tree?" I asked. "It's so pretty and it smells really good. And we have lots of tasty food if you'd like something to eat."

Charlotte stared up at her mother, saying nothing. But I could tell she was intrigued.

"That's sweet of you," Ginny said quickly. "And I think Charlotte is very tempted. But we really can't take any more of your time. I just wanted to stop by and give your mother a little Christmas gift."

"And I love it." Mom whipped out a skinny little tree branch and whisked it back and forth through the air. I figured it had to be a magic wand, since Ginny was a fellow member of Mom's local druidic Wiccan group. Mom had recently been reelected Grand Raven Mistress of the coven, and Ginny had been elected treasurer.

I had no idea what the treasurer of a coven did, but I supposed it meant that she was good with numbers.

"It's pretty." I reached out and touched the wand. "It feels good. Stronger than I thought it would be."

"It's cherrywood," Ginny said. "It has a warm, feminine energy and is good for healing."

"And it's especially excellent for detecting other magical properties," Mom added, and her eyes narrowed. "Can't wait to put that to the test."

Ginny smiled at me. "And a cherrywood wand doesn't mind being shared."

"Yeah?" I said, my tongue planted firmly in my cheek. "Maybe I'll take it for a spin sometime."

"That would make me very happy," Mom said. "But I know you're just teasing me."

I gave her a one-armed hug. "Sorry, Mom. You know it's not my thing."

She kissed my cheek. "I love you anyway." Then she

turned back to Ginny. "Now, we have plenty of room at the table and lots of food. We would love to have you join us."

"That's very sweet," she said. "But I think we're just going to go home. We've had a long day."

Gazing up at me, Charlotte whispered, "My daddy went to heaven."

"Oh no." Tears instantly filled my eyes, and without another thought, I knelt down and met the little girl on her level. "I'm so sorry, honey."

She said nothing, simply wrapped her arms around my neck and began to cry.

I was well-known for my sympathetic tear ducts, but even my tough big brothers wouldn't have been able to withstand reacting to this little girl's pain.

I wondered how her father had died, but now wasn't the time to inquire.

Ginny placed her hand on my shoulder and quietly explained, "We picked up Hank's ashes today. Charlotte wants to buy a pretty box to put them in."

"She's such a sweet little girl," I murmured.

Mom gave her friend a hug. "Why don't we all go inside and warm up around the Christmas tree. Just for a few minutes."

After another sniffle, Charlotte loosened her grasp and looked up at me. "Mommy said you have a cat."

I smiled. "I do. Would you like to meet her?"

"It's a girl cat?"

"Yes. Her name is Charlie."

She managed a watery giggle. "It sounds a little like my name, except Charlie is for a boy."

I smiled at her. "I think some girls might like the name, too."

She thought about it and nodded. "Maybe so." Without consulting her mother, Charlotte took my hand, and we walked into the house and toward the stairs. I took a quick look back at her mother and got a nod of approval.

"Your cat isn't coming to the party?" Charlotte asked.

"No, she's pretty shy. She likes to stay upstairs when there's a lot of people in the house."

"I can stay with her," she whispered.

"Okay. Let's go find her." In the bedroom, I sat down on the floor next to the bed and whispered Charlie's name.

"Is she under there?" Charlotte asked.

I nodded. "This is where she usually hides."

"Do you think she'll come if I call her?"

"Maybe," I said. "Give it a try."

Charlotte nodded, then whispered, "Charlie? Hello? Charlie?"

Sure enough, after a few seconds the cat peeked out from under the bedspread. "There she is."

She flashed me a tremulous grin. "She came out."

"She must like you," I said, then reached for the cat. "Come on, sweetie. I want you to meet my friend Charlotte."

Charlie came into my arms and draped herself bonelessly over my shoulder. I stroked her soft fur, then angled her toward Charlotte. "Charlie, this is Charlotte. She wants to say hello."

The little girl tried to follow my lead by patting Charlie's back. It was an awkward move, but the cat didn't seem to mind.

"Hi, Charlie," Charlotte said tentatively. "Hi, Charlie." She looked at me. "Will she let me hold her?"

"I think she'd like that. Why don't you sit down on the floor and lean back against the bed? I'll put her in your lap."

"Okay."

I stroked Charlie a few more times, then gently passed her over to Charlotte, who wrapped herself around the cat.

"Hi, hi," she whispered in Charlie's ear. "Hi, Charlie." She closed her eyes and swayed slightly from side to side, as though she was rocking the cat to sleep. Charlie seemed to like it, because I could hear her purring. She was such a good cat.

I glanced at the doorway and saw that my mother and Ginny had followed us upstairs. They stood by the door, watching the action, and I could see tears in both their eyes.

I quietly pushed myself off the floor and walked over to my mom. "I was thinking of getting something to eat. Do you think Charlotte would like some hot chocolate if I brought it up here?"

Ginny looked from me to Mom and took hold of our hands in hers. "You are both so kind. Thank you. I'm sure Charlotte would love it."

The little girl was still clutching the cat, so I said, "I'll be right back."

Downstairs in the kitchen, I ran into my sister Savannah. "Can I add two more for dinner? Another one of Mom's Wiccan friends and her little girl came by to give Mom a present."

"That's nice."

"Yeah. Turns out her husband just died."

Savannah exhaled. "Oh no. That's terrible. Yeah, we'll squeeze the two of them in somewhere."

"Thanks, Bug." She rolled her eyes at the nickname and went dashing off. My parents had come up with quirky middle names for each of us, and Savannah's was Dragonfly. At some point in her early childhood, "Dragonfly" had become "Bug," and we still called her that.

I pulled a packet of hot chocolate mix from the cupboard, then filled a mug with water and heated it for two minutes in the microwave. I poured in the powder and mixed it well, then I walked back upstairs and stopped when I noticed that my bedroom door was closed. Mom and Ginny stood in the hallway talking quietly.

"Everything okay?" I asked, warming my hands around the mug of hot chocolate.

Mom nodded. "Charlotte was curled up on the carpet with Charlie and fell right to sleep."

"The poor thing is exhausted," Ginny said. "We've had a long, sad day."

"I'm so sorry," I said. "Do you think she'll still want the hot chocolate when she wakes up?"

Ginny grinned. "Oh, trust me. She'll drink it even if it's ice-cold."

I turned to Mom. "Did Charlie stay with her?"

"She never left Charlotte's side."

I noticed Ginny's eyes fill again. "What a dear creature she is."

I was ridiculously proud of Charlie for keeping watch over Charlotte.

Ginny reached for the mug. "Let me hold that for you. You must want to go down and mingle with your guests."

Mom jumped in. "Yes, Brooklyn, you go find Derek and enjoy your party. We'll be down shortly."

I chuckled. "It's everybody's party, Mom. But I should go make sure everything's running smoothly."

"You've planned this party down to the matching tartan napkin rings," Mom said with a laugh. "What could possibly go wrong?"

A shiver ran across my shoulders, and I gave her a look. "Don't tempt fate, Mom."

And that's when my phone began to ring.